"Touch Me—
You Want to Touch Me,
So Don't Be Shy,"

he whispered. His voice was a seductive rumble. The brush of his beard and mustache on her skin was driving her wild. "Your skin is like ivory velvet," he murmured.

"Put me down!" she demanded hoarsely, as a car pulled up outside.

"For now," he agreed, kissing her softly. "This is a rain check. Now go put your shoes on while I greet your boyfriend for you."

DIXIE BROWNING

is a native of North Carolina. Many of her stories are born as she travels from her home in Winston-Salem to her cottage in Frisco on Hatteras Island. She is an accomplished watercolor artist, as well as a writer.

D0886296

Dear Reader,

Silhouette Special Editions are an exciting new line of contemporary romances from Silhouette Books. Special Editions are written specifically for our readers who want a story with heightened romantic tension.

Special Editions have all the elements you've enjoyed in Silhouette Romances and *more*. These stories concentrate on romance in a longer, more realistic and sophisticated way, and they feature greater sensual detail.

I hope you enjoy this book and all the wonderful romances from Silhouette. We welcome any suggestions or comments and invite you to write to us at the address below.

Karen Solem
Editor-in-Chief
Silhouette Books
P.O. Box 769
New York, N. Y. 10019

DIXIE BROWNING
Reach Out to Cherish

Silhouette Special Edition

Published by Silhouette Books New York

America's Publisher of Contemporary Romance

This is for Lou and Linda,
who are just beginning.

SILHOUETTE BOOKS, a Division of Simon & Schuster, Inc.
1230 Avenue of the Americas, New York, N.Y. 10020

Copyright © 1983 by Dixie Browning

Distributed by Pocket Books

ISBN: 0-671-53610-9

First Silhouette Books printing August, 1983

10 9 8 7 6 5 4 3 2 1

Map by Ray Lundgren

SILHOUETTE, SILHOUETTE SPECIAL EDITION and
colophon are registered trademarks of Simon & Schuster, Inc.

America's Publisher of Contemporary Romance

Printed in the U.S.A.

Thrush's Song

When the touch of love warms my hollow
bones,
Turns my song to silver, my tears to gold,
Then I'm born again, just to fly away
O'er the midnight darkness, to the light of day.

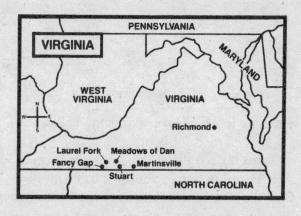

Chapter One

Aurelia covered her growing impatience with a social smile. The party was thriving, the guests were an interesting mixture, and her own date was by far the handsomest man there. She wanted to go home.

It wasn't that she was precisely bored. She had wandered around the edges of the crowds ever since they arrived, people-watching, listening to abstract snatches of conversation about butterfat content, grand slams, wine stains on a white silk dress, and the flue-cured tobacco market. The assorted guests made a colorful and attractive panorama against the backdrop of the Claiborn farm. Late summer was such a lush time here in the Blue Ridge Mountains, and Carol and Henry Claiborn were marvelous hosts. But she had been there for almost two hours, and in spite of the fact that she owed the Claiborns a lot, Aurelia could take just so much socializing before she began to fidget.

Some of the guests were playing croquet on the side lawn. Aurelia was tempted to join them, just to get away from the thicket of chattering people, but if she did that, she'd never get Chase out of there. He could party all night and never wind down. Just why Carol had thrown them together in the first place, she'd never know. They had absolutely nothing in common, other than the fact that they were both single and both lived alone.

From the edge of the patio she gazed out at the croquet players. A light breeze ruffled the fronds of the giant weeping willow, enhancing the lovely, romantic scene. Impatiently she turned away and looked for Chase's bright blond head. If he didn't come out soon, she'd walk home without him. She'd rather go alone, anyway, but that would let her in for all sorts of questions. It would mean explaining to both Chase and Carol that no, she *didn't* have a headache, and yes, it *was* a lovely party, and no, she *didn't* need anyone to escort her home. How could she tell Carol—who was not only her landlady and her part-time employer, but her best friend, as well—that she'd rather be home alone than socializing with a mess of people, however nice.

A burst of laughter cut through her thoughts. The guests were all sated by now with Carol's marvelous food and Henry's liquid hospitality. Chase was across the room talking sports to a couple of the locals; he was good for hours as long as he had an audience. Unfortunately Aurelia wasn't much good to him in that respect. She simply wasn't very interested in football and soccer—Chase's conversational strengths.

Carol waddled by with a balding man in bright pink slacks, and Aurelia heard her animated voice saying, "Not for sale, sorry. I can't help what Henry told your. . . . yes, I know your folks came from around these parts, but it's just not for sale. Have another one of those ham biscuits before they're all gone."

Aurelia couldn't imagine Henry wanting to sell any part of the farm. Even with all that corn and the acres of blue-green cabbages that looked so lovely and smelled so rank, it must have taken every bit of the Claiborn land to support Henry and his brother, Edward, and their families.

She tried to catch Chase's eye. Five more minutes— that was her limit. After that she'd invent an excuse and leave. Leaning against the railing, she breathed deeply, trying to still the familiar tension that was rising inside her. The air was cooler now that the sun had dropped behind the mountains, and the freshly mowed grass smelled like watermelon. There was practically no traffic along the nearby Blue Ridge Parkway. Compared to Atlanta, where she had been this time last year, it was pure heaven.

She glanced at her watch. Surely after two hours she shouldn't need an excuse to leave. Chase and Henry were examining a pair of the old dueling pistols Henry collected, and she watched their animated gestures and wondered at their fascination with guns. Chase didn't hunt—and neither did Henry, for that matter. Men and their toys!

Her eyes lingered on Chase's boyish profile. He was almost too handsome, and as good natured as he was good looking. Pity Carol's efforts at matchmaking had fallen on fallow ground, but after having steered clear of involvement for years, Aurelia saw no reason to change her mind at this late date.

Tucking a fallen lock of hair back into her Gibson Girl knot, she turned to smile at a woman she'd been introduced to earlier, who was addressing her.

"I understand you're a writer, Miss Kenner. My aunt once wrote a cookbook that was published. What are you writing now? Have you had anything published yet?"

Aurelia didn't mind talking about books already in print, but she never discussed work in progress. She realized she was just superstitious that way. And of course, discussing her current project was totally out of the question.

"I used to work on a trade journal, and I've ghost written a few things. Maybe I'll try my hand at a cookbook, too. How did your aunt's do?"

Over the course of some ten minutes she learned more than she really cared to know about the fine art of using up leftovers. Still, it was better than parrying unwanted questions.

"Did you read about that man who was the ghost writer for that actress—the musical comedy star? He really made a fortune on that. Imagine any woman who's done all she claims she's done wanting to tell the world about it!" The garrulous woman went on to probe avidly into Aurelia's social life, which she assumed to be rife with the famous and the infamous, and when that line of questioning produced nothing worth mentioning, she turned to finances.

"I've heard about all these million-dollar deals you writers make these days—movies and paperbacks and all that. Maybe I'll take up writing myself. We just bought a new house, and you wouldn't believe what we had to pay for four bedrooms and three and a half baths on a lot no wider than Henry's front porch. Where do you live?"

"I hate to disappoint you," Aurelia confessed, "but I live in a four-room rented house at the end of an unpaved road out in the middle of nowhere, and I work in Carol's shop part-time to make ends meet. That should give you an idea of my extravagant lifestyle." The house was a darling, complete with almost-antiques and newly painted gingerbread trim, but that was beside the point. Aurelia smiled vaguely at the woman and looked around desperately for Chase. Instead she saw Carol, and used her as an excuse to escape further questioning.

"Would you be mortally offended if I slipped away pretty soon?" she asked, joining her hostess in the patio doorway where Carol had been holding court among her bridge-playing friends. One hand rested proudly on the protuberance under her Hawaiian printed smock. Carol, at thirty-eight, was pregnant again.

"Probably, but I'll try to survive it. Just tell me one thing. What's so darned fascinating that I can't get you to stay away from that house of ours for more than two hours at a stretch? If I didn't know you were seeing Chase, I'd swear you had a man stashed away under the bed."

Aurelia's smile widened in amusement. "All I've got under my bed is one cat, a pair of crocheted slippers, and a few puffs of house moss. Did you call your mother? Is she going to be able to take over the shop?"

"Yep. If you can work full-time next week, Mama can fly down on Saturday and take over after that, and the twins can fill in any gaps."

Aurelia had mixed feelings about the arrangements. She didn't mind working part-time in the small antique shop just off the parkway—the money eked out her precarious budget. But she'd be too tired after a full day in the shop to write, and at the moment all she could think of was Jo and the letters and diaries.

Sooner or later, she admitted ruefully, she was going to have to quit indulging herself so shamefully and get on with the work she'd been contracted to do. But not just yet. Not while she could still rationalize her private obsession by calling it character research.

"Are you going to the Voncannons' annual pool-draining party? Thank goodness Mitzi agreed to hold off until after I deliver this load. I wonder if I'll be able to get into last summer's bathing suit?" Carol rattled on, not waiting for an answer to her initial question.

Aurelia was relieved. She'd been invited to the pool party, too, but she had no intention of going. Not that she couldn't handle it. She often wore shorts now, and even a bathing suit occasionally. Of course she still tried to stay out of the direct sun as much as possible, but anyone might choose to do that. She prided herself on the fact that she was perfectly well adjusted.

After all, she had launched out on her own and made a place for herself practically unaided. She had had help in landing her first job with the publishing firm, but from there on it had been her own ability that had carried her from copy girl to a position of relative independence. She had worked her way up, tackling everything from copy editing to proofreading to layout, even taking a whack at budgeting in an emergency. The ghost writing had developed along with her editorial capacity, and when her bank balance had grown healthy enough, it had been the promise of more contracts that had given her the courage to quit her salaried job, pull up stakes, and move to a place that suited her far better than metropolitan Atlanta.

Through the open doors she could hear Chase and Henry in a good-natured argument about guns. They had known each other all their lives, even though Henry was older by about fifteen years. Carol claimed to be constitutionally unable to allow a bachelor to run free, especially one as handsome as Chase Jamison. She had introduced Aurelia to him and then sat back to watch the match burst into flames. As far as Aurelia was concerned, there wasn't even a spark, and Chase had confided on their first date that he was hopelessly in love with a woman in Asheville who owned her own business. Unfortunately for him, she was more interested in developing that than in developing her lovelife. Since then, he and Aurelia had dated in a desultory fashion. Except when it came to sports, she was a good listener, and Chase enjoyed an audience. She didn't bother to tell him how much he reminded her of the brother she hadn't seen in years.

Catching Chase's eye, Aurelia signaled her intentions and then wandered down the driveway to where he had parked the car. She could have walked home, but in these heels she'd just as soon not.

Come on, Chase—please! Even though most of the party had been outdoors, Aurelia could feel the fine film of perspiration starting on her upper lip. She wasn't at her best in crowds.

A cool breeze, sweetly scented with tassling corn, blew her long polished-cotton skirt against her legs and pressed the delicate, lace-trimmed lawn of her blouse to her breasts. The blouse was one that had come into the shop in an attic consignment and it fit her perfectly. Carol had teased her about trying to slip back into the past when she insisted on buying it.

Carol had no idea how close to the mark she had come with that particular observation, Aurelia thought later as she sipped tea and gazed at Jocephus's faded photographs. She had murmured something about a headache as an excuse to cut short the evening, and Chase had dropped her off with a sympathetic word and a promise to call her the following morning to see how she was. At twenty-

nine, a year younger than Aurelia, he was a thoroughly nice boy. He'd be a thoroughly nice boy twenty
years from now. Or even forty.

She was too tired to write tonight, but she needed
this time with Jocèphus, with his letters, his diaries,
his photographs. It was almost like an addiction, and
occasionally she wondered if she weren't being dangerously, foolishly romantic. In the two short months
she had been working on the biography of Lieutenant
Jocephus Ezra Dozier Dancey of Jeff Davis's army, he
had become an integral part of her life.

"Jo, how do you like my blouse? Does it look
familiar to you? Your Mary might have worn one just
like it." The packet of letters beside her was from
Mary. Aurelia had resented them at first, but somewhere along the line she had rationalized the relationship between the two of them. The words Mary had
written all those years ago expressed in faded ink what
Aurelia had come to feel for the tall, slender man with
the melting dark eyes, the short black beard, and the
gentle smile. "Jo, why is it that I find you so much
more fascinating than I do Chase?"

She sipped her Earl Grey and ran her fingers along
the dog-eared letters the young soldier had touched a
hundred and twenty odd years ago. "It's ironic, you
know," she murmured to the sepia-toned photograph
in her hand, one taken several years after the war.
"Chase loves guns, and he's a schoolteacher. You're a
soldier, and you hate them. D'you suppose Chase and
Henry would drop everything and go to war the way
you did? Henry would hate like the dickens to leave
Carol behind, especially now—but you did. You left
Mary, even before the conscription began."

She opened one of the letters and read aloud the
familiar words, her voice soft in the small, carefully
furnished room. " 'My dearest Jo, I wonder if you will

ever read these lines. I must keep on writing just as I must keep on beleeving that one day we will be together again. I heard yesterday there was twelve thousand Yankees at Chambersburg. I am so worrit about you I cannot sleep nights. Papa has three hogs left and I beleeve we will butcher if the weather holds.'"

A love letter about hog butchering. Aurelia's throat tightened as she held the limp page away from her to focus on the spidery script. Her reading glasses were across the room. "'Thomas's youngest was kilt at Martinsburg. He was to marry the Jackson girl you know. There's many a sore heart in this valley, my beloved Jo, but none so sore as mine. There's times at night when I can hear your breething beside me in bed and I hold fast to the bolster and shut my eyes, and a powerful quietness comes down on me and I can hear you say my name.'"

Aurelia put the letters away in the tooled tin slipper box along with the diaries Max had sent her. She turned out the lamp, locked the front door, and poured milk in the basin on her back porch. She had a fluctuating cat population—sometimes half a dozen, sometimes only the one kitten, Sigh, but the milk always disappeared.

The phone interrupted her the following morning while she was engrossed in Jo's account of an unexpected meeting with a cousin in Richmond. She shut off her typewriter, muttering to herself at the intrusion, and tripped on the cord that trailed across her hooked rug. The outlets in the sixty-year-old house were few and invariably awkwardly placed.

"Hello!" The impatience was clear in her voice. She always resented being yanked back to the present when she was caught up in Jo's world.

"Who stepped on your tail?"

"Oh, Max." Some of the belligerence left her as she recognized her agent's voice. "I just tripped over the cord to my typewriter. No harm done."

"I thought you were still using a kerosene model back in them thar' hills."

"Don't cast aspersions at my mountains—or my machine, either. In case you've forgotten, I wouldn't have this commission and you wouldn't have your ten percent if I didn't live in these thar' hills," she reminded him. It was because she had just moved from Atlanta to a community near the original Dancey homeplace outside Stuart, Virginia, that Max had been able to sell her services to the man who wanted his great-great-grandfather's biography written. That and the fact that she had ghost written the story of Colonel Martha Larson's Vietnam experiences. Dancey the fourth had liked the book, and Max had tactfully kept from him the fact that A. R. Kenner was a woman.

"I called to warn you—it's about to hit the fan."

"If you mean the cat's among the canaries, then say so." Aurelia snapped. She had gotten used to Max's good-natured crudities and fielded them with ease.

"Euphemisms. We'll compromise on 'fat in the fire,' but one of these days, sweet lady, you're going to come face-to-face with four-letter reality and you're going to swoon dead away. I only hope somebody's standing by with a slug of brandy and a whiff of smelling salts."

"Max, haven't you learned by now that I create my own reality?" she teased. "Seriously, has Dancey Four discovered all?" The man's name was the same as his ancestor's, but she couldn't bear to think of him as Jo, and the rest of it was such a mouthful.

"If he hasn't yet, he soon will," the cynical Manhattanite declared. "I warned you that one of the reasons he agreed to our terms was the fact that you'd be close at hand later on. Seems the ol' Virginie homestead burned to the ground some time ago and Dancey's had it rebuilt. He plans to be in residence for the next few months, so stand by to convince him that you're up to doing the job."

"Oh, no!" Aurelia's softly horrified tones were barely audible, but Max knew very well what she was feeling. They were in it together, right up to their collective necks.

When Jocephus Dancey the fourth had first contacted Max's agency for someone to put together his great-great-grandfather's letters, diaries, and pictures into cohesive form, Max's reaction had been to send him to a vanity publisher. There was no chance that the venture would ever be a commercial success, since the man had made it plain that he wanted no liberties taken with the original material.

Max had mentioned it in passing when Aurelia had called to tell him she had finally made the break and relocated to a small Blue Ridge community in southern Virginia. At that time the only writing she had done besides her technical work were the three books she had ghosted for Max's clients, and she had considered herself extremely fortunate to be able to make a modest living at it. After all, she had only a high school equivalency certificate and ten years in various editorial positions in a medical publishing house in Atlanta as background. She had ghost written exactly three books, the last of which had been surprisingly well received by the public, but she desperately needed the job, and none of Max's other writers would bother with such a dead-end project.

"Hey, are you still there?"

"I'm quaking in my boots if you want to know the truth," she told him.

"If you've got a good first draft, what can he do? After all, we did sign a contract," Max reasoned hopefully.

A. R. Kenner had signed a contract. Max Barker had signed a contract. Aurelia Rose had lurked behind her ambiguous pen name and handed over a copy of the book she had collaborated on with Martha Larson as proof of her ability to write a soldier's story. Or rather, Max had handed it over for her.

"Uh, you didn't happen to mention that I was slightly female, did you?"

"Sorry, babe. He's bigger than I am. A hell of a lot bigger, in fact."

"Not to mention his being a male chauvinist of the first water," Aurelia added wryly. That point had come across quite clearly in Max's early interviews, which was why he had conveniently forgotten to mention the matter of her sex when Dancey Four offered a handsome advance. Handsome considering the fact that he was publishing the book as a private venture. Still, even work-for-hire writers have to eat.

"Well, don't say I didn't warn you. You agreed to tackle it, and—"

Aurelia broke in impatiently. "I agreed to tackle it purely on your recommendation. You were the one who assured me I'd have no trouble switching from ghosting to straight biography."

"And did you? You told me last week you were a third of the way into the first draft, so what's the gripe? All you have to do, my little magnolia blossom, is charm the man with that high-calorie drawl of yours. You'll have him licking sugar out of the palm of your hand in no time."

Aurelia dropped down onto a plush upholstered organ stool and twisted it around in agitation. She was well into the story, all right, but what she had written after a month of poring over Jo's diaries and his wife's love letters while she mooned over the three surviving photographs was not for public consumption. Under the influence of the strong, sensitive features that showed through his dark beard, under the spell of tender, poetic words written under the most horrific of circumstances, she feared that she had gone and committed the ultimate folly: she had fallen completely in love with a man who had lived over a hundred years ago.

Aurelia was due at the shop at one, which was just as well—her concentration was shot for the day. Three cats showed up for lunch with her resident one-eyed male kitten, Sigh, and Aurelia snapped at them as she poured out cat chow and milk. The phone rang two more times before she had to leave. The first time it was Chase, inquiring after her headache.

"Oh, it's gone, Chase," she said guiltily. "It wasn't terribly bad, anyway."

"Maybe you'd like to take pot luck with me tonight. I promise not to poison you, and after all, you have to allow some time for fun." Chase lived near Laurel Forks during the summer, but any day now he'd be moving to Asheville for the fall semester. Maybe he needed an ego boost before tackling the elusive Jan again.

"Oh, golly, Chase, after last night I don't dare take any more time off for fun," she pleaded.

If he only knew that her idea of fun was staying home with her assorted vagrant cats, her wildflower garden, and Jo. Jo liked small animals. She knew which flowers he liked best, which foods he enjoyed, and even how he liked to make love to his wife.

Mary's letters had become embarrassingly intimate once Aurelia had learned the elementary code they used for privacy.

She had poured herself a glass of iced tea and layered a slice of home-baked bread with Henry's tomatoes when the phone rang the third time. As a rule she averaged one call a week. At this rate her move to a small community for peace and quiet had been futile. She might as well have stayed on in Atlanta.

"Kenner residence," she answered reluctantly, speaking around a bite of tomato sandwich.

"A. R. Kenner, please," a terse baritone demanded.

"Speaking." She swallowed convulsively. A feeling of paralysis crept over her as she stared helplessly at the stack of manuscript on the marble-topped table beside her sleek new memory typewriter.

The silence on the other end was intimidating. "A. R. Kenner—the writer," the man enunciated, as if she were hard of hearing or weak of mind.

"Speaking," she repeated, fighting off a sense of doom. She half expected her life to flash before her eyes. And then she lifted her head as a militant determination jutted her round chin; the very worst he could do was demand his money and his material back. She'd be out a considerable sum—money already spent, unfortunately, but that could be worked out somehow.

"Miss Kenner—or is it Mrs.? This is Jed Dancey. I believe we have some business to discuss. I'll be by in half an hour."

"I'm sorry, Mr. Dancey, but I won't be here. I have to go to work." Let him stew awhile. The very thought of his being related to her Jo was totally unacceptable.

"Work? What time do you get home from work, Miss Kenner?" His voice was ominously gentle, reminding her of the purr of a carnivorous cat.

Aurelia hesitated. She was almost tempted to have it out with him over the phone. He sounded like the sort who could get violent with little or no provocation. "It varies," she hedged. If there was a customer in the shop, she wouldn't close the door on the stroke of five.

"Where do you work?"

Oh no. She wasn't carrying her fight to Carol's shop. He'd be the proverbial bull in a china shop. Max had said he was huge, and the man did have a legitimate complaint—if sexual discrimination could be called legitimate. "I'll be here after work," she said resignedly.

"I'll be there at seven. How do I find the place?"

She told him and then hung up. She made one more call, gusting a breath of relief at finding Chase in. "Chase, about tonight," she ventured.

By the time she hung up, it was arranged that Chase would pick her up at seven thirty for dinner at his house. She was using him, but she didn't care. Wasn't turnabout fair play? She had spent hours listening, commiserating, and soothing his battered ego when his calls and letters to Jan went unanswered. Besides, emergency measures were called for. Alone in the house, she didn't care to take chances with deep-voiced, fast-talking strangers. And Chase really was nice. Perhaps after she had worked this idiotic fantasy out of her system and he'd given up on Jan, they might step up the pace of their undemanding friendship.

And then again, they might not. In spite of all common sense, in spite of the evidence of her own mirror, Aurelia knew she had quite a ways to go before she was ready for any sort of an intimate relationship. And she had long since learned to ignore the cold shadow of emptiness that crept over her at odd moments.

She fished Sigh out of the desk drawer where he slept on her supply of paper, put him out, locked the back door, and changed into her working clothes. She had lost her appetite for lunch.

By six thirty she had soaked in the claw-footed tub, discarded three outfits, and finally settled on a cotton skirt of blue and green calico and the long-sleeved, high-necked blouse she had worn the night before. She had rinsed it out carefully and pressed the delicate, faintly yellowed tucks and lace edging, thinking of how ironic it was that synthetics hadn't been developed back when they were really needed. She could imagine Mary Dancey spending hours with a heavy flat iron, laboriously pressing Jo's handmade white shirts and her own layered petticoats and voluminous dresses.

Henry Claiborn had told her once that her hair was the exact color of sourwood honey. Tonight she swirled it up into a tighter, higher knot than usual. This was no time for untidy tendrils. For good measure, she put on her gold-rimmed glasses. They were reading glasses and she couldn't see much beyond three feet with them, but they added one more element of armor for the coming interview. In spite of her thirty years, her face had a dismayingly youthful look—the nose, probably. It was short and inclined to turn up. Not that her mouth was any great help, either. It had a softness to it that occasionally annoyed her. For once she wished she had a tube of scarlet lipstick instead of the pale rose shades she favored.

In the parlor she rearranged a trapunto pillow on

the cushioned settee and glanced around critically, trying to visualize the impact of the small room on a strange and angry male. She had furnished it with rejects from the shop and a few pieces from the yard sales she attended with Carol, feeling that modern furniture would be out of place in the prim little farmhouse. In Atlanta she had lived in a furnished room; when she had moved to Virginia she had had to start from scratch. It had been fun decorating even on a shoestring. She loved her small nest. She felt more secure here than she had felt anywhere in years.

Hearing the sound of a car outside, Aurelia snatched up Jo's photographs and tucked them out of sight. There was no point in waving any red flags.

The car door slammed. In less than a minute the sound of heavy footsteps crossed her front porch, and then came an impatient rap on the screened door. In a swift flashback Aurelia remembered the ghost story her brother, Adam, used to scare her to death with. "I'm on the first step," he'd drone. "I'm on the second step." Long before he reached the top step— or even the middle—Aurelia would be doubled over, her head burrowed in her lap as she begged him to stop.

"Miss Kenner!"

The commanding voice had been bad enough on the phone. It was worse in person. Bracing her shoulders, Aurelia stretched her five feet three to a possible five three and a half. She added another psychological inch or two by lifting her chin imperiously. Crossing to the closet-sized foyer that held the door to her bedroom on one side, the door to the parlor on the other, and the front screened door that was now blocked by a mammoth pair of shoulders, she schooled her voice to a semblance of control. It

was an ability that had stood her in good stead on
more than one occasion, one that had been drilled
into her by an early teacher who believed courtesy
and deportment were the keys to heaven.

"Won't you come in, Mr. Dancey?"

The vision she had was blurred by her reading
glasses and she peered unobtrusively over the tops of
them. The light of the setting sun streaming in behind
the man made it impossible to see anything other than
height and breadth—though that was impressive
enough.

He followed her into the parlor, where she had
switched on the lamp on the cricket table. Gesturing
to the settee, the only thing she had that was even
faintly scaled to his proportions, she turned to look at
the man who refused to believe a mere woman could
convincingly interpret the life of a soldier.

"Mr. Dancey," she began determinedly, and then
she caught her breath. As her glasses slid down the
short incline of her nose, she got a good look at him.
He was casually dressed in dark pants and a fisherman's knit pullover in natural cotton. Neither garment could be considered tight, yet both seemed
barely able to contain the physical presence of the
man. He positively radiated virility!

Her eyes lifted slowly to his face: black hair, like
Jo's, though windblown now, and a black beard, also
identical to his ancestor's, neatly trimmed and revealing a few threads of gray. The resemblance was
uncanny. She was dizzy from it.

And as if that weren't enough, there were the eyes.
Long and every bit as expressive as his great-great-
grandfather's, they were onyx dark and deeply set
under glowering brows. But there the resemblance
ended. There wasn't even a shadow of warmth in the

gaze that seemed intent on taking inventory of her. He seemed to have added her up and discarded the sum as negligent.

"You'd better have a seat, Miss Kenner," he growled, as if he were the host and she the guest. "We have some talking to do."

Chapter Two

The sheer physical presence of the man filled the room. His aura was a palpable force field that seemed to ricochet from the walls, leaving Aurelia feeling as if she had wandered onto a battlefield. Helplessly, she surrendered the advantage of attack and waited for him to speak.

"You're a woman!" That was his first charge, and she peered through the forgotten reading glasses to see if he was playing with her.

"I know," she admitted cautiously. The Dancey sense of humor that had touched a responsive chord in her when she first read Jo's diaries had evidently skipped the present generation.

"Don't be facetious with me!" The lean planes of his face seemed to harden even further.

"Then don't be so offensive! My sex has absolutely nothing to do with the business between us!"

"Oh, no? Then why bother to lie about it? Hiding behind your initials was a deliberate attempt to mislead me, and you know it!"

She rose to her feet in one swift movement, her arms crossed over her breasts as she glared down at him. "In case it escaped your notice, Mr. Dancey, I was signing my name A. R. Kenner long before I ever heard of you! I wasn't hiding from anyone, nor was I attempting to mislead."

He continued to stare at her skeptically, his eyes so disconcertingly like Jo's that she almost lost her train of thought. When she became aware of where her unruly mind was leading her, she rushed into speech again. "I've always taken second billing, Mr. Dancey. My ego's not at stake; I'm not that sort of writer. There was no attempt to mislead, I assure you, and besides, you read Martha Larson's story. If you didn't care for my style, why did you hire me?"

"I hired you," he told her sarcastically, "because that grifter you call an agent assured me you were one of his top writers, experienced at writing about military personnel, and furthermore, you were located not a dozen miles from the old Dancey homeplace."

Aurelia bristled. Granted, Max was due his share of the blame. He really seemed to have spread it on with a trowel, but there had been no criminal intent. He was just voicing his confidence in her ability to do the job. If Jed Dancey weren't such a throwback, the mild deception wouldn't have been necessary in the first place. "Max is a reputable agent, Mr. Dancey. If you'd care to talk to him about dissolving our contract, then do it. Meanwhile, you can take your insinuations and your outdated chauvinism and get out of my house! I'm extremely particular about the sort of people I invite into my home."

Leaning back against the hand-stitched pillow, Jed Dancey stretched out his long, muscular legs, threatening the small table across the rug from him. If he had taken Blackbeard as a role model he couldn't have looked more piratical in his black jeans and boots and the shoulder-hugging fisherman's pullover.

"What makes you think you have the necessary expertise to write about soldiering, *Miss* A. R. Kenner?" he asked, his tone suspiciously bland.

Grimly overcoming a desire to throw him out bodily, Aurelia reminded herself of the sizable advance she had already spent on her new memory typewriter, an insurance policy, and a new pair of glasses. "I write about people, Mr. Dancey. Their occupations are only one facet of their lives." Unconsciously warming to her subject, she sat down on the edge of the settee and gazed at him earnestly over the tops of her glasses. "Don't you see, neither Martha nor Jo were really professional soldiers. Oh, I know—Martha had been in the army for years, but she was a linguist, a teacher. She taught at War College, and it was only a fluke that landed her in Nam. But once there, she reacted like a civilian, like the rawest recruit, only since she was a woman, she—"

"Exactly! She was a woman!" he pounced triumphantly.

Aurelia jumped up again. "You are unbelievable!" She blazed down at him, momentarily stymied by the sheer effrontery of the man. Feature for feature, he was Jocephus's image, but under that deceptive exterior they were two different species. There was no reasoning with this man. She looked into those blazing fire-opal eyes expecting Jo's warmth and humor and instead she was met by icy contempt. Unfinished business or not, the sooner she got him out of here, the better. She couldn't stand up against someone who looked like the man she dreamed about but acted as enlightened as a Neanderthal!

Before she could focus her efforts on getting rid of him, Sigh wandered in, the red chatoyance of his single eye revealing his Siamese paternity as it lit on the strange pair of boots that had invaded his territory. Without even glancing down, Jed Dancey swept the half-breed kitten up, cradling him on one large hand while the other stroked the white fur.

"I'd like to read what you've done so far, Miss Kenner."

"No." The flat negative was immediate and instinctive. She had written almost a third of a draft, but there was no way she was going to share her intimate knowledge of Jocephus Dancey with his great-great-grandson. She had studied all three diaries, written as he escorted a dozen Yank prisoners to Belle Isle, followed his company to Cross Keys and Port Republic, and on to Mechanicsville and Fredericksburg. In the midst of all the stark horror of war, Jocephus Dancey described the beauty of a small patch of quaker-ladies on the banks of the muddy James River, a wren's nesting place in the curl of a tent flap. He found humor in a family of field mice setting up housekeeping in a crate of Sharpe's carbines. He found poetry in a fifteen-year-old soldier's description of his grandmother's collard patch, and in the middle diary he had set words to the distinctive melody of a brown thrush's song, words that had struck right to the core of her heart.

"History will record the carnage of these four tragic years," he had written in the last diary, "but how many will recall that under and over and through it all, the seasons still followed, the egg still hatched, the seed still sprouted, sending up a pair of leaves turned blindly toward the sun. I sadly fear man has a timepiece inside him that will compel him to go to war time and again, for no other reason than that the hour has struck. And each time the hour strikes again, a cause will always be found."

Jocephus had created his own reality when to have accepted any other version became impossible. Aurelia understood that only too well. Hadn't she done the very same thing herself? Didn't everyone, to some extent, shape the lens through which they viewed the world?

"No," she repeated softly, starting slightly as she returned to the present to find herself still under Jed Dancey's level gaze. "I'm not ready to show it to anyone yet."

"But you have written something?" he pressed. His eyes had a disconcerting way of putting her on the defensive and leaving her defenseless at the same time.

She backed away, trying to ignore the large, powerful hands that looked so incongruously gentle holding her kitten. And Sigh, the traitor, was purring loudly, his single eye a slit of contentment.

"Of course I've written something! I'm well into the first draft, but it's not ready for public consumption. If I were a portrait painter you wouldn't expect me to show you a half-finished painting, would you?"

"If I had commissioned you and then found reason to suspect your qualifications, I would," he said quietly. His voice registered about six on her internal seismograph.

"You have absolutely no reason to doubt my qualifications as a writer, Mr. Dancey," she told him firmly, and then to her consternation he reached out and removed the glasses from her nose, placing them on a table.

"Don't I? You're the wrong sex, the wrong age—in fact, everything about you is wrong, Miss Kenner. Just look at you!" He proceeded to rake her from the top of her honey-colored knot to the tips of her small sandals, lingering along the way to appreciate the glow of flesh that shone through the cool white lawn of her sheer blouse.

Aurelia's eyes, an unusual shade between gray and amber, snapped fire at him as she searched her vocabulary for suitable ammunition.

He didn't wait for her attack. Dismissing her anger as of no account, he shook his head decisively. "There is no way you could possibly understand the feelings of a man who saw his best friend blown apart, had two horses shot out from under him, and had a foot sawed off by the company carpenter with nothing but a belt or two of moonshine to take the edge off the pain." His mouth—Jo's mouth, but stern where Jo's was tender, hard where Jo's was sensual—that mouth curled in derisive amusement as once more his gaze followed the lace-edged tucks of her blouse over the swell of her breasts, to the narrow circle of her waist and down past the curve of her calf to her finely boned ankle. "No, A. R. Kenner. Whatever else you might be suitable for, I'm afraid you aren't up to the task of interpreting the life of a soldier."

Wracked with a strangling mixture of anger, indignation, and something that felt oddly like jealousy, Aurelia warned herself to go carefully. She could deal with her rights as a duly contracted professional writer later. The right that sent a surge of despair rushing through her now was Jed Dancey's right to take away every single thing she had of Jocephus—the pictures she had spent hours gazing at, the faded words she had read and reread until they were a part of her very consciousness.

Her eyes strayed to the mantel above the tiny, inefficient fireplace, and she wondered if he noticed the empty spot. There was a mute clock that she planned to have repaired someday, and two pieces of cranberry glass turned so that the chips didn't show. And a blank place where Jo's largest picture had been hastily snatched away.

"Why don't we just call it quits, Miss Kenner?" the tall, rangy man said evenly. "I'll take the material and save you the chore of having to bundle it up and mail it to me, and I can negotiate with your agent over the advance. You'll be paid for your time—I'm not an unjust man."

Aurelia's gaze lifted slowly to his stern face. Her eyes, large and troubled, looked far more vulnerable without the barrier of her glasses. "But I've already started. I told you, I've written over a hundred pages. I've spent weeks and weeks reading those diaries. I *know* Jo Dancey! I know him better than anyone living. I know Mary. I know about the cave Jo used to play in when he was a boy. I even know how his mother cooked shelly beans with sugar and side meat in them, just for him."

"And that," Jed sneered, placing the kitten on the settee and ignoring the drift of pale fur that marred the trim perfection of his pants, "makes you the definitive expert on the man?"

She writhed under his derision, but stubbornly stood her ground. "What do you want me to concentrate on, the gore and carnage? The—the blood and guts? The man went to war at age twenty-two with a smooth-bore gun and a mule named Hard Times! He called himself a lieutenant because everyone else was anointing themselves generals. He was a farmer, not a soldier! He knew more about hogs and horses than he did guns and fighting. Jo *hated* fighting, but he went anyway. And that only made him braver."

"Calm down, girl." Jed reached out a hand to her, as if to gentle her the way he had gentled her cat, and she brushed it away.

"Don't patronize me, you—you Billy Yank!"

He closed his eyes, looking older than the pictures of his own great-great-grandfather for a moment. He *was* older. Aurelia was struck once more by the unsettling riddle of time.

"Look, Miss Kenner, this is the twentieth century —almost the twenty first. Let's leave the territorial divisions where they belong. All right, so I grew up in New York State. I didn't graduate from VMI and I sure as hell don't flaunt the Stars and Bars, but Jocephus—Jo, as you call him—was my great-great-grandfather and my namesake. That makes me one small part Virginian, so for his sake, why don't we shelve this skirmish until tomorrow. I'd like to drive you out to—"

She hadn't even heard Chase's car drive up on the gravel outside. He called through the door.

"Aurelia? You home?"

Reprieve! She brushed past Jed Dancey, alarmingly conscious of him as she caught a warm whiff of his subtle mossy cologne. "Come in, Chase," she called a little shrilly. "I'm all ready, just let me get my purse."

She didn't bother to try and hide her relief at the interruption. Ignoring Jed's sardonic look, she made the necessary introductions with no frills, all but rushing the two men out of the house. Chase was openly curious as his eyes drifted from the tight-lipped man who slid behind the wheel to the powerful dark green Jaguar itself. Aurelia hadn't a notion of what it was—nor did she care—but Chase talked of nothing else for a full five minutes after the dust settled. If Jed had been curious, he hadn't shown it. One quick flash of his obsidian eyes had promised her that they weren't finished yet, and then he was gone.

Aurelia turned to Chase with a tremulous smile. She was determined to have a good time tonight. To that end, she primed herself to enjoy looking at his soccer team pictures and football trophies, to bear up under an evening of the bland sort of music he liked, music that affected Aurelia like an overdose of divinity fudge.

If nothing else it bought her time, and time was what she desperately needed in order to come to terms with the reality of Jed Dancey. If it weren't for his diabolic resemblance to Jo, she could handle him. As it was, every single time she looked at the man, she began to melt before she remembered. It was like looking at Santa Claus and trying to convince yourself that he was an axe murderer!

The evening with Chase was pleasant enough. They put the finishing touches on the chicken dinner together, and with any other man there might have been at least a mild sort of sexual tension. After all, they were both of age, and Chase lived alone in an A-frame on his own three acres.

There was nothing except the boyish companionship she had come to expect from Chase. There was simply no meeting ground, at least as far as she was concerned. A series of popular vocalists reached a certain decibel level and sustained it throughout the evening until Aurelia felt like strangling them. She hated to try to talk over background music, but then Chase wasn't all that much of a conversationalist unless you happened to be a sports fanatic or a gun collector.

On Saturday she went the early rounds of yard sales with Carol while the twins, Barbara and Allie, opened the shop and kept store for the first hour. Aurelia enjoyed the outing, picking up an item or two for herself that wasn't up to Carol's standards.

Carol, her bulk scarcely fitting under the steering wheel, resumed her argument with Aurelia about learning to drive.

"Carol, I know you're right, but at my age I'm not

sure I could do it. Besides, when will I ever be able to afford a car?"

"When your best seller hits the lists. And quit talking about your age. You know darned well I'm eight years older than you are!" Carol pulled into the shop's parking lot and honked for the twins to come unload their haul into the back room for later refurbishment.

"All right, we all know to what lengths you're willing to go to look young." Aurelia grinned, eyeing the smock-covered bulge. "But honestly, Carol, I wouldn't know where or when or how to start. You understand," she added helplessly.

Carol was the only person who did understand besides her brother, Adam, and neither of them knew the whole truth. After all these years, Aurelia wasn't certain she did, either. She only knew that there were too many closed doors in her life, including the one that had shut her off from the most vital years of her youth and the normal pursuits of a teenage girl—learning to drive, learning to play, learning to be a woman.

Carol grunted as she extricated herself from the driver's seat. "All right, stubborn. I'll have Henry see if he can find you a horse and cart. You can plod along the parkway to Mabry's Mill every Sunday afternoon and let the tourists take your picture."

"If either one of us is going to be a tourist attraction, it'll be you," Aurelia retorted, grinning at the tiny, extremely pregnant brunette. She opened the tailgate and began to struggle with a dubious washstand and a footlocker with possibilities. "I'd give a lot to have seen you carrying the twins."

It was almost six by the time Aurelia locked the door behind her. Using a very un-antique calculator, she had gleefully figured her small commission on the sales she had made. She worked on a combination of minimal wage and infinitesimal commission. The business didn't warrant more, but then her needs weren't all that great, and there'd be the other half of her fee for the biography when it was finished. *If* it was finished, she amended ruefully.

The walk home was always one of the high spots of the day, a far cry from dodging traffic in downtown Atlanta between the office and her bus stop. Aurelia took a shortcut alongside a field of corn that she had watched grow from knee high to six feet tall. Now the sweet, dry smell of the tassels mingled with the subtle fragrance of wild chicory and Queen Anne's lace as she followed the narrow path.

He was waiting for her. She strolled up her path, looking forward to soaking off a few layers of dust and rummaging in the refrigerator for supper. Sigh scampered out to meet her, his predominantly white coat glistening like snow in the long shadows that crept down from the mountain. The yellowish points were the only hint of his exotic paternity aside from the reddish reflection of his blue eye, and now his yellow-striped tail fairly quivered with pleasure as he wrapped around her ankles. She scooped him up and only then caught sight of the lean, broad-shouldered figure reclining in her front porch swing.

Stiffening, she demanded rudely, "What do you want?" Since yesterday she had almost managed to forget the impact the man had on her, but now her spurious defenses went down without his having to fire a shot.

"Good evening, Miss Kenner." The measured pleasantry was at odds with his cool scrutiny, and Aurelia was made painfully aware of the smudges on her yellow shirt and the road dust that stained her white wedges. After a long day spent collecting, dusting, and showing antiques, she was somewhat less than pristine, and the knowledge robbed her of what little self-possession remained.

Sigh wriggled and she dropped him. He darted up onto the porch, where Jed leaned over and lifted him up, and Aurelia was struck again by the incongruous sight of the large, darkly bearded man and the small soft animal. "I've come to take you to dinner," he announced.

Two hours later Aurelia wondered if the man had hypnotic capabilities. He had leveled her arguments without even exerting himself.

"I'm too tired," she had said. "I've been going nonstop since early this morning."

"Then you probably haven't taken time to eat a decent meal."

"I'll get something here," she had argued, and he came back with a reminder of how tired she was.

There had been more along the same lines, but she was sadly outmatched. In the end it was almost a relief to surrender herself into his keeping for the evening. He had waited in the parlor while she bathed and changed into an amber-and-mulberry-patterned crepe with a softly tied neckline. The mulberry kid belt gathered the fullness around her tiny waist, and she reached automatically for the heliotrope cologne that made her think of Jo, then replaced it unopened. She needed wits, not wiles, when it came to dealing with Jed Dancey.

As she gazed out over the valley from the glassed-in balcony of the restaurant, Aurelia's fingers tapped restlessly on the delicate handle of her coffee cup. Wouldn't you know that a stranger, someone from

New York, would come down here and promptly locate the best restaurant within miles! Aurelia hadn't even known of its existence.

"Try some of this peach shortcake, Aurelia. It's outstanding." They had both done justice to their trout and the delectably dressed salad of spinach, mushrooms, and cherry tomatoes.

"No thank you," she said stiffly. Jed Dancey was altogether too charming for her peace of mind when he chose to be—and tonight he chose. Nor could she escape the dichotomy of the senses that shook her each time she looked at him.

He was dressed casually in neutral colors again. Tonight he wore deep gray slacks, a black shirt without a tie, and a khaki-colored jacket of raw linen. Casual, totally unpretentious, and yet the effect was inescapable, unreasonably attractive. The man was simply overwhelming in his own right. Add to that the fact that Aurelia was half in love with a fantasy look-alike and it was no wonder she was reduced to ridiculous stammering whenever he asked her a leading question.

"What happened to your cat's other eye?" The sudden shift to an unexpected topic caught her off guard.

"Sigh?" Blinking, she regained her mental equilibrium and explained how she had come across the two-week-old kitten at a yard sale.

"He was under the steps looking more dead than alive, and I asked about him. The woman said she'd been after her husband to take him down to the river, so I confiscated him and left him with a veterinarian. I was told he had respiratory troubles, a badly infected eye, and he looked like he was moulting dreadfully."

Jed raised a mocking eyebrow. "And you saw something worth rescuing under all that?"

She bristled. "Obviously. You've seen the results. Sigh is intelligent, affectionate, and perfectly healthy now."

"Cy short for Cyclops, I presume."

"No—well, yes, but no," she admitted. "I hadn't gotten around to naming him when I left him at the vet's. He was there almost a week, and whenever I called or came to see him the girls called him Cy, and for some silly reason, I thought it was S-i-g-h, and I liked it. The other version didn't occur to me until someone called him Cyclops." It had been Chase, and she had thought it extremely insensitive of him.

A gleam of amusement crinkled his dark eyes. "It could have been Silas, or Cyrus, or even Psi, as in P-s-i."

Aurelia's tone remained defensive. "Well, it wasn't. It's Sigh, and that's that. Not that he knows the difference," she admitted ruefully. Her long lashes swept her cheeks as she glanced down at her watch. Who would have thought it possible that she could spend this much time in Jed Dancey's company without coming to blows? They had kept the peace by sticking to noncontroversial subjects. His own work, for instance; he had said he was in RCC, and when she asked, he explained patiently that it stood for radio common carrier. Still mystified, she decided not to push her luck. She switched the subject to food. He liked smoked shellfish and had a weakness for coconut cream pie. As for music, he admitted to being partial to Shostakovich and Sibelius, and had an unlikely fondness for Irish folk music, preferably a cappella. In spite of herself, Aurelia was fascinated by the complexity of the man.

Somehow they never got around to discussing books, and not until later did it occur to Aurelia that it might have been a deliberate omission on Jed's part. She grudgingly awarded him a mark for diplomacy.

Jed signaled for the check. "Mustn't forget how tired you are," he murmured as he held her chair for her.

Oddly enough, she felt almost invigorated now. Nor, she admitted with a tinge of disquiet, was it entirely due to the delicious dinner.

It was chilly outside, a hint that autumn was almost upon them. That would mean a steady stream of weekend traffic along the parkway as people flocked to the Blue Ridge Mountains to view the colorful spectacle. Aurelia wasn't looking forward to it.

Jed unlocked the car door and then paused to look down over the valley. Fog shrouded the lower levels, and a three-quarter moon was rising over the worn tops of the ancient mountains. "What's that peak over there?" he asked, standing so close behind her that she could feel the warmth radiating from his leanly muscled body. She was amazed to discover that he wasn't much over six feet. Somehow her initial impression had been of a formidable giant. Max had told her he was enormous, and she still tended to be easily intimidated by size—a failing she was working on with fair success.

"I don't know," she admitted, moving away slightly. "Richmond Knob, perhaps. I thought you knew. I haven't lived in the area but a few months."

"All Barker said was that he had a first-rate writer living in the area. It seems he forgot to mention several things." His tone invited her to share his wry amusement, but Aurelia wasn't confident enough of her situation yet. While it didn't seem as if the man would invite her out to dinner if he planned to strip her of her commission, so to speak, she didn't trust him one bit. She hadn't had much experience with men, and men of Jed Dancey's caliber were few and far between in any woman's experience. She was no avid, placard-waving feminist, but she knew her worth as a writer and it had nothing to do with her sex.

Jed Dancey, on the other hand, was too totally masculine to be without a tinge of chauvinism. Enlightened he may be, but he could no more ignore the fact that she was female than she could ignore the fact that he was male.

And not only male; extremely attractive, *dangerously* attractive male! And there were at least two very good reasons why she had to ignore that fact, one of which was that she was in danger of losing her professional objectivity toward Jocephus. If she wasn't careful she could very well find herself writing about the spirit of one man and the body of another.

It was on the way back to Meadows-of-Dan that Jed asked about her family. "Aren't you a little young to be on your own, talent notwithstanding?"

"I've been on my own for years, Mr. Dancey. I'm not as young as I look."

"Make that Jed, will you? Or I'll go back to calling you A.R." He shot her a quick grin as he maneuvered the heavy car skillfully around a switchback. "You look about seventeen, but I figured you must be a few years older. Tell me, how did you get started writing?"

"It just sort of evolved. I worked for ten years with a firm that published medical periodicals, doing a little bit of everything. Gradually I got to know several agents, and Max was one of them. We used mostly free-lance material, but there were so many complaints from different sources—including Max—about the regular columns by the publisher and the managing editor, that we sort of hit on the idea of their telling me roughly what they wanted to say and letting me say it."

They pulled up in her driveway and Jed switched off the engine and turned to her. By now the moon had risen high enough to cast an indigo glow inside the car. "And the rest is history," he said softly when she fell silent.

"Well, in some cases, biography." She wished the words unsaid as soon as they slipped out.

"As you say. Tell me, Aurelia, when am I going to get to read this manuscript you're guarding so jealously?"

She swallowed convulsively. "Two weeks?" she asked hopefully. "One?"

"Fair enough. Meanwhile, would it help any to visit the old Dancey homeplace? The original house burned down before I inherited the property, but I've rebuilt in about the same location. I needed a break, and besides, I hadn't seen the place since the foundation was laid, so I took off and drove down with a friend. We've been sort of camping out, but the place is fundamentally livable already."

"That would be . . . lovely," she said weakly. It would be lovely if she could manage to concentrate on Jo and leave Jed where he belonged—as merely a signature on a contract that spelled out her security for some months to come.

"Fine. I'll pick you up in the morning. The place is between here and Stuart, by the way . . . not far from what I'm told is the local Lover's Leap."

Before she could locate the latch, Jed was around the car. He held the door for her—one of the nicer aspects of his chauvinism, she admitted—and followed her up to her door.

"I know you're tired so I won't expect to be invited in for a drink," he murmured.

Which was just as well. All she had to offer was a very inexpensive white wine, and she suspected he was a touch above grocery store chic. "Thank you very much, Mister . . . Jed. I had a delightful time, and the dinner was delicious." She winced at the stiffness of her own words. Why did a simple thank you sound so darned sanctimonious?

He laughed softly, a sound vaguely reminiscent of the purring of a lion. "I'll bet you write those very proper little notes my aunt Aggie used to call bread-and-butters, too, don't you? Ten years in the business, did you say? Either you were a child prodigy or you fudged a bit on your resume when you landed the job."

"Good night, Jed," she said firmly. The last thing she needed was for him to start asking personal questions. Not that she had anything to be ashamed of. If the truth were known, she had every reason to be proud of her accomplishments. All the same, she had a niggling suspicion that once started, Jed Dancey wouldn't be satisfied until he had uncovered every item of her past, and there were some that were just too painful to be revived.

Chapter Three

Immediately on entering the small room she called a parlor, Aurelia's eyes lit on the faded oval photograph on the mantel. To her agitated imagination, it seemed as if those darkly ambiguous eyes had taken on a quiet gleam of amusement.

And then it occurred to her that Jed had waited for her in this room for almost half an hour. What must he have thought, seeing the three pictures of his great-great-grandfather displayed as if they were her property? As if Jo belonged to her and not to him? Thank the Lord she'd kept the manuscript and all the other material put away securely. He'd have had a field day tearing apart that last chapter—especially the poem Jo had written to the melody of the thrush's song. How could any two men be so different and look so identical?

She undressed slowly, then hung her dress in the wardrobe and dropped her ivory underthings into the satin laundry bag on the bathroom door. She didn't feel much like rinsing them out tonight. Thoughtfully she creamed her face, and then for the first time in ages she turned her back to the mirror on her dressing table and peered over her shoulder.

To be perfectly honest, she couldn't see any sign of the scars. All the same, she knew they were there. She had lived with them half her life now, and just because they had faded sufficiently not to be visible in the inadequate lighting of her bedroom didn't mean they had magically disappeared. Burns of that magnitude, and the skin grafts required afterward, leave permanent marks. Even if by some miracle her back and the backs of her thighs could be made flawless again, the scars inside her would always remain. She had heard too many stories about people who had large, crooked noses made beautiful by plastic surgery but could never manage to escape the "old nose" personality.

It had been years since she had allowed herself to dwell on it—the fire that had taken the lives of both her parents. Aurelia had accompanied her mother and father to a seminar where her father, head of the philosophy department of a small Alabama college, was a speaker. It had been during the banquet that the fire had broken out, and Aurelia, small for her age, had been torn from her parents by the terrified crowd. She had never seen them again.

The full knowledge of her loss had been kept from her for weeks; under the circumstances it had been easy to do. After she recovered from smoke inhalation, she had been sedated until the worst of her burns had been brought under control. Even afterward, when she had been told the truth, it hadn't seemed quite real. The following period was an endless blur of pain. The loss of her father and mother was at the aching core of it all, but after a while the pure physical agony of endurance had cast a merciful veil over her losses. Her world had been circumscribed by the perimeters of the Burn Center.

It had been a heartbreakingly slow process, the grafting of new skin to her back from the backs of her thighs. Over and over she was told it was a blessing that neither the front of her body nor her face had been touched, but she had felt anything but blessed; it had seemed as if her whole identity had been wrenched from her. She was forced to spend an eternity on her stomach, in spite of all the latest suspension techniques. While she was there, the rest of her high school class graduated and drifted off to college or jobs or marriage. To allay the endless tedium more than anything else, Aurelia studied for and passed the high school equivalency tests.

After that she had read anything and everything she could get her hands on. She had taken out some of her seething hostility and resentment toward fate by ruthlessly correcting every typo and error in spelling and grammar she came across, and in some of the smaller publications they were rampant.

It got to be a joke. And then some of the student nurses began to bring in papers they had written and asked her to look them over. After a while doctors and therapists started challenging her to crossword puzzle duels, and she had won a surprising number of them considering the difference in educational backgrounds. All that had laid the groundwork she was to build on later.

Adam came as often as he could. He had moved to Birmingham four months before the fire. Adam had been twenty-two then, Aurelia almost fifteen. By the time the last of her tedious plastic surgery had been completed and healed sufficiently, she was seventeen and Adam was newly married and living in Birmingham, where he worked in the news room of a local television station. There had been nowhere else to go but to him. The insurance had gone to cover her catastrophic hospitalization and there was nothing left. Her home on Faculty Row had long since been re-occupied by a family of strangers, and her brother was her only living relative.

Adam's new bride resented her. Aurelia hadn't discovered that for over two years. She had been too busy coming to terms with the new reality of her world, too busy trying to figure out what she could do with the rest of her life. At first she had been coddled, but gradually she had taken over almost all the household chores so that Diana could work. Since the house was a rundown five-bedroom post-Victorian with all the attendant inconveniences, she had thought she was making a genuine contribution. Both Diana and Adam were saving every penny to put into remodeling before starting a family.

And then she had overheard them. It was obviously an old issue, one they had discussed before—the fact that since the second month of their marriage they hadn't been alone in their own house for a single day, and even with both of them working it was impossible to feed and clothe three people and have anything left over.

And on, and on, and on. Aurelia, out of sight in the laundry room where she had been pressing the new dress Adam had bought her for her birthday, had been shattered. She had listened to it all and then quietly made up her mind. Diana was right. She was not only putting an unbearable strain on her brother's marriage, she was doing herself a disservice as well—unless she wanted to be an unpaid domestic all her life.

She had gotten in touch with the dearest friend she had made during those unending months at the Burn Center. Dr. Grainger had arranged for her to move to Decatur and board with his widowed sister, paying a reasonable rate while she worked at a small medical publishing firm in Atlanta. Aurelia went about making her arrangements with stoic efficiency. Not for the world would she ever let anyone know she was aware of Adam's helpless frustration, of Diana's bitter resentment, but it would be a long time before she'd be able to forget that conversation. Full of her own frustrations, Diana had raged that she hated her sister-in-law, hated the lack of privacy, and hated the man who was insensitive enough to saddle her with a pathetic wretch who didn't say half a dozen words from one day to the next and was forever scurrying out of sight like some hideous pink mouse.

Aurelia reached for her nightgown and turned out the light. If she had been silent all those years ago, it had only been because she had tried to be as unobtrusive as possible. She was no longer a hideous pink mouse—nor had she ever been, not on the parts that showed. There was nothing at all wrong with her looks. Her hair was long and thick and lustrous, and her complexion, thanks to having followed the doctors' orders and avoided prolonged sunbathing, was flawless. Her features and her figure were sufficiently attractive to have caught the attention of more than one desirable man, and if she didn't happen to be interested, then that was no real tragedy. Diana had unwittingly done her a favor all those years ago in forcing her out. She now had a satisfying career that enabled her to live where she wanted to. She had a home of her own, good friends, and as much social life as she wanted. If it hadn't been for that bitter outburst overheard ten years ago, she'd still be drudging away in someone else's house, growing more miserable and introverted with each passing empty year.

The small sound of Sigh's claws in the bedspread

reached her ears just before she felt his warm weight settle down on her legs. One of the nicest things about cats, she thought drowsily, was that they liked to sleep on people.

Sunday dawned sapphire clear. Aurelia breathed deeply in sharp appreciation as she noticed the wine-red tips of the sourwood and a cluster of pink-tinged dogwood leaves. Last night's mist was this morning's diamond sunburst as it glistened on every spiderweb in sight. She put fresh food and water out for Sigh and his transient friends and selected a plump, mountain-grown peach for her breakfast. Not for the world would she admit her eagerness; nevertheless, at nine she was bathed, brushed, polished, and dressed in a becoming navy scoop-necked blouse with a camel-tan skirt and a harmonizing paisley scarf belt.

No time had been mentioned, and she didn't want to be discovered sitting on the front porch swing, eagerly awaiting Jed's arrival. She forced herself to sit down at the typewriter instead. For the past few days she hadn't done much, and she really liked to get at least ten pages a day under her belt.

"Let's see, where were we, Jo? Observation balloons," she mused, scanning her notes. The use of observation balloons for seeing behind enemy lines had been one of two developments of the period that had intrigued Jo. The other had been photography. The two earlier pictures of him in his uniform might even have been taken by Mathew Brady. "Hard Times is gone," she muttered, finding her place, "and you're up on that moon-eyed roan you liberated from a Yankee cavalryman at Buffalo Gap."

She re-read her last half chapter, checking against the diary and her notes to see if she could include anything more military. Darn it, it had started already! She could practically feel him peering over her shoulders, criticizing her every word!

The crunch of a car on the gravel outside actually came as a relief. After putting Sigh outside, she checked to see that the stove was off and grabbed up her purse and a shawl. She'd just as soon not lay herself open for a review at the moment. He had said he'd give her a week but she didn't care to push her luck.

"Good morning," she called out from the porch with determined cheerfulness. The air smelled like crisp mountain apples—it was undoubtedly full of the proper sort of ions. Now, after the painful self-evaluation of the past night, she felt as ready as she'd ever be to deal with Jed Dancey as one reasonable adult to another. On a businesslike level. Today's outing, she reminded herself, came under the heading of research.

By the time she reached the car he still hadn't bothered to get out and hold her door. How quickly one became accustomed to such niceties, liberated or not, she thought wryly. She opened her own door and swept her skirt under her as she slid inside, and only then did she see that the driver was not Jed Dancey. The car had been parked with the passenger side toward the house, and with the low angle of the roof, she simply hadn't noticed.

"Morning," came the brief greeting from the sophisticated woman who slapped the steering wheel impatiently with a pair of pigskin driving gloves. "Jed sent his regrets. He couldn't make it. I'm delegated to show you the works."

Aurelia was more dismayed at her reaction than at the actual change of plans. Why should she be so disappointed? She was going to see Jocephus's homeplace, wasn't she? And without the disconcerting presence of his look-alike relative.

"Well, thanks. I'm Aurelia Kenner. I guess Jed told you I'm doing his great-great-grandfather's biography."

The woman scratched two bits' worth of gravel off the driveway as she accelerated. "How do you do. I'm Rae Craver. You're not at all what I expected, you know." She reached the intersection of Highway 58 in a cloud of road dust and turned toward Stuart with scarcely a look in either direction. Aurelia gripped the edges of the leather-covered bucket seat and took a deep breath. Evidently Miss Craver considered country road traffic no threat at all. Aurelia only prayed she wouldn't round a curve and come upon a hay bailer plodding its laborious way from one field to another.

"How'd you get the job?" the other woman asked after several minutes of silence. She seemed to be a superb driver in spite of a certain unnerving lack of caution.

"You mean writing? Through my agent. Jed read my last book and liked it. And the fact that I lived here didn't hurt." She was dying to ask who Rae Craver was and what her connection to Jed Dancey was, but she couldn't think of a way to phrase it that wouldn't sound overly curious—which she was. Desperately so. Under the guise of watching the landscape roll past, she studied the dark-haired woman. She was as dark as Aurelia was light, with an elegant cut that allowed her short glossy hair to swing freely. She looked tall but it was hard to judge. Her clothes were expensive, and her profile was both beautiful enough and arrogant enough to be thoroughly intimidating. Aurelia only hoped she was Jed's sister—or someone else's wife.

"Satisfied?"

"Oh, sorry," Aurelia muttered, caught in the act. "Jed never mentioned that he was—that you were—" She broke off helplessly.

"There's a lot Jed never mentions, even to me. For instance, he never mentioned that you were a little Alice in Wonderland type with nothing to say for yourself."

"I have plenty to say for myself," Aurelia asserted quickly. Only most of it goes unsaid, she added silently. She was great at mental dialogue and smart afterthoughts.

Rae grinned, looking slightly less intimidating. "He'll walk all over you, you know. The only reason we've lasted so long is that I stand up to him. He respects me as an equal as well as a woman, and believe me, in these days that's what counts."

Which told her absolutely nothing. "Is it very far?" Aurelia asked, trying for an attitude of careless sophistication instead of the plain old garden variety envy she actually felt. Rae Craver was everything she herself had striven to be over the past ten years.

"Not far. We turn off just past the next curve and it's a quarter mile or so around on the other side of the hill—Dancey Hill, I think it's called in these parts." She flashed a quick, speculative look over her shoulder, and Aurelia noticed for the first time that her eyes, an unusually pale shade of blue, seemed almost expressionless. Beautiful, though. The lashes were thick and long and dark enough to look almost artificial.

They turned off onto a steep grade and Rae geared the powerful engine down accordingly. And that was just one more thing that made Aurelia feel totally inept. Everybody drove in this day and age! Children around these parts drove tractors before they were as high as the hind wheels. First thing in the morning she was going to investigate taking a driver's training course.

Second thing. Tomorrow started her full-time work at the shop. Carol was nearing term and Henry wouldn't allow her to be on her feet more than an hour or two at a time. But at least she'd look up a driving school and make the appointment.

"*Voilà!*" Rae exclaimed, pulling onto a paved circle rimmed with yew trees.

Aurelia looked around for the house. The original had burned to the ground, of course, but Jed said the restoration was almost complete. "Where?"

"Up there," the other woman told her, obviously enjoying herself.

Aurelia leaned out the car door to look up the sheer cliff and she saw it. At least she saw something. A massive edifice of rock and glass that seemed to grow out of the side of the mountain. Turning back into the car, she faltered, "I thought we were going to the original Dancey homeplace."

"This is the original Dancey homeplace. The original *Jed* Dancey homeplace, that is. How do you like it? Jed hired a top architect, then proceeded to tell him what to do and how to do it. Typical of the man. He'll drive me crazy one of these days, if I don't watch it. Come on, we'll drive up the rest of the way. I just wanted to give you a preview. Looks terrific from here, doesn't it?"

During the few minutes it took to finish the climb along a narrow paved driveway lined with mountain laurel and rhododendron, Aurelia sorted through the bits and pieces of information she had picked up from Max and Jed about the Dancey property. The old homestead had burned, but it was being restored.

Or was it being replaced? Surely no discerning

person would replace a lovely old antebellum home with such an aggressively modern structure. It would be totally out of keeping with the spirit of the place.

Rae pulled the car up under a low-roofed porte cochere attached to a solid rock wall and opened her door. "Come on, I'm ready for coffee. What about you?"

With one last desperate glance over her shoulder, Aurelia followed her. She had half hoped to see a tall, white-columned structure across the small clearing, but there was nothing to see but woods and rocks and a cloudless sky.

The massive front door was painted Chinese red. The contrast with the weathered gray native stone was striking and, she had to admit, attractive. The interior was even more striking. It was practically devoid of furniture.

"Kitchen through here. Wander around if you want to. Jed's around somewhere." Rae disappeared behind a monolith of stone that could have housed a family of cliff dwellers in the gaping fireplace.

So Jed was here. So why couldn't he have picked her up? A lack of interest? A particular point he wanted to get across? Maybe he had simply slept late.

Her unruly mind wondered fleetingly if he had slept alone. The references Rae had made to their relationship were somehow both pointed and ambiguous.

Aurelia's footsteps sounded overloud on the slate and hardwood floor as she crossed to gaze out a glass wall over the valley. The view was spectacular, both interior and exterior: glass walls, some with mitered-glass corners, separated by stone piers. Obviously no one here suffered from acrophobia. At night one could probably see the lights of Martinsville. She turned away and glanced at the single piece of furniture—an enormous sofa covered in gray-sueded pigskin. A small smile lifted the corners of her mouth. It was perfect for the room and perfect for the man.

She glanced into a pair of back-to-back bathrooms, then opened the next door and closed it again immediately. It was furnished with one rumpled double bed and an open suitcase. Her hand was on the knob of the next door when it opened and she was unexpectedly confronted by the solid wall of Jed's bronzed and furry chest.

"Oh, I'm—"

"Good Lord!" he exclaimed, reaching for her as she backed away. As he caught her upper arm, something clattered to the floor and she looked down, startled to see a crutch lying between them. Her eyes moved to the feet that were only inches from hers—one bare, exceedingly masculine, and about a size twelve, the other covered by an Ace bandage of an incongruous shade of pink that left only the toes protruding.

Before either of them could speak, Rae's voice sang out. "Coffee! Come and get it!"

Aurelia retrieved the crutch over Jed's protests. "Forget it! It's not necessary."

She held it awkwardly, wondering where and how to attach it to him again. He was shirtless, and all she could see were acres of glistening skin, like tan satin, and the crisp dark hairs that swirled into two flat circles before narrowing down his lean, hard stomach. Never in all her life had she been so overwhelmingly aware of the difference between the sexes. "Here, you'd better do it," she squeaked, poking the thing at him and turning away.

His laughter raked down her spine, and color flooded her face as she all but ran toward Rae and safety.

Over coffee she learned that Jed had twisted his ankle badly only that morning. "I thought I'd scout

out Jo's cave for you, see if it was still accessible. I had a general idea of where to look, but I hadn't counted on the rocks being so damned slippery with dew."

Aurelia's eyes widened at the thought of what might have happened. There were some drops around this place that could easily have been fatal. "Are you sure it's only a sprain?"

"Not even that, according to Dr. Craver here," Jed said dryly. "I hobbled back up the hill and got her out of bed and she drove in to Stuart on a mercy mission. Managed to locate the bandage, a couple of ice packs, and some aspirin. The crutch was strictly her idea, but after discovering how unexpectedly mortal I am, I didn't turn it down." He grinned wryly. "Living on the vertical is going to take a bit of getting used to. I've spent too many years on flat concrete and thick carpeting."

Aurelia held her coffee cup in both hands and stared unseeingly through the wide window. What could she say? Jed had obviously been attempting to do her a favor when he fell. As it was, she probably wouldn't get to see the cave, wouldn't get to explore the Dancey property, and as for a restored home-place, she was increasingly certain that this was the only house Jed had built here. On such a slope there weren't all that many suitable, accessible sites.

Rae's shapely bare legs intruded on her vision as the other woman casually crossed one over the other. The three of them were seated on the sofa facing the window. The coffee things were on a plank resting on two wooden nail kegs.

"You're a doctor, Rae?"

"Good Lord, no!" The brunette laughed shortly. "I know enough first aid to tell the difference between a sprain and a break, but actually I'm a management analyst. My office is one floor below Jed's and I've been after him for ages to let me clean up his corporate act for him." She rested a flawlessly manicured hand on Jed's thigh and Aurelia averted her eyes. It was as if the nerve endings in that hand were hers, as if the feel of those hard muscles beneath the restless fingers burned into her own consciousness.

She couldn't think of a single thing to say. Somehow, with the space on the deeply cushioned sofa equally divided, Jed and Rae were a pair, and she was odd man out. Her mind flew back to the years when she had tried to make herself small so as not to intrude on Adam and Diana any more than necessary.

"I—um—if you don't mind, then, I'll just wander around outside. Is this the site of the original house?"

Jed moved restlessly and Rae's hand dropped from his thigh. "Just about a hundred feet farther east you'll see a heap of rocks and one standing chimney. That's all that's left. As a matter of fact, I understand that the only part of the original house was the rock work and an old freestanding kitchen. The rest had fallen in years ago, and what burned was the remains of the old kitchen."

Rae stood up and collected the three mugs. She was tall, as Aurelia had suspected. Five feet ten, at least. Standing between them, Aurelia felt Lilliputian. She wished she'd worn higher heels, even though they wouldn't be exactly the thing to go clambering around over the rocks. She had envisioned wandering through the rooms of a newly restored, high-ceilinged house and mentally furnishing it with four-posters and blanket chests and Chippendale mahogany.

"Thank goodness you had sense enough to have the necessities of life installed first," Rae stated, striding around the rock divider. "A dishwasher and a microwave oven. How did the pioneer women manage without them?"

Aurelia was at the door when Jed called to her. "Hey, Aurelia? Stick close to the house, will you? This thing"—he indicated his injured ankle—"is only a twist, not even a sprain. I'll be in shape in a few days to give you the guided tour. I'd hate like the devil to have to crawl out and fish you off a ledge somewhere. You don't strike me as the outdoor type."

"I'm perfectly capable of looking after myself," she retorted, rather more sharply than she intended. It wasn't Jed's fault that she felt inadequate around so much self-confident physical perfection. Even with one foot wrapped in flesh-pink elastic, he threatened her composure by his sheer masculine vitality. Before she had much more to do with Jed Dancey, she'd better cultivate a few basic skills—not the least of which was keeping her mind under strict control at all times.

She gave up on trying to locate the cave. It wasn't all that important. None of this was, actually. She told herself as she picked her way through milkweed and goldenrod that given the proper materials, she was perfectly capable of writing a comprehensive biography of a man without having to tread in his footsteps. Nor did it occur to her that her attitude toward Jo's biography was undergoing a subtle change.

Before Rae drove her home, Jed invited her to bring her typewriter and work on location if the idea appealed to her.

The idea not only didn't appeal—it frightened the bejabbers out of her! "As a matter of fact, I won't be doing too much writing for the next week or so," she said rather cautiously. "I promised to work at the shop full time until my employer's mother comes to take over. She's expecting a baby any day now." She glanced quickly away from the sight of Jed's lowering brows and blurted nervously, "Carol—not her mother. The baby, I mean."

Rae, waiting with ill-disguised impatience outside the door, said, "I hope to God you write a little more coherently than you talk. It wouldn't make it, even as stream-of-consciousness."

"I'm paying you to write that biography," Jed reminded her grimly.

"And I'm writing it! Only I do have another job, you know," Aurelia snapped. "I'm not independently wealthy, nor is the sort of writing I do all that lucrative!" If he wanted to take that as a dig at the size of the advance he had offered, then let him. It was no more than the truth.

"If you need more money, then say so," he grumbled, lurching slightly as the door swung under his weight.

At the reminder of his handicap, Aurelia relented slightly. "I don't. But thank you for today, and for the coffee," she added grudgingly as she turned away. Her lips tightened ominously as his laughter followed her to the car, and she jerked her skirt viciously clear and slammed the door.

His words came clearly through the open window of the car. "Bread and butter again, Aurelia? I'll bet Mama was proud as punch of her shiny, ruffled little lady, wasn't she?"

Chapter Four

The third time Aurelia forgot to add on the sales tax she knew she was going to have to take herself in hand. There was absolutely no reason why she couldn't apply herself to making a modest profit for Carol and an even more modest one for herself. At the moment, her own was shrinking rapidly. The forgotten tax, a perfectly good Imari creamer dropped and broken; two things to be deducted from her salary at the end of the week, and this was only Monday.

By the middle of the week she was bone tired. As fall approached, traffic along the parkway increased, and the drop-in trade picked up to more than twice its normal level. She was often open until almost seven, and as she was too tired to post the books, that meant coming in early the following morning. And if she was there and customers drove up, she simply couldn't turn them away.

Jed called on Wednesday night. "Where the hell have you been? I've been trying to reach you for two days!"

"I've been at the shop and here at home. Did you need me for something?" She was standing in the middle of the floor in her stocking feet, her belt hanging from its loops and her hair unknotted and tumbling around her shoulders. The phone had started ringing as she came in the front door and she was so tired she had almost ignored it.

"You sound terrible. What's wrong?"

"You don't sound particularly great yourself, Mr. Dancey. And now, if that's all, I'll say good night. It's been a long day." She waited for the outburst, unable to bring herself to hang up on him. "Well, damn and blast," she muttered plaintively when her ears were assaulted by the crash of the other phone being slammed into the receiver.

She was almost too tired to eat, but she was too hungry not to. Chase might have provided a solution but he had left Monday morning for Asheville. The twins started school next week, too. They were caught up in a round of last-minute social activities and weren't able to help out much in the shop. Today she hadn't even had relief at lunchtime. Carol had called to say that they couldn't make it and to insist that Aurelia close the doors and take an hour or so off, but somehow the afternoon had progressed and she hadn't gotten around to it.

Her stomach had reminded her of the skipped meal long before the last customer went out with her trivets, her butter churn, and a really good Liberty Boy doll. Henry had been by and left a basket of tomatoes and okra on her porch. She didn't feel up to frying okra, but a tomato sandwich and a cup—a potful—of rich coffee would be heavenly. The tomatoes were stunted now, the last of the crop, their sweetness concentrated just under the tough skins.

She soaked first, with a handful of herbal bath salts thrown in for whatever obscure benefits it might bring. She could do with any boost—even a psychological one. Sigh came to perch on the rim of the basin and watch her, his single eye unblinkingly attendant.

"What, no dinner guests? Where's that nubile tabby I saw you with last night?" She pulled the plug and stood up, snatching the towel higher as the kitten swatted its fringe. There was really no point in getting dressed—she'd probably fall asleep at the table. She reached for her nightgown and then, following an impulse she didn't even try to comprehend, she got out a voluminous Indian cotton print instead. It was a favorite and had seen long and arduous wear, but it was soft and comfortable—and safe.

She grimaced. Just the sound of Jed's voice over the phone had rattled her enough to send her scuttling for the dubious security of a long-sleeved, high-necked, completely opaque garment. Call it delayed adolescence, midlife crisis, or early senility; whatever it was, she'd better pull herself together before the next time she saw him.

She had never been able to tell the difference between the sounds of tree frogs, crickets, and cicadas, but tonight the chorus was sufficiently loud to blanket the sound of the approaching car. The first she knew of a visitor was the solid thud of a closing door. It was definitely not Henry's pickup.

Reluctantly leaving her coffee honeyed but uncreamed, she reached the front door just as Jed's hand was lifted to knock. She had no trouble recognizing him. Who else had shoulders that threatened to spread the doorjamb? Besides, if the truth were known, she wasn't really all that surprised.

"Good evening," she murmured stiffly, willing her voice to steadiness as she held open the door.

"Good evening," he echoed, his greeting pure mockery. "Now, would you mind telling me just why you've been avoiding me all week long?"

That was the wrong approach. "Avoiding you! Was it avoiding you to answer the phone just now and have it slammed down in my ear? Was it avoiding you to open the door and let you inside my house when, quite frankly, you're the last man on earth I want to see right now?" She was rashly, rudely overreacting. Knowing it, she was still helpless to do anything about it. Dredging up all the composure her years, if not her experience, could provide, she made herself gesture to the settee.

"Would you care for a cup of coffee? I was about to have a sandwich. If you haven't eaten yet, I'll be glad to make you one, too."

Some of the aggressiveness seemed to drain from him then. His eyes swept over the softly faded rust, ivory, and violet print gown that swept the tops of her bare feet, and then returned to her scrubbed face. He looked almost as tired as she felt. Once more he was wearing the open-weave fisherman's jersey with the close-fitting black jeans he had worn that first day she had met him, but this time she saw beyond the piratical surface to something more complex, something far less obvious, and at the same time, far more dangerous.

"I'd like that fine," he said softly. "And coffee, did you say? What I'd really like is milk, if you have any. I've been living on coffee all week."

He watched her as she broiled bacon and made a stack of bacon and tomato sandwiches, his steady scrutiny grating on her nerves until they began to fray. She poured milk for Jed and coffee for herself. The caffeine might or might not be a good idea; she was too tired to stay awake and too stimulated to go to sleep.

Jed devoured three sandwiches while Aurelia polished off one thick one. There was something insidiously beguiling about sitting across the small kitchen table from a man. No, not just any man. Chase didn't affect her at all, but sharing the informal intimacy with Jed, having her knees occasionally bump against his, was enough to render her all but witless. As soon as they finished, she put the dishes in to soak and herded her guest into the parlor. At least there she could keep him a safe distance away.

"How's the biography coming?"

"Fine," she parried cautiously. "How's your ankle?"

"Good as new. It was only wrenched. Hurt like the devil for a few hours, but no permanent harm done. About the book—"

She broke in irritably. "I told you I had to work in the shop this week. By the time I get home I'm too tired to do more than glance over my notes. Anything I wrote under these conditions would only have to be rewritten. I know that much from experience."

The light from the table lamp limned the side of his face, throwing into prominence the sharp cheekbones, the slightly crooked bridge of his nose, and his high, intelligent forehead. He was Jo—and yet not Jo. The looks were essentially the same, but in Jed's case the personality far outweighed the physical arrangement of his features.

"What? I'm sorry . . ." She had been caught woolgathering.

"I said I want you to give up your job and move to my place and spend full time on the biography," Jed said with perfect equanimity.

Aurelia came to her feet in one fluid movement. "You *what?* Are you out of your mind? Look, Mr. Dancey, you hired my skills as a writer; you didn't buy me! For all you know I could be working on half a dozen books at once. Lots of writers do, you know. Unless you're turning out best sellers on a regular basis, it's a pretty iffy way to make a living."

"Are you?"

"Am I what, turning out best sellers?"

Biting off an impatient oath, he said, "Working on anything else!"

"No. That's why I have to work part-time at the shop—Carol's Antiques. Aside from helping her out, it helps me make ends meet."

"Oh, hell. Look, I don't have the least idea what a writer's supposed to earn. After the first meeting with Barker, my lawyer handled all the contract arrangements with him. I assumed it was more than fair, since he seemed eager enough to sign."

Darn it, how had they gotten off on this subject? Aurelia sighed heavily. "It was. Frankly, I'm not all that experienced a writer, and it was a work-for-hire deal. It's not as if you were going to make a bundle on the book, anyway. In fact, I don't know why you didn't just have photocopies of the diaries and letters made as they are and let it go at that. What do you propose to do with it once it's finished?"

Jed took out a thin cigar, glanced around him at the lack of ashtrays, and put it back in his pocket. Aurelia left the room without a word and returned a moment later with an unmated Wedgwood saucer.

"Go ahead. It's just that I don't."

He lighted up and blew out a thin stream of fragrant smoke as if relieved to have something to do with his hands. He was totally out of place in her small, prim room, and he was obviously as aware of that fact as she was.

"I guess a drink would be too much to ask," he suggested hopefully.

"After three sandwiches and almost a quart of milk?" she marveled. "If you can take a four-dollar-a-gallon white wine that's been opened for three months, then you're welcome to it. I cook with it and I'm afraid that's the best I can offer."

His lips twisted expressively. "I'll manage without, thanks. I'd manage better if you didn't ask awkward questions."

What questions? Aurelia wondered. Aloud she said, "I can't imagine your being thrown by any questions, awkward or not. You'd simply ignore them."

"Normally, yes, but under the circumstances I guess you rate an answer as to why I commissioned you to do the book. You see . . ." He reached out a hand to knock the ash from his cigar and Aurelia followed the gesture, unwillingly admiring the strength and grace of his hands. She instinctively judged a man by his hands, his eyes, and his shoes. Jed passed on all counts.

"Until a couple of years ago I didn't even know about Jocephus. Then, when a distant cousin died leaving no closer heirs, I inherited the Dancey property, a tax lien, and a box of personal papers. I was involved in some expansion at the time, so I turned the details over to my lawyer. It was some time before I got a chance to come down to look the place over." He tugged thoughtfully at his beard in a way Aurelia had often imagined Jo's doing, and she caught her breath. Her fingers curled as if they were experiencing the texture of the glossy, vital growth.

"Go on," she prompted a little breathlessly.

"To tell the truth, it slipped my mind—my inheritance. Remember, I'd never heard of these Virginia Danceys. As far as I knew I was strictly New York—

and a pretty tough product, at that. For reasons I won't go into, family ranked pretty far down on my priority list." There was no discernible emotion in the words; they were strictly informative. Aurelia wondered what lay behind the steely composure of such a man. "So here I was, ready to claim my heritage: a hundred acres or so of unusable land, mostly vertical, a heap of burned-out rubbish, and one standing chimney. I understand any valuable bottomland had all been sold off years back. Not a whole lot to show for a hundred and fifty years of Dancey stewardship, was it?" His eyes strayed and Aurelia followed his gaze. He was studying Jo's picture on her mantel.

"Not a lot, no," she murmured, her thoughts fleetingly touching on her own circumstances. Was she any better off than he was as far as family was concerned?

"No," he echoed thoughtfully. "Well, I glanced through the papers. A few bills, a few picture postcards from Luray Caverns, signed Aunt Tilly—that was about it, except for the bundle of diaries and letters and the pictures of old Jocephus. According to the lawyer who handled the estate, my great-aunt Tilly had intended to do something with them, but she'd kept putting it off and then one day it was too late. She was gone—the unknown cousin was gone. End of the line." He leaned forward, resting his arms on his thighs and studying his clasped hands. "It occurred to me, Aurelia, that it was a damned shame for a man to have no more to show for having lived than Jocephus had. Evidently I'm the only one left. I've got no brothers or sisters. My mother ran off when I was ten and my dad died a couple of years later. I hustled myself an education, and since then I've been too busy building a business to think about what's laughingly called posterity." The word was disparagingly spoken, but the glance he shot her was oddly unsure.

"Who's laughing?" she asked softly. Silently she willed him to continue.

"Hmmm. Well, at any rate, I got to thinking about the matter of continuity. Don't laugh. For some reason it just seemed important not to let things simply end there. Five generations ago a man cared enough to write down his thoughts and feelings, and now, somehow, the whole burden has landed on my shoulders. Maybe I'm nuts. Maybe I'd just been working too hard for too long, or maybe I'd had too much to drink at the time. At any rate, I felt obligated to do something about it. I flew down last March and looked the property over again, contacted an architect and told him what I wanted done. We went a few rounds over it, I don't mind telling you," he added in an aside, his long, obsidian eyes gleaming with amusement. "Once I got the actual construction under way, I set about finding someone to take on Jocephus's papers and do something with them. Enter A. R. Kenner."

Aurelia glanced at the mantel, where the ornate black metal clock with its brace of silver gargoyles gazed back silently. Propped against it was the oval picture of a darkly bearded man in a Confederate uniform. "There's still a lot of information I don't have, you know." She set the bentwood rocker in motion and tucked one bare foot up under her. "That's why I've approached it the way I have instead of chronologically. I've been able to piece together a lot of Jo's earlier life from his reminiscences, but there are gaps. For instance, I don't know the date of his marriage or the birth of his children—or even how many he had. He seldom mentions them, and that's odd, don't you think? Maybe when he wrote the diaries, he and Mary were newly married. Goodness knows they sound like it."

Turning to look directly at the man across from her, she conquered a ridiculous impulse to ask him all the questions she had wanted to ask Jo. The resemblance was disconcerting, even now that she had more or less come to terms with it. Instead she said, "Roots are in style now, probably because we're such a transient society. At any rate, one of these days your own children will appreciate all you've done."

It was a deliberately leading question, but he chose to ignore it. Instead he asked, "What about your roots, Aurelia? What sort of soil did they grow in?"

She stirred restlessly. On the verge of offering to make a fresh pot of coffee, she was sidetracked by the phone. "Excuse me," she muttered, jumping up to hobble across the room with a feeling of having escaped something. Needles and pins shot through the foot she had been sitting on.

"Aurelia, it's Chase."

"Chase! I wasn't expecting to hear from you so soon." She wriggled her toes experimentally.

"Hey, look, I'll be coming back for another load of stuff this weekend. How about saving Saturday night for me. I want to talk to you about Jan. I've seen her already, and I'm more screwed up than ever. Please . . . say you will."

She said she would. What else could she say? With Jed sitting there openly listening to every word on her end of the conversation, she wanted only to get off the line. Somehow he was beginning to insinuate himself into her personal life as deeply as his great-great-grandfather had done, only this time there was a difference. She didn't take time to examine that difference, but all her instincts urged her to chalk a magic circle around herself and keep him on the other side.

"All right, Chase, I'll see you Saturday about seven. 'Bye for now."

Jed stood up as she turned away from the phone and her eyes flew to him apprehensively. An hour ago she had been exhausted. She hadn't wanted to see him, and now she didn't want him to leave. Her mind and her emotions were on a par—both about as steady as a weathervane!

"How is young Lochinvar?" he jibed, and then, before she could object, he asked, "Doesn't this place ever give you claustrophobia? Come on, let's go try out that swing of yours," he grumbled, flexing his shoulders as if they had been physically cramped.

"It's late. I was really planning to go to bed early," she parried.

"At nine o'clock? Honey, there's only one reason to go to bed at this hour, and I seriously doubt you're issuing an invitation at this point in our relationship." His eyes were gleaming, his grin a wicked flash of white against his dark beard.

Aurelia's head swung back defensively. She was going to have to learn not to let herself be disarmed by his rugged, offbeat sort of charm. "You're being unnecessarily crude, Mr. Dancey," she said coolly. "If you'll let me know how to reach you, I'll mail you a copy of the first draft when it's finished. You can make any—"

He caught her by the arm, moving her the few steps to the minuscule foyer. "What is it about you, Aurelia Kenner? You're an extremely attractive woman in your own way, but you act like something out of the last century. Hell, even your face still looks as if nobody had lived in it. Is that the problem? Mama's little lady isn't allowed to play with the big boys?"

She froze, jerking her arm against his grip. It wasn't a painful grip—merely unbreakable. "Jed, will you please—"

"Unhand you?" he teased.

In spite of herself, Aurelia thawed slightly. He was right, of course. No matter how hard she tried to loosen up, she always gave the impression of being reserved, if not actually repressed.

"Come on, sit with me for a few more minutes and then I'll leave you to your virginal bower. There are still a few points to be cleared up." He urged her to the oak swing and sat down beside her.

Aurelia held her feet off the floor until he had set the pace, and then, as the rhythmic creak of the chain broke the late summer silence, the last vestige of resentment subsided, to be replaced by a tremulous sort of wariness. She could barely see him—just the outline of his bearded profile against the parlor window. It wouldn't take much imagination to pretend she was sitting out here with Jo.

And that sort of foolishness was going to have to stop! Look at where it had already got her: to the point where she couldn't look at a man—at Jed—without thinking of certain passages of Mary's letters and wondering what it would feel like to have a man's hands—Jed's hands—"climbing the hills to discover the sweetest berries, wandering past the little round pond, over the pasture and down into the valley to where the thick bush grew, to plant a tree that would spring up wondrous tall."

"Better stick to hog butchering," she muttered under her breath, and Jed turned to her inquiringly.

"Hmmm? By the way, you didn't tell me how you liked my house," he prompted. His arm extended along the back of the swing so that Aurelia could feel the warmth of it against her neck.

She sat up straighter. "I . . . it's overwhelming. Not at all what I was expecting."

"You were expecting maybe honeysuckle and magnolias climbing up white columns, or maybe a quaint little log cabin? That was then, honey—if ever. This is now."

"I wasn't criticizing," she muttered defensively. His arm brushed against the coil of hair she had hastily bundled up at the back of her neck, and without being obvious about it she didn't know how she could ask him to remove it. His stated opinion of her wasn't very flattering, as it was; no point in underlining it.

"I wasn't criticizing when I said this place of yours gives me claustrophobia, either. I happen to need plenty of space around me. You need a snug little nest to hide away in. Just the difference in personalities, I guess." The observation was completely impersonal and yet it hurt. It made her seem cowardly—as if she didn't have what it took to meet the real world head on, and that simply wasn't true. Look at where she was today, living life on her own terms. That didn't come free in a box of popcorn. It took—what was that word Max used? It took moxie!

Jed's hand came down on her shoulder, his long fingers sliding the fabric against her skin in slow, sensuous strokes. "I didn't mean to hurt your feelings, girl. Maybe I'm just thinking out loud, trying to figure out what you're all about." His voice seemed softer, lacking its usual high-energy delivery—or maybe she was getting used to it. "You're a new experience for me. Remember, I was expecting to deal with A. R. Kenner. Miss Aurelia takes some getting used to."

"You didn't hurt my feelings, Jed," she said quietly, reacting to his touch with a breath-catching awareness. "Your sort of house is just right for you, mine is for me. As you said, we're completely different kinds of people."

"And some of those differences are quite intriguing," he murmured. Using her shoulder as leverage, he quickly turned her so that she half fell across his lap, her face momentarily burrowed in the hollow of his shoulder.

"Jed, don't—" she protested angrily, lifting her face to glare at him, and he silenced her protest in the most efficient way possible.

As sweet and compelling as his mouth was, Aurelia's defenses were instinctive; the barriers flew up automatically and locked into place. Teeth clamped tightly together, she sealed her lips against his invasion, trembling rigidly with the effort to resist. He was physically stronger; she couldn't fight him on that level, but her will was more than a match for his.

Within moments, though, the doubts began to seep in. Her will might be a match for his, but was it a match for this wild, bittersweet yearning that was infiltrating her very bones? She wasn't armed against this! The very foundation of her carefully ordered existence was threatened by a force that was totally alien to her.

Jed's hands were warm and hard on her body, tracing the delicate bones of her shoulder, shaping the concavity of her waist, moving inexorably upward. And then he was cradling her breast in his palm as tenderly as if it were a baby bird. She felt her flesh respond to his touch. The feel of his beard and mustache on her face was hopelessly erotic, and her fingers curled against an overwhelming desire to burrow into the dark pelt she had seen that day when she had surprised him at his bedroom door.

Steely fingers gripped her chin and tugged downward. "Open your mouth, you thorny little rosebud. Don't be so stingy," he growled against her lips.

Sensing the insidious power of his words, her mind frantically rejected them. She fought against the intoxicating wine that was beginning to flow through her body, warming her, melting her, thawing great blocks of ice. *Thorns and roses*—words Jo might have used. But Jo was kind and loving and understanding. Jo could never hurt her as this man could; that much she knew instinctively, for the hurt was starting already. The clash of mind against emotion, of fantasy against relentless reality, was tearing her apart.

Jed gained the prize he sought and his tongue invaded the vulnerable warmth of her mouth. Aurelia heard a low whimper escape her. The taste of him, the scent of him, acted on her nervous system like a drug, dulling her powers of reason.

"Jed, please—" she managed to gasp when his lips rolled away from her mouth. His breath was sweet on her face as he answered her hoarsely.

"Jed, please *what*, Aurelia? Tell me what you want from me."

She twisted and managed to pull away from him. He released her reluctantly, and she was embarrassed to discover that he seemed to have recovered himself much quicker than she had. Her own pulse was beating like the wings of a startled hummingbird and her breath was clearly audible.

When she could manage it, she said, "That was totally uncalled for!" And then she thought, Oh, God, he's so right about me! I sound like something out of a nineteenth-century melodrama.

Jed sighed heavily and leaned back against the corner of the swing. "Okay, honey. One outraged protest registered and duly noted," he said tiredly.

"Forget it. Just call it honeysuckle madness. Meanwhile, to get back to business . . ."

The feel of his muscular thigh brushing against hers, the scent of his body mingled with the powdery sweetness of wild autumn clematis, joined to form a potent intoxicant. A flush of hot color rose to Aurelia's face as she fought against a rush of unlikely urges. One unsteady hand lifted to the cascade of hair at her nape just as the last hairpin gave way. She poked at it vainly and then gave up, allowing its weight to fall heavily to her shoulders.

"The—the book . . . I should be through at the shop by Saturday. Carol—Carol Claiborn, that is—I work for her, you know. It's her shop," Oh, Lord, Rae was right; she *was* incoherent! Taking a deep, steadying breath, she gathered what little composure she could scrape together and did her best to ignore the solid, virile warmth emanating from the man beside her. "Carol Claiborn and her husband," she continued, simulating a calmness she was far from feeling, "own both the shop and this house, and since Carol's having a baby any day now, I agreed to help out until her mother gets here."

"So?" His voice sounded utterly disinterested, and she winced. So he was already bored with her; at least he could have the courtesy not to show it.

Aurelia made herself go on in an unemotional tone while all in the world she wanted to do was crawl off somewhere dark and safe to lick her wounds. "So I'll be able to devote full time to the book after that. Well practically full time. I'll still work a few mornings a week and an occasional Saturday," she replied evenly.

He stood up, setting the swing into violent motion. "I've wasted too damned much time as it is. Look,

Aurelia, I didn't get where I am by drifting along with the prevailing tides. By trial and error I worked out a foolproof system. First I decide what I want, and then when, where, and how I want it. Then I set about making it happen in the most efficient way possible. I've decided the book should be done by the end of the year. If that means working full time on it from now until then, then that's what you'll do." He glared at her for a full minute and then went on to remind her that she had signed a contract.

"Who do you think you are, the king of I-am? *I* decided this, *I* decided that! Well, let me tell you something, your highness, *I* gave Carol my word," Aurelia seethed, "and that's as binding as any contract."

She struggled to overcome a wobbling chin. So much for romance! If that didn't accomplish his ends, it was back to threats and coercion!

"Are you in shape to take on a breach of contract suit?"

The warmth that had risen to her face suddenly fled, leaving her feeling shaken and cold. "You wouldn't! Not over something so—so petty!"

"Don't try me. I wasn't sold on having you do the job in the first place, remember, and so far you haven't produced a single bit of evidence that you've even started the project. For all I know, you make a practice of accepting advances for books that never materialize."

She couldn't have been more shattered if he had struck her. Against the chilly hollowness that opened up inside her, Aurelia was intensely conscious of the sweet scent of clematis and the cool, gritty feel of the painted floor under her bare feet. They were both standing now, facing each other in the dim light that flowed through the window. She felt his eyes on her face, saw them move to the mass of hair that fell untidily to her shoulders and drop slowly down her body to her naked toes. And then his hands came down heavily on her shoulders.

"Get your hands off me! You have absolutely no right—" she began angrily, attempting to fling him away, and he interrupted her.

His words were harsh, but at least the scathing contempt was missing. "You're right. That was both unfair and uncalled for, and for what it's worth, I'm sorry as hell. I do know you better than that, Aurelia, but to be perfectly frank, I'm beginning to wonder if I know myself." His short bark of laughter was notably lacking in humor. "After pretty much calling the shots for as long as I can remember, I find myself having trouble adjusting when things don't go according to my plans. To tell the truth, I seem to be stepping out of character entirely too much for my peace of mind just lately." His gaze focused somewhere beyond her, and Aurelia had a sudden urgent desire to know what he was seeing. "I had my whole life all neatly arranged, laid out on a priority basis, one through ten. Only something's not adding up."

She sagged under the weight of his hands, no longer angry, no longer even worried about her commission. "What, you too?" she murmured in acrid amusement. Jed wasn't the only one who'd been acting out of character. For the past ten years she had thought out every move with the deliberation of a champion chess player, carefully considering all eventualities before making the next move. She had set her goals and purposely constructed the sort of lifestyle she wanted. It was a bit like furnishing a dollhouse down to the last tiny detail. The only thing missing was the dolls.

"Maybe we have more in common than either of us realized," she ventured skeptically. "We certainly both like to run things our way." And those ways clashed on every level. About the only thing they really had in common was that each of them had chosen to make a home here in the Blue Ridge Mountains. Jed's was built solidly into the side of a mountain, but hers seemed lately to have been founded on shifting sands.

Chapter Five

*D*rewry Claiborn was born at four twenty-three the following morning. Henry came into the shop just after one looking red-eyed, unshaven, and jubilant.

"It's another girl," he announced to Aurelia and the two women who were poking through a basket of old buttons.

"Are you disappointed?"

"Hell, no! Started out with a mixed pair, drew a matched pair, and ended up with three of a kind. That makes a full house, and believe me, this is as full as it's going to get. Can you believe those twins are already talking about the car I'm supposed to give 'em on their sixteenth birthday?"

Aurelia would have liked to visit Carol at the hospital at Stuart and see the new baby, but she hated to ask Henry to take her. She had heard the corn picker rumbling by early that morning, so she knew he was in the middle of harvesting. One more reason why she needed to get on with learning to drive.

Half an hour before closing time Jed arrived. Aurelia recognized the sound of his car, the solid thud of his slamming door. One hand flew to her hair, the other to the top button of the silky, pumpkin-colored blouse she had unfastened in deference to the heat.

"Hi! About ready to call it a day?" His grin was as wide and as guileless as if they had parted on the very best of terms instead of on a note of mutual wariness.

"I haven't posted the books yet, and another customer might come in," she parried.

"The books can always wait until tomorrow, and another customer might *not* come in," he riposted.

Clamping her lips shut, Aurelia opened the drawer of the small quartered oak desk, pulled out the ledgers, and slammed them onto the counter. She reached for the neat stack of sales slips and switched on her calculator. When the numbers blurred before her eyes, she fumbled in the pocket of her navy blue skirt for her glasses and rammed them forcefully on her nose.

"Need some help?" Jed offered, putting down a copy of Flayderman's antique firearms catalog.

"Thank you, I'm perfectly capable of doing simple arithmetic."

His thick black brows lifted and he moved quickly around to stand behind her. She was caught against the waist-high counter, and there was no escaping without making an issue of it—which was probably just what he wanted; an excuse to ridicule her again. The warmth of his breath on her nape stirred the tendrils there and sent a rush of goosebumps tumbling like dominoes down her flank.

"If you don't mind!" she bit off impatiently, elbows tucked closely against her sides to avoid touching the arms that reached around her to brace against the counter.

"Just thought I'd help you out so we can get away sooner. I'm pretty good with figures."

"I'll just bet you are," she seethed, and then could

have kicked herself for refocusing his remark. She suffered his eyes to travel the length of her body, lingering on all the hills and valleys along the way, and then she pushed his hand from the counter and strode past him to the door. "If you're through browsing, Mr. Dancey, I have work to do."

He shrugged, stretching the soft fabric of his gray shirt over the muscular width of his shoulders. "I wasn't offering anything more compromising than dinner and maybe a drive along the parkway. Are you afraid your tame boyfriend will object? He doesn't strike me as having a whole lot of personality, Aurelia. What is it—are you a sucker for a pretty face? Or maybe he's warm enough in the pocket to keep you from getting bored with him."

The sarcasm curled around her like a withering frost. "You're the most offensive man I've ever met, Jed Dancey. We have absolutely nothing in common, so thanks for your invitation, but no thanks. The further away from me you stay, the better we'll get along."

The small outburst might cost her her commission, but at this point she didn't care. As much as Jo meant to her, his image had been hopelessly blurred by the more powerful one of his look-alike descendant.

For an uncomfortable eternity he glared at her, and Aurelia was unexpectedly reminded of a little boy refused an expected treat. "Just remember," he said, shattering her illusion, "I gave A. R. Kenner two weeks to get that manuscript ready for my approval. The first week is almost up."

Biting her bottom lip in frustration, Aurelia watched the flash of movement as he strode from the room, lithely took the two steps as one, and swung himself under the wheel of his powerful car. She almost wished he had told her to forget the darned book. As it was, sooner or later she was going to have to learn to deal with the man—strictly on a business-like basis, of course. But better later than sooner!

Henry's brother Edward phoned shortly after Aurelia got home, and offered to pick her up on his way to visit his new niece. She changed clothes, grabbed a bite to eat, and dashed out to pick a bouquet of ageratum, orange marigolds, and a few sprigs of silvery rabbit tobacco, which she found an attractive addition to the arrangement. She scratched Sigh's ears, retrieved the rubber ball he had wedged under her blanket chest, and put out enough fresh food for him, the visiting tabby, and a battered looking marmalade that had turned up on Monday.

Drewry Claiborn, all six pounds, two ounces of her, was a red-faced mite who vaguely resembled an Eskimo. At the first sight of her, Aurelia's hands lifted instinctively toward the plate-glass viewing window and she sighed wistfully. She followed Ed to Carol's room, where she listened to a comparative resume of ounces and inches and then briefly filled the new mother in on sales and consignments at the shop. On the way out she made Ed stop by the nursery window for one more look.

All during the drive home, while Edward rambled about the tobacco market and the price of feed, Aurelia thought about that odd lurching sensation that had afflicted her just for a moment when she had first seen the infant. A delayed maternal instinct? Lord help her, she hoped not! There was no room in her scheme of things for sentiments of that sort, now when she had finally arrived at the independence she had worked so hard for.

All the same, perhaps she would write to Adam. Or better yet, this time she'd direct her note to Diana. That way she might avoid stirring up the old in-law animosity. They exchanged birthday and Christmas cards, and that was about the extent of it. Maybe it was time to mend a few fences and get acquainted with her niece and nephew.

On Friday she mailed the short, impersonal note to her sister-in-law. Moving with a briskness that reflected the autumnal feeling in the air, she took the shortcut to the shop, past stubbly cornfields rimmed with goldenrod, black-eyed Susans, and rampant morning glories, and unlocked the front door, propping it open with a flat iron. She set out the cast-iron pot of pine cones and a wooden cask of apples, and then she looked up the number of a driving instructor in Stuart, promising herself she'd call soon and make an appointment. By ten she had the books up to date, and by lunchtime she had showed a superb pair of Coalport urns and sold an R. S. Prussia tureen.

A familiar car pulled up in front of the shop with a fine disregard for the dusty gravel parking space. Subduing a quick rush of excitement, she braced herself to withstand Jed's alternating charm and sarcasm. Instead of Jed, however, it was Rae Craver who slid out and sauntered across the wide porch, looking stunning in khaki trousers and a pokeberry silk shirt.

"Hi! Anybody home?"

"Hello, Rae. It's nice to see you again." Aurelia brushed a fleck of imaginary dust from her skirt, obscurely glad she had chosen to wear one of her nicer dresses today. The navy blue was relieved by a delicate collar and cuffs of ecru lace, and the simple styling made the most of her narrow waist and high, full bosom.

"Ye gads, this place would drive me up the wall in five minutes! How do you breathe?"

Aurelia elected to take her literally. "Asthmatically, at the moment. It's the loveseat and chair—they were delivered just before I shut up shop last night, and evidently they needed a thorough airing out first. I'll open another window."

The tall brunette paused to finger a tray of old jewelry, none of which was particularly valuable. "Look at this! Can't you just see it? Evening in Paris perfume, patent-leather hair, an open-topped roadster, and me with pounds of jet beads down to my navel and little else. Hmmm, might be fun."

"Might be chilly, too. I like the opals—those dangling earrings. They're really just doublets, of course, but the color's nice."

They discussed the jewelry, but Aurelia was quite certain that neither of their minds was really on the collection of garnet pendants, jet beads, and opal earrings. She rearranged an incomplete set of lusterware while she waited for the other woman to come to the point of her visit.

"Has Jed been making a nuisance of himself lately?" Rae asked idly, dusting her hands on a monogramed linen handkerchief.

"A nuisance?" Aurelia repeated blankly. That was hardly the term she would have used.

"The way he's been acting, I thought—oh, well, I should know his moods by now. God knows he has them, and lately he's been impossible. I suppose you were bowled over by him," Rae speculated, slanting a glance from her unusual pale blue eyes.

Lifting her chin imperceptibly, Aurelia replied, "Not noticeably. I think I held up my end fairly well."

"Your end? You mean you fought?" The look grew even more probing. "I don't see any signs of blood, and I can assure you, people don't usually walk away after a fight with Jed Dancey. He's big as a bull and about as opinionated as they come, in case you hadn't noticed."

Something about the tiny smile that flickered across Rae's flawlessly made-up face reminded Aurelia of Sigh. "What does a management analyst do, Rae? Do you work for Jed?" She had had enough of the other woman's gentle inquisition.

"Don't I wish! My office is in the same building, and I've been trying to land him for over a year—as a client, that is. He's got this outmoded idea that he doesn't need an outside expert coming in and telling him how to run his business, and I can't seem to get through to him."

Aurelia marveled that anyone would even try. She gazed up at the taller woman silently, admiring her style as well as her nerve.

"On a personal basis," Rae continued casually, "no problems. He's stubborn, but believe me, he's worth the trouble." Again that catlike look of satisfaction that set Aurelia's nerves on edge. "I think I can handle him as a husband well enough, but . . ." Here she paused to light a cigarette, blowing out a thin stream of smoke that exactly matched her eyes. "It was a tough decision to make, whether or not to try marriage. You're a professional woman, Aurelia, you know how it is. But marriage or not, I don't plan to compromise a damned bit. I promise you, one way or another, I'm determined to bring that man to heel. If I don't manage to land a contract of one type or the other with him before the year's out, you'll see fireworks."

Rae left soon after that with a breezy promise to drop by again before she left for New York. Aurelia tried to drum up a little enthusiasm for the prospect and failed miserably. By all rights she should be applauding the other woman's spunk. Jed treated women as if they needed a keeper beyond the safe confines of the kitchen and bedroom. The overbearing oaf was just asking for someone to yank him up into the twentieth century, and let's face it, Aurelia herself didn't seem to be much of a match for him. Nor did the irony of her thoughts occur to her.

Saturday she was rushed off her feet. The twins came in at eleven and stayed until almost four. Allie was a crackshot at math and handled the sales slips while Barbara wrapped, leaving Aurelia free to discuss the various pieces with prospective buyers.

"Whew!" she whistled, taking a rare opportunity to lie back on the moth-eaten loveseat and put her feet up. "If we're this busy in September, what's it going to be like in October when the leaves are in full color?"

"Still better, I hope," Allie replied. "To hear Daddy talk, you'd think one more mouth to feed was going to scuttle the good ship Claiborn. Every time we even show him a car ad, he starts muttering about having two girls in college at the same time, and another one coming up through the ranks!"

A station wagon load of women with avid gleams in their eyes sent the three of them to battle stations again, and it was after six before Aurelia closed the door on the last customer. She was hot and tired and her feet felt like chopped steak, and she'd have given her week's pay not to have to go out with Chase tonight. Quiet by nature, she was willing enough to listen to other people's problems and offer an occasional word of advice, but she had heard Chase warbling Jan's praises from the first date, and at the moment she couldn't drum up a whole lot of sympathy.

The cats greeted her, Sigh's single Paul Newman-blue eye staring at her balefully. "Thought you were going to miss dinner, didn't you, boy? Come on, call your friends and I'll treat you all to a can instead of the dry stuff."

She made her way through the house, strewing her belongings as she went. There hadn't been time for a lick of housework all week, and it was beginning to show. Chaos! Sigh's toys, a coffee cup, the week's accumulation of junk mail, two pairs of her shoes, and a scarf that looked slightly clawed.

But it was *her* chaos, and it welcomed her like a pair of loving arms, wrapping her into its warm security. She was answerable to no one, and if Chase, who leaned more toward easy-care vinyl and chrome than to early miscellaneous, objected, then he could take his heartbreak to Dear Abby.

Feeling vaguely guilty over her lack of patience, she hung her clothes on hangers over the curtain rod to air out before she put them in the cramped wardrobe. "I'm just bone tired," she growled, tossing in the last of the herbal bath salts. They hadn't performed any noticeable miracles during the week; on the other hand, it was relaxing just to soak for a few minutes in the old claw-footed tub while she inhaled the balsam and rosemary, or whatever esoteric mixture the salts contained.

Before climbing into the inviting bath, she poured herself a glass of wine and laid out her clothes, deciding on a simple little gray print with a grape-colored belt and a jacket of violet mohair in case it got cooler later on. Lacy gray lingerie, nylons, and a pair of gray suede sandals that were old enough to be comfortable completed the ensemble.

Knowing Chase, jeans would have done as well. They'd probably go only as far as the nearest restaurant, which wasn't much to brag about, but Aurelia enjoyed pretty, feminine clothes and managed to indulge her small vice by shopping carefully at sales. What lay beneath all the window dressing was no one's business but her own.

The wine was flat, but it helped ease the tension that ached in her shoulders. She promised herself a bottle of really nice Madeira the first chance she got—as a reward for learning to drive, perhaps. Not that she'd be any more mobile for having a slip of laminated cardboard in her purse, but when she finished the Dancey commission—if Jed didn't take it away from her, that was—she'd be ready to take on another project, and that meant another advance. With a bit of careful juggling, she might be able to afford a small secondhand car.

Sipping the wine, she flexed her toes and slid down a bit farther in the tub. The strappy shoes with four-inch heels she had worn that day were a crime against nature. Thank goodness the week was up and she could get back to her typewriter. At least when she was writing, the burden of her hundred and three pounds was distributed over a slightly larger area.

She was struggling with the back zipper when she heard Chase arriving. He *would* be early when she was running late! She padded to the bedroom door in her stocking feet, opened it, and reached out to unhook the front screen. Quickly she darted back to the safety of her room, closing the door to a mere crack as she recognized the breadth of Jed's shoulders silhouetted against the gold and magenta sunset beyond.

"What are you doing here?"

"Good old southern hospitality—you can always count on it," he mocked as he let himself into the tiny foyer.

"This has nothing to do with hospitality! I'm expecting someone. We're going out to dinner, so will you please get out of my house and let me finish dressing?" She blew a strand of hair from her forehead and glared at him furiously. "You can't come in here!"

"You unhooked the door for me. I'd consider that a legally binding invitation, in spite of your outward show of reluctance." He strolled into the living room, and Aurelia opened her door farther to stare helplessly after him. The man was a master of timing! He always seemed to turn up when she was expecting Chase; although to be honest, there had only been a couple of times, and the first one had been her fault.

"Look, if you want to read the manuscript, then take the blooming thing and go!" She'd rather take the risk than have him spoiling her evening. His very presence had already shattered the tranquility of her home.

"No hurry. Get dressed and come on out and we'll discuss it," he said with maddening nonchalance.

Reaching around behind her, she tugged impotently at her zipper. The blasted thing was stuck halfway and wouldn't go up or down! "There's nothing"—she yanked and swore under her breath—"to discuss! The manuscript is in that metal box on the table. Take it and go!"

"Having problems?" he called out, and she slammed the bedroom door. If it were possible to do it without ripping the seams out, she'd wriggle out of the dress and wear something else, but it wouldn't go over her head or her hips. Heaving a sigh that was partly from frustration, partly from exertion, she smoothed the skirt and reached for the jacket. She'd worry about the zipper later.

"All right, what's the idea of barging in on me when you know very well Chase is coming any minute? You were here when we made the date, weren't you?

You're deliberately harassing me to make me so mad I'll tell you to tear up the contract. Well, go ahead! Tear it up! I don't need your old commission!" Her bottom lip jutted angrily and she bit it in an effort to keep it from trembling. No one—*no* one had affected her this much in ten years!

He was beside her in an instant, moving with the deceptive languor of a jungle cat in his prime. The hands that came down on her shoulders were as gentle as a kitten's paw, but she was acutely aware of the claws that lay sheathed under the velvet touch.

"You're all upset," he purred. "I told you you shouldn't be trying to work and write at the same time."

"And I told you," she came back, steeling herself against the unthinkable urge to move one step closer, "that when or where I work is none of your business. Your book will be finished on schedule, and that's the extent of your concern."

His ripe olive eyes found hers and burrowed in, unearthing all sorts of unsuspected weaknesses, and she twisted her shoulders in an attempt to get away. Already she could feel a fine film of perspiration breaking out on her forehead and down her spine.

"You're letting yourself get all hot and bothered over nothing," he soothed, not troubling to disguise his amusement. He was playing with her—cat and mice games!

"Look, don't you have something better to do than to badger me? Where's your girl friend? Did she let you off the leash for your evening run?" Was she actually taunting him? Timid, cautious Aurelia Rose? God, she must be insane! What was there about the man that drove her to such reckless lengths?

"Don't worry about Rae." Not by a flicker of an

eyelash did he react to her taunts. "She'll be there when I want her—if I want her."

"I can't believe what I'm hearing," she marveled slowly. "Do you know your great-great-grandfather was more enlightened than you are? He respected women. If he'd treated his wife the way you treat your fiancée, she'd have—"

"Whoa, there." His hands actually seemed to lift her slightly off the floor. "Back up and go over that again. My what?"

If only he'd put her down and go sit on the other side of the room, she could think a little more clearly. The man was a menace! He should be labeled by some agency as hazardous to any woman's peace of mind. "Rae. Your fiancée. The woman who came down here from New York with you. Is she planning to help decorate your new house, or is it just that she knows you can't be trusted out of sight? If I were her, I'd keep you on a much shorter leash."

He waited for an agonizing moment before he asked, "Are you finished?" An unholy gleam narrowed his eyes as the planes of his face shifted subtly. "So you'd keep me on a tighter leash, would you? Purely as a matter of abstract interest, how would you go about it?"

"How would I . . . ? Well, that's beside the point. I have an idea Rae can keep you in line when the time comes, although for the life of me, I can't imagine her even wanting to."

"Can't you? Maybe Rae knows something you don't," he suggested softly.

"I suspect Rae knows a lot of things I don't," she snapped back, trying once more to free herself from the tender prison of his hands. "That doesn't mean I—"

He stepped closer, bringing his body only a whisper away from hers, and her blood slammed through her body at breakneck speed. "That doesn't mean you what, Aurelia? What don't you know? Are you afraid of knowledge, or are you just not interested? Let's see, shall we?"

Even as he spoke, he was lowering his head to hers, and she, like some foolish, light-blinded doe, waited helplessly for disaster to strike. When it came, it came with melting, deceptive gentleness. His lips brushed over hers with a series of featherlight kisses—sweet, moist, beguiling caresses that lulled her senses, robbed her of the will to resist. He lifted his face to smile down at her and then brought his mouth back to her parted lips in a kiss that was strangely like a gift, blessing both the giver and the receiver.

When the tip of his tongue sought entrance, she opened to him willingly. Pure pleasure flowed through her with liquefying force, and she wasn't even aware of his hands under her jacket, inside the half-open zipper of her dress, moving in circles over the skin of her back. Gone was all the old awareness, the constant knowledge of how her back had looked that time so long ago when the doctor had proudly held a mirror for her to admire his handiwork.

"See? Almost as good as new," he had said, and she had seen, seen and cried out and then wept silently for days. Her back had resembled a patchwork quilt done in a dozen shades of pink and red. It had been years before she had steeled herself to look again, and in spite of the fact that the scars were now barely visible, her mind was imprinted by that earlier vision . . . the newly healed burns, the first small grafts, the trails of rose-colored lines that welded together her very flesh.

Now blindly following newly awakened instincts,

her fingers curled on his chest and crept through the opening of his shirt to comb through the crisp pelt on his hard chest. She felt him stiffen, heard him catch his breath as her fingertips encountered the tiny masculine nipples, and she snatched back her hand as if she had touched a hot stove.

"No, don't stop," he uttered harshly. "God, sweetheart, your touch goes through me like a bolt of lightning."

Her jacket had fallen to the floor unnoticed, and her dress was hanging around her shoulders, dipping dangerously low in front. She wedged a hand between them and tugged it higher.

"Stop acting like some Victorian maiden," he whispered, capturing her hand and moving it back to the opening of his shirt. "Touch me. You want to touch me as much as I want to touch you, sweetheart, so don't be shy."

His voice was a seductive rumble, the slight movement of his mouth causing his beard to brush sensuously against her temple. One of his hands had closed over her breast, and she could feel the electrifying pressure of her nipple tightening against his palm. His lips moved slowly over her eyes, down her cheek to the corner of her mouth, and he whispered her name softly, once more driving her wild with the brush of his beard and mustache on her sensitized skin.

He swung her up in his arms and began to move toward the foyer. *This was impossible. She was stark, raving mad!* He swung the front door closed and shouldered the bedroom door open, burying his face in her throat.

"Your skin is like ivory velvet," he murmured.

Whether it was the choice of words, the sound of a car outside, or the crash that came from the bathroom, she never knew. The effect was like falling out of bed in the middle of a warm dream of love. "Put me down!" she demanded hoarsely.

"For now," he agreed, lowering her slowly down his body until her feet touched the floor. "You're an intriguing little morsel, Aurelia Kenner. Thorny as a cactus, all full of defenses and contradictions." His hands moved up over her shoulders, tactilely appreciating the delicacy of every curve and hollow. They slipped sensuously up along the sides of her throat, and she stood there, helpless under the tantalizing spell of his familiar-unfamiliar face. He tilted her head and brushed his mouth slowly over hers. "This is a raincheck, love. Now you go put your shoes on and fasten up your dress while I greet your boyfriend for you."

Chapter Six

$\mathcal{A}$urelia took one look at the shattered wineglass on the bathroom floor and closed the door on it. Sigh now owed her two glasses, one Wedgwood cup, which had been minus a handle anyway, and an assortment of scarves and pantyhose. Inside her bedroom she slipped off the jacket and belt and twisted her dress around so that she could see the jammed zipper. From the parlor she could hear the murmur of masculine voices, which only added to her agitation.

Finally, with only one broken nail and a slightly harried look, she emerged from her room to greet Chase. For all the attention she received, you'd think she was the intruder instead of Jed. It seemed that he had gone to engineering school on a football scholarship, which made him and Chase all but blood brothers.

"Are we ready to go?" she prompted a little impatiently.

Jed glanced up with a suspiciously guileless smile. "What was the crash?"

"Sigh broke a glass in the bathroom," she snapped,

moving closer to the front door as she shot Chase a laden look.

"It's the one eye," Jed informed her sagaciously, ignoring her none too subtle hint. "No depth perception. I notice the glass thingamabobs on the mantel are chipped, too. Either you're going to have to get an unflawed cat or settle for owning a lot of flawed glassware."

Frostily she retorted, "I don't have to *settle* for anything. I prefer Sigh to any other cat, regardless of the number of eyes, and if I don't mind having chipped glass, then I don't see why it should bother you!"

He shrugged, his massive shoulders moving easily as he hooked his thumbs under his belt. "Matter of preference, I suppose. But then, our tastes run counter in several areas—interestingly enough."

His obviously ran to perfection, she thought rancorously, as witness his singleminded drive to arrange his life in what he considered the proper order. As witness Rae Craver. A more perfect example of the modern woman would be hard to find—she had brains, courage, style, and undisputed beauty, and what's more, she was likable!

Jed was staring at her, as if waiting for her to snatch up his words and throw them back at him. His eyes moved slowly over her features. What was he looking for—a brand? A mark of possession on the lips he had so recently kissed, the face he had held and caressed? Maybe he was looking for perfection, comparing her with Rae. His eyes had narrowed at her instinctive stiffening, at the lift of her small, rounded chin. Perfection! Let him buy plastic glasses if he couldn't stand flaws!

The barriers were up again, clanged shut and bolted down. Aurelia turned to Chase, who was grinning admiringly at Jed's football hero physique. He *would* be impressed by all that brawn. It wouldn't matter if most of it was between the ears, either! "Chase, if you don't want to go out, that's fine with me. I'd just as soon stay home and work. But if we're going, then let's go. Mr. Dancey was just leaving, anyway."

Chase turned his eager, toothpaste-ad smile on Jed. "Say, why don't you come with us? We're just going down the road a few miles to eat. I'd like to ask your opinion about the chance for a scholarship for a kid I know."

She could have strangled him! And then, when Jed declined the invitation with benign condescension, she wondered fleetingly if the penalty for double homicide was worth the double satisfaction.

"I'm pretty well out of touch with the sports scene these days, Jamison, but if anything occurs to me, I'll let you know. You two run along and have a good time. Aurelia's been working too hard lately. She could do with an exciting evening on the town." His beaming, bearded face was positively avuncular. It changed imperceptibly as it turned from Chase to the door, where Aurelia stood seething. "We'll finish our business later. I can wait."

Her mouth fell open at the sheer effrontery, and as he let himself out the front door he paused long enough to lift a finger to her chin and close it ever so gently. The smile he poured over her like a benediction held more than a glint of pure deviltry.

Dinner was an ordeal of monotonous food and an endless monolog. All during the tasteless soup and overdone roast beef, Chase dredged up bits of esoteric information about a quarterback named Dancey who had made headlines for his school ten or twelve years back doing whatever it was football players did—and doing it better than anyone else, according to Chase. Over the soggy-crusted apple pie he moved on to the mystery of Jan's defection. How could any female in her right mind prefer an aging, out-of-work pilot over a gainfully employed athletic coach from one of the better prep schools, who had been told he could make a fortune as a male model anytime he wanted to switch jobs?

"And on top of all that," he added in an aggrieved tone, "I own my own home. Frankly, I think this women's lib thing has shoved some of 'em over the edge. Jan's not even thinking rationally these days!"

It was all Aurelia could do to keep a straight face. The poor boy was perfectly serious. Actually, his frank self-appreciation was one of the more endearing things about him—when it wasn't boring her to tears. But she much preferred boredom to the disturbing complexity of someone like Jed Dancey—someone who was entirely too physical, entirely too cunning for her ever to feel safe with. He was dangerously attractive, and her immunity had already been undermined by her exposure to Jo.

"—not as if she was against marriage per se. We talked about it, and she fully intends to combine marriage with her career once the store's on its feet."

Poor Chase, with his Prince Charming looks and his engaging egotism. He had probably proposed to Jan on the first date, after earnestly showing her his bankbook and letters of reference from his pastor and his high school coach.

"Chase, has it occurred to you that you don't really want Jan after all? Maybe you're only piqued because she didn't fall on her face the first time she saw you. Think about it. Could you really respect a woman who hasn't the good judgment to appreciate all you have to offer?"

A frown marred his high, clear brow. "Maybe you've got something, at that," he mused. "Hey, I think you've hit on it! It was just a conditioned response with me. She ran; I ran after her." He grinned and signaled for the check. "Boy! If she's just been playing hard to get, she's flat out of luck. There're plenty of women out there just as good looking and twice as smart!"

Grace Bradham, Carol's mother, picked up the shop routine with surprising ease. Aurelia worked with her for one morning, but it was evident that the older woman was accustomed to running things. What she didn't know about the stock when she walked in, she would before she walked out again. A new grandchild was a pleasant occurrence, but to a woman who had raised nine children and had already accumulated seven grandchildren, the novelty was gone. The shop provided much more of a challenge to her adventuresome spirit.

"Carol mentioned a consignment from some estate in Richmond," Mrs. Bradham said as Aurelia was gathering her things to leave. "She'll call you about it tonight. Now don't you worry about a thing here. What I don't know, I can figure out. Thank the Lord I was blessed with common sense."

It was past noon and Aurelia was hungry. All the same, she decided to walk the extra three quarters of a mile to the Claiborns' house and take another look at the new daughter. So far she hadn't even held her, and she really did need to talk to Carol about the Richmond thing. Carol obviously couldn't go, and Mrs. Bradham wasn't qualified.

Getting around would be a hassle. She didn't know Richmond at all. Drat! She had gotten busy and forgotten all about the driving lessons. Not that it would help her this time, but her past negligence was proving to be a big handicap.

Carol greeted her at the door with a speculative look. "The grapevine has it that you've been seen around with a tall, dark, handsome stranger. Is something coming to a boil in the romance department?"

Feeling the swift rise of warmth to her cheeks, Aurelia muttered, "Just my temper at silly gossip!" She crossed to the ruffled bassinet and shot Carol a pleading look. "May I?" Then, lifting the infant, she murmured, "No wonder Henry's putting in more cabbage and less corn next year. I'd go looking under cabbage leaves myself if I thought I'd find something this sweet."

Carol resumed her task of folding laundry. "He's in a mood to try the tooth fairy next. The darned picker's had it. Do you have any idea how much one of those mechanical monsters costs these days? Here, take the rocker while I put these in the twins' room."

The women shared a pot of tea and a plate of sandwiches while Carol filled Aurelia in on the estate of the Richmond merchant that was finally open to private bids. "Go for the Flow Blue and the Belleek," Carol instructed her. "Mitzi Voncannon will buy every piece of Flow Blue we can find, and I think I've got a sale for the Belleek, even the newer pieces. The place will be swarming with dealers, of course, but you've got an edge. Henry went to VCU—it was Richmond Professional Institute back in those days—with Cordell Hughes, who's handling the estate, and I'm not above using any amount of influence to compensate for the fact that I can't be there in person."

"Okay. I'll feel like Daniel in the lion's den, but I'll give it a try. Better write down all pertinent addresses and phone numbers and I'll check out bus schedules."

She wasn't looking forward to it, but she owed Carol a great deal. Besides, she could use a little distance at the moment. Maybe with the perspective of time and space she could put those intrusive, disturbing thoughts of Jed Dancey back where they belonged— wherever that was.

"Don't bother," Carol said, reaching out for her daughter, who was to be christened Drewry Bradham Claiborn unless something more euphonious took precedence over family ties. "Edward has to go to Richmond on business and he doesn't mind going a day early. He'll drive you there tomorrow morning and bring you back the next afternoon. Can do?"

Reluctantly handing over seven pounds of red-faced, screaming femininity, Aurelia sighed. "Can do, I hope. I warn you, though, I tend to panic when I'm in a bind."

Carol's dark eyes softened as she lifted them to the younger woman. "I know, honey. But you're a big girl now. This will be good for you. They're only antique dealers, you know. Not armed guerrillas."

Strolling slowly along beside a stubbly cornfield a few minutes later, Aurelia flashed back to the fading nightmare. And *they* had only been college professors, but she had seen them turned into a mob by sheer terror.

Her pace quickened impatiently. That had been ages ago! She couldn't spend the rest of her life cowering every time half a dozen or more people started shoving at her. Good Lord, she'd even panicked in a ticket line two years ago and missed out on a marvelous concert for her foolish fears. For years she had done her Christmas shopping in midsummer rather than subject herself to throngs of last-minute shoppers, most of whom seemed to be both taller and broader than she. The minute she was surrounded by people, unable to see her way clear over their heads, the familiar choking sensation started again.

It was a form of claustrophobia, she had been told. Under the circumstances it was ironic that she preferred living in a tiny house. That hadn't occurred to her until Jed mentioned it. Still, she hadn't actually minded all the empty space of his house. It had been rather nice, once she had accepted the fact that she wasn't going to see a reproduction of Jo's old homeplace. In fact, the only thing about it that bothered her was Jed himself, and that had nothing to do with what had happened fifteen years ago.

Or had it?

The following afternoon Jed stalked angrily from one end of the small front porch to the other, pausing each way to bang on the front door. She had said she was through working at that damned antique shop. Probably lying to keep him from forcing the issue. Where the hell was she? With no car, she couldn't go far, and Jamison had gone back to school. He scowled at the varnished swing, the trellised vine that shaded it, and the half-grown tomcat who gazed at him unblinkingly from one blue eye.

"What's the matter with you, Cyclops?" he grumbled. Then, ramming his hands into his hip pockets, he added, "More to the point, what the devil's the matter with me?"

He couldn't recall the last time he had met a more infuriating woman. From the very first, when she had had the brass-bound gall to tell him she was perfectly capable of writing about a soldier, she had rubbed him the wrong way. Something about the very way she stood there, not backing down an inch in spite of the fact that the top of her head didn't reach his shoulder, had got under his skin. If he'd been smart he'd have bought her off on the spot. The woods were full of writers. He'd have found another one who'd jump at the chance. In fact, the damned biography didn't have to be written, anyway. Who the hell would read it? His children? His grandchildren? A few old die-hards who haunted the hallowed halls of local history?

"The devil with her," he growled, swinging down off the porch and striding out to the car. He impatiently switched on the engine, then paused for a moment in thought.

Rae. What was he going to do about Rae? He must have been out of his mind to invite her down here, although come to think of it, he didn't recall actually issuing the invitation. Rae had been talking about a prospective client she had been courting and had mentioned the fact that he was summering at Roaring Gap. Jed had already told her about the house he was having built in Virginia, and one thing had led to another. It was a relatively short drive from Stuart to the small, exclusive resort in the North Carolina mountains where her quarry, Paul Anderson of Weeks-Anderson Pharmaceuticals, was relaxing with flyrod and golf clubs. Jed wouldn't give a tinker's dam for his chances of escaping this time. He'd be off guard and no match at all for Rae's particular brand of coercion.

Jed patted the pocket of his chamois shirt for a cigar and fingered the lighter as a gust of wind blew a flurry of yellowed leaves across the highway in front of him. One more summer spent. What had he to show for it? How long had he been seeing Rae now? Several months? He had started by parrying her half-teasing assaults against his corporate entity—as if he needed any outsider to overhaul his operation. Especially a female outsider.

They had taken it from there, and it had gotten to be a habit, a pleasant enough one, to be sure. Working in the same building, it was easy to get together for drinks, dinner, and a show or a bit of dancing. And when it led occasionally to something more, they both enjoyed it. Neither of them had any attachments to preclude a relationship, and if Rae was inclined to be a little too aggressive to suit him at times, he was more than a match for her. She was good company, and Lord knows, his ego didn't suffer for being seen with her. In fact, he had even considered the possibility of . . .

No. Oh, hell no!

Clamping his teeth on the cigar, he accepted and rationalized certain facts in an instinctive reaction. Item: Lately he had been feeling an unaccustomed urge to procreate. Typical midlife restlessness, no doubt. Item: He had fleetingly considered Rae as a possible partner. Physically she was highly desirable. Hell, physically she was perfect! She was more than a match for him in that department, but some inner radar kept holding him back from making the next move. She knew it. He knew it. It was as if they were playing a game of nerves for the sheer thrill of the sport. Which was precisely what made her an expert in her field; she had the type of mind that could engage an opponent, swiftly search out his weaknesses, evaluate his strengths, and act on the information, usually before he knew what had hit him.

Fortunately—or unfortunately—he had the same sort of mind. Not that it had been functioning with enviable brilliance lately. "A. R. Kenner," he muttered, gearing down as he approached a sharp, inclining curve near Lover's Leap. With her prim manners and her sanctimonious attitude, she had practically dared him to break through that invisible cellophane wrapper she wore and find the flesh-and-blood woman inside.

And he had accepted her dare. Damn, that had been a close call! But she was so unexpectedly soft and sweet and enticing. There was something almost vulnerable about her.

Vulnerable as a she-cat, he argued with himself. Your imagination's acting up again, Dancey. Soft? She was about as soft as a cactus! Besides which, she was decidedly peculiar when it came to old Jocephus. The way she had his pictures plastered all over that doll's house of hers, you'd think they were lovers.

The woman had no business getting under his skin the way she did. She was pretty enough . . . hell, she was lovely in her own way. Big, haunting eyes the color of cairngorms, skin like whipped cream. She looked as if she'd never been out in the noonday sun.

He turned into his driveway and then pulled over at the halfway place to stare up at what he had built. Aurelia had tiptoed around those empty rooms looking like a wide-eyed kitten, peering into doorways, gazing out the windows at the sheer drop. The place should have dwarfed her, and yet it hadn't. Now, with Rae off for a few days bearding her lion in his summer lair, it was empty. He had sat there until almost midnight last night, enjoying the peace and quiet while he attempted to visualize the way it would look when it was furnished. After the second drink something had begun to nag at him, as if he'd forgotten something important. After the third whiskey it occurred to him that it was the first time he had had the place entirely to himself. There'd always been carpenters or stone masons about—and then Rae.

But it wasn't Rae's presence he was missing, he admitted to himself halfway through the fourth and last drink. Oddly enough it was Aurelia's. It wasn't

the absence of Rae's astringent remarks and her
sexual expertise that was making him restless. He was
bothered by a more elusive protagonist, a softer
presence that fingered the edges of his mind with
annoying persistence. A. R. Kenner, damn her!

   Edward Claiborn drove her by the shop to unload.
He had taken the van to Richmond in case he was able
to locate the machinery part he needed, so there had
been no problem in making room for the various
boxes and crates. She had gotten all the Belleek and
most of the Flow Blue, plus a collection of open salts
she knew Carol would like. What she was less certain
of was the German bisque doll and the wicker peram-
bulator. There had been no excuse for that weakness,
but she comforted herself with the thought that there
had been at least three other dealers after them, and
Carol could always pass them on at cost.
   "Give you a lift to Henry's if you like," Ed offered
after carrying in the last of the boxes. Aurelia couldn't
resist poking about in the packing material to admire
the translucent creaminess of the Irish china and the
smug innocence of the tissue-wrapped doll. She considered his offer. It was suppertime and she hated to
turn up looking hungry—which she was—but she did
need to report to Carol, and she wouldn't mind
getting her hands on that baby for a few minutes.
   After I wash them, she grimaced, looking at her
black fingers, then sliding in beside the burly driver.
"Look how filthy I am. You'd think nobody in that old
mausoleum ever washed a dish."
   "It's the newspapers you packed all those doodads
in. I'd have waited for you to wash up if you'd asked."
   "Never mind. I will take you up on your offer,
though. Carol's bound to want to know how much this
binge cost her, although it might be safer to tell her

over the phone." She gazed out at the sunset-glazed houses, their white paint looking pink against the hazy blue of the wooded mountains. "I guess Essie will be waiting supper for you."

"She'd better. I called her that last stop we made. Told her to spread the butter on the biscuits, I'd be home before it melted."

They crossed under the parkway overpass and turned into the Claiborns' long driveway. Aurelia shuffled through her purse for the sales slips, business cards, and scribbled notes she had made. "Edward, I do appreciate all your help. It would have been awkward having to depend on taxis and arranging shipping for all that loot. I only hope I didn't take up too much of your time."

"Think nothing of it, honey. If it means Carol's going to make a dollar or two extra, we'll be that much closer to paying off the new corn picker. Damned interest rates eat a fellow up these days." Edward farmed with his brother and lived with his wife in their parents' old house half a mile farther on. "Henry'll give you a ride home with your bag."

And Henry did, after she had been fed and had brought Carol up to date on the business transactions made on her behalf. Aurelia rocked the baby while she described the German bisque doll she had succumbed to and the French one she had reluctantly passed up, and Carol grinned knowingly.

"Nesting urge. I warned you, you know. It happens to all of us sooner or later. Good Lord, look what it did to me! I was all set to be general manager of Cooper's Wholesale Produce House when Henry showed up with his jeans riding low and that irresistible leer on his face."

"Yes, well, urge or no urge, I've got a book to finish and I'd better get at it."

"Hey, speaking of urges, I almost forgot—some man's been trying to reach you. It wasn't Chase, so I can only suppose it was your tall, dark, and mysterious stranger. Are you still sticking to your story that there's nothing going on?"

For a moment Aurelia couldn't speak past the sudden paralysis that constricted her throat. Jed! So much for the benefits of time and distance; the first reminder and he was back again, muddling up her blood pressure and turning her brain into so much Swiss cheese! She tried unsuccessfully for a coolly disinterested note. "It's probably just the man who commissioned the biography I'm working on. He keeps insisting on checking up on my progress."

All during the short drive home her fingers kept twisting on the handle of her purse. Henry carried her overnight bag up to the porch and Aurelia thanked him politely, then fumbled frantically with the key when the phone began to ring inside the house.

It was her brother. "Adam! What's wrong? Are the children all right? Has something happened to Diana?"

"Hey, hang on there, hon. Everything's fine, just fine! I've been calling you off and on all day. I'm on the road, heading up your way. Going to Washington, actually, but I thought I'd take the long way up and stop by for a visit. I was afraid I was going to miss seeing you."

Aurelia dropped her purse and stepped out of her shoes, then hooked the organ stool closer and sat down. "Didn't Carol tell you where I was?"

"Carol who?"

Of course. Adam wouldn't know to call Carol. "Never mind. Where are you now?"

"Place called Fancy Gap. I knew you were somewhere along the parkway and I figured I'd better climb aboard before I got into Virginia so as not to miss you."

Aurelia gave him specific instructions for finding her house. It would be easy to miss a small place like Meadows-of-Dan in the darkness, but Adam had always been good at following instructions. Hanging up the phone, she decided she'd have time for a bath and then she'd see what she could put together in case he hadn't taken time to eat along the way.

"You look wonderful," she told him later, standing back after the bear hug he had given her. He'd always been attractive, and age only enhanced his red-headed, green-eyed good looks. Even with the graying sideburns and the slightly thicker middle, he was the same Adam who had tried to be father, mother, and brother to her all those years ago.

"So do you, little sister. You're looking smart and pretty and all grown up. How's the writing business?"

It was as if the devastating quarrel and the subsequent years of caution and restraint had never occurred. They discussed her writing and his work as general manager of the television station. He brought her up to date on the children, and then, a bit hesitantly, she asked after Diana.

"Frankly, she feels guilty as hell, honey," Adam admitted over a third cup of coffee. They were in the parlor, where Aurelia had made up the settee for herself after insisting that Adam take her room. "She was young then, and we hadn't been married all that long, and she was . . . I don't know. Jealous, I suppose. I was so concerned about you after everything you went through—only natural under the circumstances—but Di got this crazy notion that she took second place with me."

"But that's ridiculous!" Aurelia was sitting cross-legged on one end of the settee, nibbling on bits of the salad Adam had left. He never was one for grazing, he had apologized.

"I know. It was my fault, mostly. I was so damned busy worrying about you, about propping up the station's ratings, and about money in general, that I just didn't see what was happening until all hell broke loose. You heard us that day, didn't you? I finally figured that much out after you'd gone. You changed about then—all tight and sort of clammed up, smiling for all you were worth whenever I asked you anything, and so polite to Diana any fool should have been suspicious. I guess I was just hoping it would blow over."

She shrugged. It was all ancient history now, without the power to hurt her. "Diana was right, though. If I'd stayed, I'd never have known what it was to hold down a job, much less do so well at it I could afford to chuck it all and try something as risky as writing. Honestly, Adam, it was the best thing that ever happened. It just hadn't occurred to me to get out on my own. I actually thought I was—what do they call it?—fulfilling my potential by being a live-in housekeeper. I would have taken over the raising of your children like some destitute maiden aunt—which I was." She grinned ruefully.

"And still are," he added. "Only not destitute, I hope. When are you going to come visit them? They don't even know what their one and only aunt looks like."

"Well, we're even. You're not very good at sending pictures. The last ones are over a year old," she reminded him.

"They're hellions, but you'll love 'em. Di's still working and we have a woman who lives in, does the housework and keeps us all in line."

How ironic. If she'd stuck it out, she might have

been that woman. "I really do want to pay you all a visit, Adam, but I've got a deadline on this book I'm doing, and I've been spending far too much time lately on other things."

"Are you happy, honey? Is this what you want out of life?" He gestured vaguely around her small, carefully furnished parlor, with its yellow painted walls and dark varnished floors, the hand-stitched cushions and the assorted antiques she had gleaned from the shop and various yard sales.

She followed his glance, looking for the charm and warmth she usually found there. "Of course I'm happy," she insisted, puzzled by the unexpected core of emptiness that cropped up inside her to mock her words.

Adam insisted on leaving soon after breakfast. "I've got an appointment with a man from the FCC and you've got a deadline, remember? We'll get together again real soon, honey, I promise."

"And you'll write? And you'll remember to send me some up-to-date pictures of the children? And you're really sure Diana won't mind if I pay you a visit soon?"

They were standing out in the yard beside Adam's late-model sedan. It had started raining sometime before daybreak but it had slacked up enough for Aurelia to see him off without getting drenched. "I will and I will and I'm sure," he teased her, pinching her short nose affectionately. "It's going to be okay from now on, honey. You get on back in the house now—it's starting up again."

And it was. A cool, blowing, autumn rain, the first one of the season. Aurelia threw her arms around her brother's neck and he swung her up and kissed her quickly before putting her down. "Scat!" he ordered, grinning. He slid in the car and started the engine, backing away so she'd get in out of the rain when it became evident that she was going to watch him out of sight.

It was only then that she noticed a long, low sports car farther along her drive. Jed's car. The engine was running; she could hear the rumble from here, but he wasn't moving. Adam slowed to pass him, and only then did Jed begin to move.

Aurelia stood there as if hypnotized, getting wetter and wetter until Jed pulled up before the house and stopped. He swung out of the car and strode the few feet to where she stood. He wore black again—black trousers that delineated the lean lines of his flanks and his long, powerful legs with devastating faithfulness. In a dark knit shirt that dampened and clung to his broad chest like a second skin, with wetness glistening on his ebony hair and beard, he looked enormous and angry and even more stunningly beautiful than she remembered. There was no confusing overtones of Jo this time. This time he was all Jed, and that was enough. That was more than enough! She gazed up at him mutely, her arms wrapped around her against the chill of the early morning rain.

"That was a touching send-off," he snarled. "Tell me, what does a man have to do to get past the bread-and-butter stage with you?"

"I don't know what you're talking about."

"The hell you don't! I get a mealy-mouthed little 'Thank you very much for the dinner, Mr. Dancey,' and your redheaded Adonis gets the full treatment— bed and board and a tender, loving farewell!"

Chapter Seven

"Get in the house!" Jed ordered, his fingers biting into Aurelia's arm as he hurried her up the steps. The rain was coming down relentlessly by now and she could feel chill bumps rising on her body. She refused to believe it was a response to Jed's touch on her arm or the way his eyes seemed to burn right through her clothes. As she'd overslept, she hadn't taken time to dress. While Adam shaved, she had quickly cooked him a hot breakfast, most of which had gone uneaten. He was in a hurry to get on the road, and she had come outside to see him off still wearing her gown and robe, a matched set done in café au lait cotton with flounces of eyelet embroidery. They were a limp and sodden mess now.

As soon as the door slammed behind them, Jed spun her around. "Who is he? Where the hell have you two been? Off for an unofficial honeymoon?"

She started to speak but he cut her off, his voice rough with anger as he said, "You damned well haven't been home, because I've been trying to reach you all day! I finally called your landlady and she told me you were out of town. By then I'd pretty well figured that out for myself," he added with a bitterness she couldn't begin to understand. In fact, she couldn't understand the reason for any of this tirade. He hadn't reacted this strongly even when he had discovered her gender for the first time.

Shivering in earnest by now, she was nevertheless burning up with anger, and where Jed's large hands still gripped her shoulders, the heat struck through the thin layer of wet fabric. "How do you know who my landlady is?"

"Mutual friends," he snapped. "That's beside the point! The point is, what the hell do you mean by taking off overnight with some man and then bringing him home with you like another of your damned stray tomcats? You're supposed to be working for me!"

"I don't believe you," Aurelia marveled slowly. "I don't believe what I'm hearing." As her indignation increased, her words gathered force. "How dare you barge into my house—into my *life*—and try to tell me what I can do and—and who I can see! Who do you think—"

"I'm not trying to tell you a damned thing!" he yelled. His fingers tightened on her shoulders and she winced, sagging under the pain. Instantly he released her, a fleeting look of concern lowering his fierce brow even farther than the scowl it replaced.

She was not to be disarmed so easily. "You listen to me, you carpetbagging bully! You can take your blasted ancestor and your Simon Legree tactics and get out of my house! I don't need you. I don't need anybody telling me how to run my life. I bought that privilege for myself, and I'll buy it again if I have to—I'll pay back every cent of the money you advanced, and if you set one foot in my house again, I'll call—"

At the crash, they both turned to face the kitchen.

"Oh, no," Aurelia groaned under her breath. Almost relieved at the distraction, she hurried to the kitchen door and then stopped abruptly at the sight of Sigh, delicately picking his way amidst the debris of broken china, silverware, and food on the floor. Pausing only to lick a crumb of bacon from one fastidious paw, he sidled behind a table leg and peered warily up at her with his one good eye to await reprisal.

Oh, good Lord, what next? For a day that had started out so promisingly, this one had deteriorated beyond belief! Suppressing a hysterical urge to giggle, Aurelia turned away and plowed into the solid fortress of bone and sinew behind her. Jed's arms closed around her before she could back away. She flung up her head to protest, but he was too quick for her. Uttering what sounded strangely like an oath, he lowered his mouth to hers, at the same time bringing one hand up to the back of her head to hold her prisoner to his punishing kiss.

She didn't stand a chance. Caught off guard, she was no match for the skill and determination of his assault. After an all too brief struggle on her part, a subtle change shaded the forced intimacy, and when his tongue invaded her mouth to wreak havoc on her senses, her own anger faded so swiftly that she soon forgot all about his. His lips moved persuasively over hers, their incredible sensuality at odds with their usual firmness. The last fragment of reason left her; it was as if she had been conditioned to respond to him the very first time he had touched her. Every nerve in her body was impressed with the feel of him, hot and hard and aggressively masculine. Her mind shuddered under a stunning sensory overload—the soft, bristly texture of his beard against her face, the intoxicating taste of him on her tongue. The scent of his healthy male flesh, enhanced with a subtle touch of mossy cologne, assailed her nostrils to stimulate her beyond all reason, and she flowed unconsciously into his body, fitting softness to hardness. Entwining her arms around his waist, she allowed her palms to curve over the powerful muscles of his lower back and her fingertips dug into his spine.

"What *is* it about you?" he groaned, dragging his mouth from hers to bury his face in her hair. "I look at you and I have to touch you. I touch you and I have to have you—" His voice roughened. "And you're still warm from his lovemaking!" His hand slid inside her robe and closed over her breast, his fingers rigid with tension. "Tell me—did he do this?" He brushed his thumb slowly over the hardened nub of her nipple, causing her to gasp at the streak of pure pleasure that lightninged through her body. "Or this?" His other hand moved down over her hips to lift her up and hold her against him so that she was stunningly aware of his desire. "What did he do to you, Aurelia? What did you do to him?" His voice was harsh with the burden of some overpowering emotion, and Aurelia, still suspended against his lean frame, tried to push away.

"Jed, no—you don't underst—"

"Shut up," he grated against her throat. "I don't want to know! But I promise you this, A. R. Kenner. When I make love to you, it will damned well show on your face. I knew the first time I saw you with Jamison that you'd never been in his bed, but this one, whoever he is, is a different matter." His face lifted and he stared down at her, his eyes burning slumbrously, like dark coals. "But he hasn't broken through to you yet, has he? He might have slept with you, but he hasn't found the key to unlock you. You're still holding back, aren't you, Aurelia? Still covered in cellophane." His voice was a rumble that registered on the base of her spine like an enormous pipe organ. There was no sign of anger in it now, only a mixture of curiosity and determination and something else—something that frightened her far more than his volatile temper.

"Jed, about Adam . . . he's—"

"Hush! I told you, I don't want to hear it. He's gone. Forget him. Forget Jamison too—not that he seems to have any restraining effect on your behavior. You're going to concentrate on me from now on, understand?"

The intensity of his unfathomable eyes gave his words the power of a command, and it was several seconds before Aurelia could free herself from his spell enough to respond.

"Will you please put me down?" She pushed against his shoulder stiffly, hating her helplessness before his superior strength and size. It was impossible to sound firm and authoritative when one's feet were dangling a good six inches off the floor.

He put her down slowly, still not releasing her gaze, but before she could summon the words to tell him where to go and how long to stay, he turned away and strode to the door. One hand on the knob, he paused. "If I stay here now, I'll end up taking you to bed. That's not what I came for—this time," he added with a tight smile that Aurelia found peculiarly unsettling. "But in case you think I'm finished with you, take heart—I'm only postponing the inevitable. I make it a policy never to act in anger, but in your case I came pretty damned close to making an exception. Now go take a hot shower and hop into some dry clothes and spend the next few days getting that manuscript ready for me to look over!"

He let himself out, closing the door behind him firmly. Aurelia stood there for several moments, ignoring the ingratiating purr of the cat twining around her ankles. "Well, hell-damn-blast," she uttered in soft exasperation. She wasn't given to profanity, but for once she wished she had cultivated a more expressive vocabulary.

All wrong! Damn it, he had handled it all wrong! He had called her yesterday with the perfectly reasonable intention of working out a mutually agreeable timetable for finishing the book. She'd been out and he had tried later on, with the same results. By the time he'd thought to ask Bill Voncannon if he knew who owned the antique shop near the parkway where she worked, the fuse was getting dangerously short. It was all he could do to be civil to the Claiborn woman when she refused to tell him more than the bare fact that Miss Kenner was out of town.

Not that he could blame her. He wasn't noted for his party manners under the best of circumstances, and if Aurelia was a friend of hers, she probably thought she was being protective. He could have explained himself, but by then he was in too foul a mood.

When the whine of the powerful engine reached through his preoccupation, informing him that he was taking out his frustration on the accelerator, Jed eased up, deliberately shelving the problem with the discipline of long practice. He was overreacting. Blame it on the state of his gut; he had charged out with no breakfast; in fact, dinner the night before had consisted of two stiff drinks and a slab of cheese, hardly a soothing diet.

He drove on into Stuart and bought a costly and ill-assorted supply of groceries, appreciating more than ever the very efficient woman who looked after his Gramercy Park apartment and managed to remain practically invisible in the process. On the way out of town again, he considered stopping by Voncannon Electronics. He'd met Bill Voncannon the first time he'd come down here on a flying trip and had made a mental note to follow up on the meeting. V. E. was a new firm, and everything Jed had seen of the plant indicated sound backing. Besides which, Voncannon had both the business and the technical background to make a go of it. It was an interesting possibility, leapfrogging from Trenton, his southernmost branch, to Virginia. Before he put out any more definite feelers, he'd better call a session with Rassmussen and someone from legal, probably Belvins.

Drawing up close beside the massive rock wall of his house, it occurred to him that his pleasure in the beauty and seclusion of his Blue Ridge retreat had paled somewhat in the last day or so. He put the groceries away haphazardly and prowled restlessly through the echoing rooms, ending up before the wall of glass in the living room to stare down into the hazy valley. It was scarcely ten thirty; the whole damned day loomed before him. He simply wasn't accustomed to unstructured time, having worked his tail off for as long as he could remember.

He could kill an hour or so tinkering with the ancient Jeep that had been a part of his inheritance. He'd got the thing running and it was legal as of yesterday, but inspection or no, he'd hate to tackle some of the more rugged terrain around these parts in it. Rae had eyed it speculatively, her gaze moving from the Jeep to the Jag and back again.

"Oh, no, you can just forget it," he had declared. "If you want wheels, rent 'em. I'm not planning to hole up here until you get back with Anderson's scalp hanging from your belt, and I value both our necks too much to entrust them to that relic."

She had rented a late-model sedan, passing a few

choice remarks at the lack of selection, but he hadn't relented. It was one thing to share your home briefly with an attractive female guest. It was quite another to share a piece of sensitive machinery for an extended period.

Rae was still at Roaring Gap. He didn't know whether he was glad or sorry. At least when she was here, she kept his mind off certain other matters. He bit off the end of a cheroot and raked a match across the rock flank of his fireplace wall. The problem was . . .

The problem was, he just wasn't cut out for so damned much freedom! He had worked like a galley slave for years to build an early fascination with crystal sets into a tightly constructed radio telephone business. Competition in the field was murderous, especially in metropolitan New York, where he had started. He had opened his fourth branch last year. The challenge of expansion had waned after that, and he had applied himself to developing some highly innovative ideas for rural fire and emergency services. That done, he had begun to hone his management team to a fine edge, and now, somewhat to his chagrin, he found it functioned almost too smoothly.

That wasn't what was chewing on him, though. Management had never interested him as much as the creative end of the business. Give him a problem to solve, any problem, and he was off and running. But just lately—just since he had come south, in fact—he had found it increasingly difficult to concentrate on business problems of any sort.

"Damn it, communications is my life's work! So why the hell can't I communicate with one stubborn, straightlaced, pint-sized female writer without jamming every frequency in my brain?" He reached for the bottle and then drew back his hand. He'd been doing too much of that lately—another mark against the woman who irritated him all out of proportion to the importance of her role in his life.

Oh, sure, she was pretty enough, but he was accustomed to a high standard of beauty. With all due modesty, he didn't underestimate his attractiveness to women, although he was inclined to attribute it more to his highly successful business than to any personal charisma.

It had to be the peculiar relationship between them. He was used to people who either worked for him or not—none of this halfway business! He paid top wages and demanded top performance; it was as simple as that. Balancing firmness with fairness, he had seen his policies proved out over and over in the labor market, but when he began to apply the same logical, systematic approach to his personal life, things went haywire. It just didn't compute.

He stabbed out the half-smoked cheroot on the virgin hearth. Damn it, he had mapped out a flawless plan for his future. With the business practically running itself, he set out to acquire himself a home and a family. It was long past time. Other men had something of the sort to work for, to enjoy their free time with, and he could certainly afford to indulge himself at this stage.

Applying what he considered an eminently reasonable approach to a simple matter of personnel, he had screened his little black book—which in his case was a personal computer. The list was extensive and brought a few smiles of reminiscence as he scanned it, but no one name stood out. When Rae had hinted for an invitation to Virginia, he had taken it as an omen. Candidate number one. He rather suspected nothing would come of it, but it was against his policy to prejudge. Besides, he enjoyed her company.

By the time they had got as far south as Richmond, he had known it was no good. They were too much alike. They'd never make it over the long haul, and he suspected Rae knew it as well as he did.

He slammed out the front door and prowled the grounds restlessly. There was a cave around here somewhere. He'd more or less promised to locate it and show Aurelia where the old man had played as a boy. Damn it, even here on his own territory that woman intruded. He didn't owe her anything! He'd turned over a box of diaries, letters, and photographs to Barker, leaving it up to him to find a writer to put it all together into readable form. Barker had then commissioned A. R. Kenner, who had ended up plastering the pictures all over her house and doing Lord knows what with the rest of the stuff! Either she was adding to her collection of antiques or she fancied old Jocephus. Damned if he could figure out which. And now she had the temerity to refuse to let him examine her work!

Well, he could cancel the damned project anytime he chose. He didn't need to justify his existence by paying homage to the past—or by insuring the survival of clan Dancey, for that matter. He didn't owe anyone anything! His personal experience of family life so far was certainly no glowing testimonial to the establishment.

After his mother had run off, his father had more or less opted out of his responsibilities. He'd been ill even then, it later turned out. Jed had migrated to a relative of his mother's who, with her husband, ran a small shirt mill in Troy, New York. Aggie Phelps had taken one look at his build—he'd been husky, even as a child—and taken him in.

There had been no sanctimonious flap about family duty from old Aggie; he'd been expected to pay for his lumpy bed and skimpy board by putting in as many hours as was physically possible in the mill. Only the fact that Charlie Phelps had been an armchair jock had enabled Jed to play football in high school. Jed had always been grateful to Charlie for that: he'd won a two-year scholarship on brawn and determination alone, and when that ended, he'd worked his way through two technical schools, earning his degrees the hard way.

As relatives go, his weren't much to brag about, at least not on the maternal side. He'd left home, or what passed for it, the day he'd graduated from high school, and he hadn't looked back. For a long time he hadn't recognized the ever present feeling of rootlessness that had followed him from Troy to the midwestern college he had attended, and then back to New York, hanging over his shoulder, sneaking a quick jab now and then when he was exhausted and feeling particularly mortal. Maybe that was why he had latched on to the Dancey heritage when it had presented itself.

Oh, hell, he hadn't thought of old Aggie for years. Charlie had drunk himself to a timely death, leaving her the richer by one insurance policy. The firm's legal department kept tabs on her, assuring him that she wasn't in need, but beyond that, he owed her nothing. He'd paid his debt by enduring six years of twenty-hour work days, short rations, and harsh words.

Meanwhile, there was Aurelia. He hadn't made allowance for her anywhere in his plans, and it bothered the devil out of him to have her screwing up the works. He couldn't categorize her, and that disturbed his sense of order. She worked for him, but he seemed to have no control over her whatsoever. Hell, she wouldn't even let him read what he had paid her to write. And to complicate matters even more, he couldn't seem to keep his hands off her. She was unlike any woman he had ever met. He couldn't get a handle on her. *Face it, Dancey. She's a challenge, and you've never backed down from a challenge yet.*

At the end of three days Aurelia ripped another page of stilted drivel from the typewriter, screwed it up into a ball, and tossed it across the room. Sigh leaped down from the mantel and obligingly swatted it into the foyer.

"Oh, *blast!*" She had worked so diligently, forcing her mind to a rectitude that had been hard to maintain; she refused to allow it to dwell on Jed and the disastrous effect he had on her. Theirs was a business deal, purely and simply. If he seemed to forget that fact now and then, it was merely the nature of the beast. She might not have had all that much personal experience with men, but she wasn't stupid, nor was she uninformed. And she had fielded a few passes in her years in Atlanta—caught a few, as well. But she never ran with them; she always dropped them when the breathing got heavy.

She tucked the pitifully thin stack of pages away in the tin box with the others. Not much to show for three consecutive eight-hour days, either in quantity or quality. Her dubious muse had deserted her. Jo stubbornly refused to come alive for her, either in her mind or in her heart.

Not even re-reading Mary's letters had helped. Repetition had dulled their effectiveness. Words. Just so many words in brownish, faded ink, the archaic spelling and dated phrasing completely devoid of the charm she had found there in the past.

With an uncharacteristic lack of charity, she wished Grace Bradham would grow tired of shopkeeping and go home—not that that would solve any real problems. Still, even postponing them might help. She needed all the objectivity time could buy her, not to mention full-time employment if Jed decided to unhire her. At the rate she was producing, he very well might. Nor could she blame him.

Spinning around on the organ stool with a sigh of frustration, she stared at the dim photograph propped against the clock, seeing not Jo's lean, sensitive face, but Jed's. She had to admit it; there was just as much sensitivity there, if of a slightly different sort. There was warmth in Jed's darkly brooding eyes, too, a warmth that could swiftly reach flash point with devastating results. And she had even caught glimpses of tenderness. There was tenderness in the large, capable hands that had looked so alien against Sigh's soft white fur. And Lord knows, she remembered all too well the tenderness of his touch on her face, in her hair, on her body.

Suddenly Aurelia ached with a desolation she hadn't felt in years, a hollow sort of pain she thought had been left behind her. Blame it on monthly tension, or the rainy spell, or the uncertain economy —and hers was certainly uncertain enough. Blame it on the fact that she had staked everything on her ability to make it as a writer and she was falling flat on her face at her very first solo effort.

"Darn it, what's happening to me, Jo? You're a wise man—you tell me what I'm supposed to do now." She stared accusingly at the darkly bearded face in the photograph, but there were no answers there. Nor was there the familiar glow of pleasure she usually experienced when she looked at the photographs, or at Jo's spidery handwriting in the musty old journals.

"It's all over between us, isn't it, Jo? You're not going to help me out with the answers, are you? I might have known I couldn't count on anyone but myself." She picked up a forgotten cup of cold coffee and frowned at the skim on the top. She had counted on him for more than answers, unfortunately. He had been her bread and butter, the roof over her muddled head, and now he had turned his back on her.

"Damn it, Jo," she exclaimed in an unusual burst of exasperation, "I *need* you! Don't just stand there with that blasted sword strapped to your side, looking like a pious pirate! You had the courage to leave your wife and go to fight for what you believed in. The least you could do is help me when I'm in danger of losing—of losing my—"

Of losing her what? Her career? What was one measly career in the cosmic scheme of things? Of losing her home? It didn't even belong to her, and anyway, there were plenty of people in the world without jobs *or* homes. At least she had her health and a moderate degree of ability.

She knew very well what she was in danger of losing, and it was too late for Jo or anyone else to help her.

Sigh wrapped around her leg, inviting a caress with an arched back and a quivering tail. He couldn't help her, either. When the phone rang, she reached for it as if it were a lifeline. It was Carol.

"Last chance for a splash before Mitzi pulls the plug," she announced gaily. Drewry was howling in the background.

"What last chance? What splash? What plug? And what are you doing to that baby?"

"The Voncannons' annual wingding—you remember! It's tomorrow, rain or shine. Wear a raincoat over your bathing suit and bring a blanket for afterward in case that cold front goes through tonight."

"Oh, Carol, I don't think—"

"You're *not* going to be a pool party pooper! I won't allow it! You've been cooped up there working like a navvy and if you don't come up for air, you're going to go stale. Besides, I could use some help with Drew."

"You said the magic words." Aurelia laughed. Hanging up a few minutes later, she felt inordinately better. She *had* gone stale. That was all that ailed her. She'd been cooped up in here for days, plowing through airless old volumes trying to breathe life into a dusty subject, and she was *stale*.

Besides, she could play dolls to her heart's content while Carol swam.

Not once as she covered her typewriter and rinsed out a basin of hand laundry did it occur to her that her attitude toward Jo's story had undergone a vast change. Much less did she permit herself to delve into the possible reason.

Henry and Carol stopped by for her in Henry's new sports car. Aurelia wedged herself into the back seat and held out her hands for the baby. "My turn, little mother. Oh, darn, she's asleep, isn't she?"

Henry chimed in with a comment about certain small females who couldn't tell day from night, but Aurelia's attention was already taken up by the delectable bundle in her lap.

The party was open-ended, and it was in full swing when they got there. The whole area around the oval pool was swarming, and the decibel level declared the affair a howling success.

"Three gin and tonics and one short milk, coming up," Mitzi sang out, shoving a chair toward Aurelia. "Park yourself for a minute and I'll locate a basket or something for the baby."

"Don't bother, thanks, Mitzi. I'll hold her until

she's ready to have a nap and then I'll make her a nest in one of the bedrooms, if it's all right." She wasn't about to give up her chance to play dolls yet. Carol and Henry had come prepared to swim, but Aurelia had the perfect excuse this time. She had worn a crinkled cotton peasant dress in shades of russet and gold, and she hadn't brought a bathing suit. As unofficial baby sitter, she could sit on the sidelines and enjoy the whole affair.

Bill Voncannon arranged an umbrella over a chaise lounge, and after assuring herself that Aurelia really didn't want to swim, Carol joined Henry and the others in the pool. Drew's unfocused blue eyes seemed to follow the noisy, colorful scent for a few minutes, but then she rammed her tiny knuckles in her mouth and fell asleep, unbothered by shouts of laughter or the stereo that held forth from the den nearby.

The sun fell across the foot of the chaise, warming the crisp mid-September afternoon, and Aurelia slipped off her shoes, pulled her skirt up above her knees, and settled deeper into the cushions. Drew, lightly covered, was asleep on her breast, feeling warm and damp and smelling faintly cottage-cheesy. Aurelia patted the tiny back softly and laid her face against the bald head. There was something so bliss-fully satisfying about holding a sleeping baby. Career woman or no, she wasn't about to deny it. She might never have one of her own to cuddle, but there were plenty of babies in the world she could reach out to. Perhaps she might even adopt one; restrictions against single parents were a lot more relaxed than they used to be.

The cheerful blend of laughter, screams, and music faded into the background as she felt her own eyelids droop. This was precisely what she needed—to get away from that darned typewriter, away from the bearded face on her mantel that had lately seemed more than a little accusing.

Drew hiccoughed in her sleep and Aurelia's eyelids drifted up lazily. Smiling, she closed her hand over a doll-sized foot, squeezing ever so gently. With some idea of locating Mitzi and arranging a place in one of the downstairs rooms, she focused her eyes on the colorful scene beyond her own shady spot and began to search. She had covered half the crowd when her eyes encountered a darkly enigmatic gaze that brought color to her face and a quick gasp of disbelief to her lips. She blinked and then looked again, but he was still there. Jed was across the pool, leaning up against a portable bar, listening to something Bill Voncannon was saying, but watching her with a perfectly baffling expression on his face.

Chapter Eight

*H*e continued to watch her. It was Carol who insisted that Aurelia put the baby down for her nap. Aurelia, stricken with an acute attack of awareness, found herself holding the small, sleeping form in front of her like a shield until common sense intervened. She was going to have to face Jed sooner or later, and this was as good a place as any. At least he wouldn't do anything drastic in a crowd of people—although how he came to be a part of this crowd was beyond her.

Turning her back on the gaze that raked over every sensitized nerve in her body, she reluctantly handed over her burden. It wasn't right for a grown woman to hide behind an infant, and besides, her dress was sticking to her with perspiration where Drew's hot little body had rested on her breast.

"Go change into your suit and take a dip," Carol ordered as she relieved her of the small, limp burden.

"Maybe I'll just settle for something tall and cool to drink."

"Honestly, Aurelia, sometimes I swear the twins

are more adult than you are! Now change your clothes and jump into the pool and stop being silly!"

"I'm not being silly, Carol. I just don't particularly enjoy swimming. Not that there's room to swim in that mob—one more body and the pool would sink." Aurelia plucked at the scoop neck of her dress and tried not to be aware of the prickling feeling along her spine. It was silly to be so self-conscious. He had probably lost interest by now, anyway. With women of every size, shape, and state of undress cavorting around the pool, why should she think he'd be interested in watching a nondescript female in an unexciting cotton dress? "I'll stick close to the window so I can hear Drew if she wakes up. Meanwhile, I'm going to grab a bite to eat. What's that chunk of spread that seems to be disappearing so fast, some kind of cheese ball?"

"It's smoked salmon with walnuts, and don't think you're fooling anyone by changing the subject," Carol retorted astringently. "You're letting yourself turn into a first-rate idiot about something you should have outgrown years ago! Now go on. If I can peel down to my postpartum flab and Mitzi can bare her freckled all, then you ought to have the courage to break out of that shell you've been wearing around all these years. You're not a turtle, you know!"

For a moment it was almost like being back at the Burn Center. There had been an extensive session of rehabilitative counseling, and it had worked, after a fashion. Of course, she hadn't been quite as secure as she had thought, as evidenced by her reaction to Diana's outburst, but she had picked herself up and taken the next step, and then the next, until she was completely recovered from both the physical and the emotional trauma.

Aurelia accepted Carol's chastisement as a measure of their friendship. Another time she might even have given in, but with the possibility of Jed's examining eyes on her, she'd sooner march down the parkway stark naked. So she was being silly about it. It was no one's business but her own, and the doctor *had* warned her against getting too much sun. And this time of year, when it was hot in the sunshine, cool in the shade, it was easy to overdose. Best to be on the safe side.

"Maybe later," she sidestepped. "First I'm going to eat."

And then there'd be the traditional pause for digestion. And then her lack of a suit. She knew better than to argue with Carol, who occasionally treated her with the same maternal impatience that she did the twins. She also knew when to smile and nod and go her own way. And her own way did not include stripping down and baring herself to Jed's scathing scrutiny.

When Carol continued to eye her suspiciously, Aurelia fished out another red herring. "By the way, do you happen to know a good driving instructor who wouldn't mind tackling a real challenge?"

"Hallelujah! What brought that on?"

"A certain basic lack of mobility, mostly," Aurelia admitted ruefully. "That's the one thing I really miss about Atlanta. At least I could get around there without a car." They had strolled toward the house, and she waited just inside the door while Carol bedded Drew down in a makeshift crib.

If only she could think of a legitimate excuse to stay inside, away from those mocking black eyes of his! What was he doing here, anyway? How had he wangled an invitation—and why? "Carol, the man with the black beard who was talking to Bill—do you happen to know him?"

"No, but if you smell anything burning, throw me in the pool, will you? He's so divine he's *got* to be fattening! D'you think he might have noticed my new figure? Do you know I graduated from an A to a B cup with Drew? With the twins, I went from minus zilch to A."

"Does Henry know about your roving eye?" Aurelia murmured as they wandered back to the party. Her own eye was roving—unobtrusively, she hoped— as they rejoined the group around the picnic table.

Carol reached for a drumstick. "Henry doesn't worry about my eye as long as the rest of me behaves. We have a pact. Lookee, but no touchee." She bit into the fried chicken with an appetite that belied her wiry ninety-nine pounds. "Good party, hmmm? Wonder who he is? We don't see all that many strangers around here—at least not gorgeous bearded hunks like that one. Now aren't you glad I twisted your arm and made you come? I'll wangle us an introduction."

Aurelia swallowed a small surge of guilt. Why didn't she just admit she knew him? She was magnifying the whole episode all out of proportion! Any minute now, Jed was going to wander over and speak to her and Carol would give her a *look,* and she'd feel like a perfect fool!

"Don't bother. It is a good party," Aurelia replied belatedly. The guests were about equally divided between Bill's business associates and Mitzi's bridge-playing, antique-hunting friends. It was a congenial crowd. Aurelia had gotten to know the women quickly in the few months she had lived there, in spite of the scattered nature of the several nearby communities. Ordinarily she would have been perfectly comfortable with them, but under the circumstances she wished she were anywhere else in the world.

While they were settling the baby, Jed had peeled down to a pair of brief trunks. He wore a towel draped around his neck, and Aurelia's eyes dropped compulsively from the ends of the towel down the tanned hardness of his flat middle. Her gaze snagged on his narrow, black-clad loins and she tore it away, letting it linger, instead, on the clean lines of his tightly muscled legs. Curly dark body hair glistened on his taut thighs, his well-shaped calves, and she wondered fleetingly if it had the same crisp-soft texture as the flattened pelt on his chest.

He was a striking figure, standing several inches taller than most of the other men. At the moment he was talking to Bill Voncannon, both men nursing a drink beside the pool. Aurelia found it virtually impossible to drag her eyes away from all that virile magnificence. The man looked as if he'd run naked in the jungle half his life! Marvelously fit, his lean, sinewy physique was a target for every female eye in the group, and Aurelia felt a quick surge of pride.

Which was absurd! As if he were hers to be proud of. Arranging a bright smile on her face, she murmured something to Carol about the array of food, and then she took a deep, steadying breath and slipped back into the throng around the table. Carol was entirely too shrewd to miss Aurelia's preoccupation, and too inquisitive not to ask several rounds of pertinent questions if she discovered that Aurelia had been deceiving her. The more uncomfortable Aurelia became, the angrier she grew with Jed. How dare he show up here among her friends to make a fool of her!

Absently filling her plate with an unlikely assortment of food, she searched for a place where she could escape the crowd until Carol and Henry got ready to leave. The party seemed concentrated in the pool area, but at the other end of the Voncannons' long ranch house there was a stone bench beside a sliding door that was half shielded by a hedge of nandinas.

Forcefully, she restrained herself from making a twenty-meter dash. Smiling, nodding, she moved from one cluster of half-familiar faces to another, edging farther and farther away from the small group composed of Jed, Bill Voncannon, Henry Claiborn, and another man, whom she vaguely recalled having seen somewhere before. It was impossible to miss the curious and admiring female glances that swung in Jed's direction like so many magnets. By the time she had gained sanctuary, she was thoroughly out of sorts with the world in general. Silly women! It was a wonder their husbands didn't provide them with blinders. She plopped her plate on the bench and grimaced at it. What on earth was she going to do with all that food? She'd choke if she tried to swallow a bite.

Catching an unexpected reflection in one of the sliding glass doors that opened out onto the patio, she paused, the untouched plate forgotten on the bench, and stared at the mirrored scene. Even here, there was no escape. Beyond her was the party—a colorful, constantly shifting panorama against a backdrop of blue-hazed mountains. In the midst of all that was Jed. Even seen in reflection, he stood out in the crowd.

He was so darned *beautiful!* How could a man be so intensely masculine, so impossibly, outrageously, *outdatedly* chauvinistic, and still make her bones go limp with a single look?

Worse yet, how could a woman of thirty, of independent, if somewhat limited, means, with a fascinat-

ing career just now getting off the ground and a
backlog of reasons for not getting too closely involved
with any man—how could such a woman fall in love
with such a man?

With her back to the noisy group around the pool,
Aurelia continued to stand there. A gust of wind blew
her sheer cotton dress against her body, emphasizing
the perfection of her small, rounded figure. She was
oblivious to the reflection. The low angle of the
September sun glistened on her thick, honey-colored
hair, but she was unaware of its beauty. She saw none
of the loveliness in the delicately molded face, in the
clouded gray-amber eyes or the softly vulnerable
mouth.

Oh, God, how could you? she grieved silently. Of
all the hopeless, idiotic things she could have done.
She'd have been far better off sticking to a fantasy
affair with Jo. She'd certainly been much happier—
not to mention safer—indulging herself in that harm-
less daydream.

The empty years ahead drifted to the surface of her
mind like a wisp of fog that cleared to reveal her
hollow future. There'd be a succession of cats—
maybe even a dog, as well. The books she had kept of
her father's would be joined by an increasing number
of A. R. Kenner titles, and the rooms would gradually
fill with almost-antiques. She'd have the mantel clock
repaired one of these days, and as Sigh got older and
less adventurous, she'd augment the chipped cranberry glass with a few nicer pieces. She might even treat
herself to a small oriental rug if her common sense
ever deserted her.

But how long could she fool herself into thinking
any of it really mattered? Jed would soon tire of
playing whatever obscure game he was playing and go
back to his career—and his usual standard of women.

If Rae was any example, and she obviously was, the standard was formidable. Certainly Aurelia could never hope to meet it.

Oh, maybe someday she'd consider marrying. Even now, when she had everything any sensible woman could want, there were times when she'd give a lot for another human presence in the house—someone to appreciate it when her baking turned out extra well, someone to laugh with over Sigh's antics, to indulge her occasionally with coffee in bed. Somewhere there was bound to be a congenial man who valued companionship and was tolerant enough to overlook certain shortcomings. Not all men would look at a piece of cranberry glass and see only the flaw; it took a perfectionist like Jed to ignore the fact that it was ninety-nine percent beautiful.

The party waned as cooling shadows crept down over the eastern slopes of the mountains. Mitzi insisted on showing Aurelia the new display shelf for her Flow Blue, and they were still inside when Carol dashed in, diaper bag under her arm, and said, "Oh, here you are! Aurelia, Henry and I have to go pick up the twins. They spent the night with some friends at Groundhog, and the Spencers were supposed to deliver them, but the car's got an ulcerated doojigger and they can't locate a mechanic until tomorrow. I've fixed a ride for you with someone else, okay?"

She was as cheerful as a breakfast food commercial, and Aurelia took one look at those glassy, chestnut-brown eyes and knew she had been done in. She also knew there wasn't a particle of use in protesting. When Carol was up to something, the angel Gabriel shook his head and backed off!

"Carol, I don't mind riding down to Groundhog with you." It was a lost cause and she knew it. All the same, she had to try. She knew beyond all doubt who was waiting to drive her home, and it wouldn't be Claude and Polly Banner, who had to pass right by Aurelia's road on their way home.

"Oh, but with the sleeping bags and the twins and—well, you know how it is. We should have driven the station wagon instead of Henry's toy, but you know how men are. He can't stand to drive my car and he can't stand for me to drive him."

There was more, but Aurelia wasn't listening. Jed appeared in the doorway, dwarfing the comfortable family kitchen with its cozy, low ceilings. He nodded to Carol, offering her a suspiciously bland smile, and turned to his hostess. "Nice party, Mitzi. Thanks for having me. Ready, Aurelia?"

Casting her friend one last accusing glare, Aurelia followed Jed out into the amethyst evening. "The Banners could have given me a lift. You didn't have to bother."

"Glad to oblige. I'm in no particular rush to get back home." He ushered her outside to where he had left his car, bestowing a benevolent smile on her as she stalked beside him.

She waited until he lowered himself into the driver's seat. "You call it home? I thought it was just a summer place. I thought you'd be back in New York by now."

"I'm in no hurry. It's been years since I've had a real vacation, and things are running well enough without me—probably better. I have a tendency to want to run the whole show." He grinned, maneuvering skillfully between several remaining cars.

"I can well imagine," Aurelia muttered in a repressive tone, and he laughed outright.

They remained silent until they were back in Meadows-of-Dan, and then he said, "I'd invite you out to dinner, but after seeing the plate you loaded up and scurried off with, you probably won't be hungry for a week. Maybe a cup of coffee . . ."

He made it a question, but Aurelia ignored it. So he'd been watching while she stood there heaping her plate with mounds of potato salad, congealed salad, cocktail sausage, baked apples, brandied fruit, curried fruit, smoked ham, and marinaded shrimp—to which she was allergic, anyway. She hadn't eaten any of it, and she was suddenly starving, but she'd wither away to dust before she asked him to feed her.

As for coffee, maybe she'd offer him some and maybe she wouldn't. It depended on how well she had herself in hand by the time they reached her house. She still had to deal with the newly discovered—or rather the dimly sensed, but newly admitted—fact that she was in love with the man. And having him there beside her didn't make it any easier.

Dust rose from the road behind them. "Needs rain," Jed observed laconically.

"It rained just the other day," she reminded him, and then wished she hadn't. It had been raining the morning he had watched her saying good-bye to Adam. Why had her silly pride kept her from admitting that Adam was her brother, not her lover? She searched for a casual way to tell him now, but it was no good. The words just wouldn't come. It would only sound as if she were clearing the field for him—which she was. "Where's Rae?" she asked instead.

"Roaring Gap. Rented a car and drove down to visit a friend who owns a pill factory."

She eyed him curiously as he switched off the engine. "Don't you mind?"

"Not particularly. He's old enough to fend for himself."

"That's not what I meant," she muttered irritably as he reached past her to unlatch her door. For a moment she thought he wasn't going to come in, and her heart sagged in disappointment. Then he swung out and came around to take her arm, ushering her solicitously up her own front walk.

"About that cup of coffee," he suggested, and she surrendered silently. Unless she watched herself, she'd end up giving him not only coffee, but anything else he wanted, as well. When she was hungry her resistance was low, and she was getting hungrier by the minute! She'd do well to fortify herself as quickly as possible.

"I baked an apple cake last night. It's good with cream cheese and coffee," she confessed as he followed her into the kitchen.

He prowled while she set the water to boil and laid out plates, cups, and silver. Sigh scratched the back screen to come inside and Jed opened the door and scooped him up.

"Why don't you move into my house to finish the book? Don't you think it would be inspiring—being on the scene, so to speak?" Jed murmured as he helped himself to another slab of cake some time later. He hadn't voiced his opinion when Aurelia had cut herself a three-inch wedge and smeared it with the softened spread, but the gleam of amusement in his eyes had been expressive enough.

"There's no earthly reason why I should close up my house and move into yours," she retorted. "I haven't noticed any lack of inspiration right here where I am."

One dense black eyebrow lifted quizzically. "So I've observed. Tell me, how do you like old Jocephus?"

She sweetened her already sweetened coffee and

stirred it vigorously. "Fine. I like him just fine," she declared.

"Is that why you keep his pictures out where you can see them?"

Her head lifted indignantly. "What are pictures for but to look at? Was I supposed to keep them under wraps and sneak a quick peep at them on alternate Thursdays?" She took a hasty gulp of coffee, made a face, and put it back down on the table.

Jed spooned more sugar into her cup. "Here, you probably forgot to sweeten it, didn't you? Now, about the possibility of your moving into my house for a spell—"

"No chance. Forget it! I don't take my coffee preserved—and if you're through with the cake, I'll put it away." She glared meaningfully at his half-empty cup and he adjusted his position as if settling in for a lengthy stay.

"Pretty good cake, Aurelia. Almost as good as the cake I get from my favorite bakery back in New York." He beamed at her, looking rather like a benevolent pirate, and she tried to accept the dubious compliment graciously. Tried and failed.

"I'm sorry," she muttered grimly. "If I'd known you preferred store-bought bakery goods, I'd have offered you a box of saltines instead!" She stood up and snatched her plate and cup, and he caught her off balance and toppled her into his lap. "Watch what you're doing! I almost dropped these dishes!"

Warm amusement simmered just under the dark surface of his voice. "You watch what I'm doing, honey—I'm going to be too busy doing it."

Using her wrist as leverage, he held her so that her head had no place to go but the hollow of his shoulder. Then, with all the subtlety of a sumo wrestler, he held her immobile as he placed the dishes back on the table. He lowered his face and waited; she stubbornly refused to look up. He was physically stronger, and he had a formidable weapon he wasn't even aware of, but she wasn't going to make it any easier for him.

"Kiss me, Aurelia."

"Don't be absurd!"

"Feisty little thing, aren't you?" he murmured, burrowing his chin into the swirl of hair on top of her head.

Was she? She hadn't really thought about it. If anything, she would have considered herself meek and complaisant, if not actually cowardly. Perhaps it was only Jed's effect on her. Lately she had noticed all sorts of new wrinkles in the personality she had lived with for years. She might have just waked up after a Rip Van Winkle–sized nap!

Jed's right hand was resting lightly on her thigh. He could have enforced his will easily enough, but for some reason he didn't. It was as if he was playing some sort of game with her. The fact that she didn't even know the name of the game, much less the rules, made her merely a pawn, a cipher, and she didn't care for that position at all!

His unnatural stillness made her glance up at him warily, and that was a tactical mistake. Jed bent to close the few inches between their mouths, and the touch of his beard on her face was electrifying. She caught her breath, and then his lips closed over hers and she was lost.

Every nerve in her body vibrated to his personal rhythm. When she felt his tongue invading the soft warmth of her mouth to engage hers, she found herself clinging to his shoulders, twisting around on his lap to press her breasts against the hard wall of his chest. He wore a soft white cotton safari shirt, and her fingers, clumsy in their haste, began to work on the buttons.

It took only the contact of her fingertips on his taut flesh to bring them both to flash point. The tension had been building from the first moment she had looked across the swimming pool and seen him—since long before that, really. Not once had she met his gaze that afternoon, for whenever she dared slide her eyes in his direction, he was looking somewhere else. And yet she had felt his eyes on her. He had been as aware of her as she had of him; he *had* to be! The force field that shimmered between them, that had built to the present exquisite state of tension, couldn't have been generated by one person alone.

One of his hands was on her thigh, sliding sensuously over the pale, velvety flesh as it pushed her skirt higher. His lips were nibbling the line of her eyebrows, pressing butterfly kisses on each eyelid, and it wasn't enough. She was hungry for him, thirsty for him; she wanted his mouth on hers, his hands on her breasts. She wanted to be *in* and *of* and *around* him. She wanted the weight of him bearing her down, endlessly down, until she was lost to everything but the compelling world of sensation.

"Come live with me while you finish the book, Aurelia," he whispered against her ear.

Cold reason shattered the fragile spell, and she stiffened and pulled away. He allowed her the space of a few inches between them. When she lifted accusing eyes, he smiled down at her, and her breath caught in a quick, painful gasp. That wasn't passion glistening in the inky depths of his eyes; it was amusement. It was pure devilment. He *was* playing with her!

"Didn't I warn you, love? When I want something,

I can be as tenacious as all hell. You may as well give in gracefully and spare us both the agony." One of his hands lifted with slow deliberation and his forefinger burned a circular pattern on the bodice of her dress.

As a frantic message was telegraphed to all the vital parts of her body, Aurelia looked down in dismay. Her nipples were standing out in full relief against the crinkly cotton gauze. She watched, stunned, as Jed's hand came up to cup the small globe, and then, deliberately, he did it again, and again the drums pounded out their primitive message. She lifted her gaze strickenly. "Damn you, Jed Dancey. For the last time, will you leave me alone?"

"No."

"Why are you doing this? What do you want from me?" She had the small satisfaction of seeing a flicker of uncertainty cross his face, and then, grasping her opportunity while he was momentarily distracted, she escaped. With the width of the kitchen table between them, she confronted him. "If you're trying to get me to void our contract, then—"

"Damn it, Aurelia, forget the contract! Do you think this is the way I generally conduct my business affairs?"

"What would I know about the way you conduct your affairs—business or otherwise?" Bitterness accented the ambiguous word. "I only know I'm not going to be one of them!"

"Nobody asked you to," he snarled.

There was no sign now, in either his voice or his eyes, of amusement, of passion, or even the odd look of uncertainty—which Aurelia decided must have been a misinterpretation on her part. If there was one thing that characterized Jed Dancey, it was sureness. Sureness to the point of arrogance.

"I think you'd better leave," she said quietly. The

innate dignity of her bearing had nothing to do with her small stature, the less than tidy mass of hair that was slowly sliding down her nape, or the naked vulnerability of her unusually pale face. Her lipstick was gone, leaving her lips with a soft, slightly bruised look.

Tilting his head back threw Jed's face into shadow, and Aurelia could read nothing at all in his voice when he asked her if she'd be all right.

"I'll be perfectly all right—once you're gone."

"Aurelia, if I—"

"Good night, Jed. Thank you for bringing me home." Inwardly she was quaking; outwardly she was perfectly composed, evincing a firmness that left him no option but to go. After shooting her one long, searching look, he did.

For the next two days Aurelia forced herself into a miserable regime of ego-punishing work. She re-read all she had written, scoring the manuscript viciously in red ink as she went. It was awful!

No, not really awful, she concluded objectively. It was biased. She had been living in a dream world when those chapters had been written, willing herself back to a time when she could pick and choose her version of reality. She had chosen to empathize with, and to write about, the poetic, sensitive side of the man, a man who had been determined not to allow the carnage around him to shrivel his soul.

In a sense she had done precisely what Jo had done. Both had cultivated a selective vision that enabled them to shut out whole areas of life. In a vast sea of circumstance, when they were in constant danger of drowning or being savaged by their fellow creatures, each had clung to a small life ring and called it reality.

The seas had subsided, and both of them had been cast ashore. Jo's diaries had ended while he was still a soldier, but he had gone home again; of that she was somehow certain. Had the war finally crept into every crevice of his life, drying up the very springs of his gentle nature so that the love he and Mary shared had withered and died? Looking back, it seemed to Aurelia that that would have been the ultimate tragedy, for when all was said and done, what was more important than love?

Closing her mind to further speculation, she forced herself to pick out the hard facts from among the diaries. Dates, places, battles, casualties, the introduction of new and cleverly revised weapons, the wildly improvised tactics of a handful of farmers and blacksmiths and merchants who suddenly found the tides surging against them.

These she noted in a chronological list—a difficult task, since Jo had a way of weaving raw facts into a gentler fabric, mentioning at random things that had happened months earlier, things that he had only later heard of, or had deemed unimportant at the time.

The third day she started drafting her facts into shape. It was a little like being back in Atlanta, cross-checking medical data, names, sources, references, dates—not to mention spelling—and then proofreading the lot with each additional bit of information. By the time she was two-thirds done, she was exhausted.

"After this ordeal I'm going to stick to fiction," she told Sigh, rubbing the bridge of her nose where her reading glasses perched. "It might tax my imagination, but at least my posterior won't be so numb." She made herself stop to eat, scavenging the last of a baked chicken and her no longer very fresh vegetables. She needed to go grocery shopping; she usually went with Carol, but she hadn't heard from her since the party. Which was unusual. As a rule, either Carol or Henry checked on her every day or so. Henry still couldn't convince himself it was safe for a woman to live alone, even in a place like Meadows-of-Dan.

After stacking her new pages neatly and placing them in the tin box, Aurelia put away the two diaries she had gone through and placed the last one beside the typewriter. She opened a new box of paper and aligned it with the edge of her table and then set the mustache cup containing pens, pencils, and erasers at an angle of relative geometric perfection. She'd have a long, hot soak in the claw-footed tub—most of it lying on her stomach—indulge herself with a small glass of Madeira, and then work for two more hours before calling it a night. When—and if—Jed demanded to see what she had done, she was going to be ready for him.

Chapter Nine

Raking aside the colorful blanket of damp leaves, the tip of the stick made a single vertical mark on the red earth. Only when it moved to another position and formed the number 2 just below, did the first mark take on an identity. A 3 was etched in the gravelly clay beneath the first two numbers, and then Jed leaned back against the granite ledge and sighed, tapping one booted foot with the muddy tip of the stick.

He stared at the numerals, and the engineer in him willed a schematic to appear beside them. Damn it all, he needed a set of plans—something. Anything! He was rapidly being driven around the bend by that woman, and he didn't even have so much as a road map.

It was one thing to make a rational, level-headed decision based on known data. It was something else to try to implement that decision only to discover that cool logic didn't apply. As witness his recent decision to acquire himself a wife and a son, in that order. Item: As the last male member of his family, he owed it to his great-great-grandfather, if to no one else, to insure its continuity. On less altruistic lines, it was a known fact among statisticians that married men had a longer lifespan. Item: He had drawn up a mental list of specifications for a suitable mate, based on his considerable experience with the opposite sex.

Item: Nowhere in those specs did it say anything about an ornery runt with an exaggerated sense of independence and a look about her that made him want to hold her in his two hands and—for want of a better word—*cherish* her!

Whipping the stick against the leg of his corduroys, Jed stared unseeingly at the rim of mountains beyond the valley. It had rained the night before, and against a cloud-softened sky of deep gray, the damp colors of autumn glowed incandescently. He felt uneasy, and the feeling was beginning to rile him. Under similar circumstances he'd been known to get mean. It was a good thing he was a fair fighter. He never underestimated the enemy, but he never overlooked an advantage, either.

As a visual memory of Aurelia the way he had last seen her rose before his eyes, he swore softly. What *was* there about that woman that affected him this way? He wanted her—God, yes! His fingers curved inward at the thought of her small, perfectly made body. But he had wanted women before, wanted and had them. This was different. *She* was different. The others, Rae included, had filled a certain void in his life. They had satisfied his physical needs, offered a degree of congenial companionship without making any undue demands. They were all pretty much of a standard when it came to looks, intelligence, and independence; all capable of standing alone and looking after their own interests. Sometimes he had been the one to break away; sometimes they had moved on. In no case had there been any untidy emotional ends.

So what was so different about Aurelia R. Kenner? She was a mature woman of somewhat better than average looks. If she lacked anything in brilliance, she more than made up for it with dogged persistence. She did have a certain quiet style about her—a womanly quality—that was pleasing, and she was obviously doing well enough in her chosen field to enable her to support herself. Besides which, she currently had at least two men in her life that he knew of.

Not that there was anything going on that level with Jamison. If there had been, he'd have felt it.

Felt it, hell—he'd have stamped it out! And that was the point where all his calculations began to go haywire—he had never been bothered by feelings of possessiveness before. With all his other women, the knowledge that there were other men discreetly in the background had been welcome. Somewhere in the recesses of his mind had lingered that old saw about safety in numbers. With Rae, he was one of several. It didn't bother him. He had been attracted to her mind as well as her body, and when the novelty wore off, there was still a mild pleasure to be found in watching her play the next victim. It was over between them, had been for some time, but since neither of them had any particular commitment elsewhere, they'd let it idle along. At least, that had been his rationale. He was reasonably certain hers had been something like that.

So what *was* so different about A. R. Kenner? What was there about her that had made him feel like tearing that muscle-bound redhead limb from limb that morning when he had witnessed his leavetaking? The kiss hadn't been all that fervid, although it had galled him to watch her throw herself into his arms like some overaged groupie. What had really burned him, though, had been the suitcase—clear evidence that they had spent the night together.

And after all that, she still came across like a damned virgin! Even when she was practically tearing the shirt off his back, there was something different about her, something oddly hesitant. Something that held out, held back. Like her prim little bread-and-butter manners.

And what the hell difference did it make, anyway? He had contracted her to do a job for him. Period. Granted, he had made a pass at her once or twice, but then, what man wouldn't under similar circumstances? He had never claimed to be a Boy Scout. If she wasn't interested, then she wasn't. He could survive the occasional rebuff. Lord, it wasn't the first time he'd struck out, and it wouldn't be the last, although with all due modesty, he could admit to a pretty impressive batting average.

What bothered him right now was the sure knowledge that he was going to risk his neck again. He hadn't the foggiest idea why, except that even as a boy he'd been fascinated by puzzles. It had always annoyed him to leave one half solved for a few minutes and come back to find that someone else had finished it for him.

Was that it? Was he simply resenting the thought that another man might get to her before he could solve the riddle of Aurelia Kenner?

Possibly. One way or another, he knew he was going to figure out just why she affected him the way she did before he left these hills. And he was just mean enough to use the information he had recently come across to his own advantage.

Damn it all, he was almost forty and he'd long since lost count of the women he had taken to bed! So why did the mere thought of making love to her affect him this way? Look at him—he was worse than a sixteen-year-old kid at his first X-rated movie!

Carol called on Friday morning. "Hi! Want to go to Stuart with me? I've got to pick up a part for Henry. Actually," she gurgled, "it's for the tractor. Henry's parts are all in good working order. We can have lunch somewhere and pick up groceries on the way back. I'm breaking in a part-time baby sitter for Drew for when I go back to work."

"My cupboard's so bare I thought you were going to let me starve just to teach me a lesson," Aurelia quipped.

"What lesson is that?"

"Forget I mentioned it." Carol would be avid to know what happened with Jed, and Aurelia didn't want to talk about it. She didn't even want to think about it, but these days she didn't seem to have much control over her thoughts.

"Obviously not your driving lessons. Have you started yet? No, you can tell me all about it when I pick you up."

They collected an odd-shaped parcel from the implement dealer and stopped in a place that had absolutely no atmosphere but boasted marvelous hamburgers. Carol hadn't yet brought up the subject of the Voncannons' party and Jed, but Aurelia braced herself for the questions she saw rising to the surface of her friend's elfin face.

"So what's been going on with you since the last time I talked to you? Been seeing much of our tall, dark, and handsome stranger? And before you perjure yourself all out of shape, I know the basics."

"How?" Not how did she know, but how *much* did she know.

"His name's Dancey, right? You're writing about a

reb named Dancey who used to live around these parts, right? Rumor has it that a Dancey from up north has been building a monster of a house on Dancey Hill where that old shack burned down a few years ago." She stirred her iced tea and sipped noisily through the straw. "So what I want to know is, how come you pretended you didn't even know him? And it had better be good!"

Carefully picking over an assortment of possible phrases, Aurelia told her that there had been a certain amount of dissension because of her sex. "He's the prototype for the male chauvinist—hit the ceiling when he discovered he had accidentally hired a woman to write about his soldier ancestor. Honestly, Carol, he accused me of deception just because I use my initials instead of signing my work Aurelia Rose! I've had to fight tooth and nail to keep the commission, and I've felt like throwing it back in his face at least a dozen times since he turned up on my doorstep!"

"So why didn't you?" Carol asked practically.

"Do you refuse to sell an expensive antique to a man just because you don't like the cut of his jib? I need the money, that's why not."

"I can't say I agree with you about the cut of his jib. Me, I like the cut of everything I've seen about him, Henry or no Henry. I've been man-watching since I was about fourteen, so that makes me a connoisseur." She attempted a sultry look, gave it up, and took a giant bite of her hamburger-all-the-way. "So maybe your agent has something else you could tackle instead," she mumbled.

Aurelia blotted her mouth fastidiously. "You don't know just how dangerously we writers live. I've had a plot for a mystery simmering in the back of my mind for ages now, but launching out into fiction is about like taking a swing at the commodities market, only riskier. I'm Max's only ghost writer, and that sort of thing comes along now and then, but there's not usually much money in it—not unless you get to write the memoirs of some rock star or a famous madame."

She finished off her burger, declined the homemade pies without yielding to the temptation of asking whose home they were made in, and continued. "The sort of thing I'm doing now is really a vanity press job, except that most of those don't require an outside writer. Frankly, I think Jed's crazy to spend so much money on a dead-end project like this, but who am I to argue?"

Carol insisted on picking up the check and Aurelia felt herself flushing. "I wasn't hinting, Carol," she muttered as they left the café. "I'm not destitute, you know!"

"You mean you're not flat busted, like me?" The small brunette tapped her modest bosom and made a wicked moue. "So take me to dinner in Paris when your mystery hits the top of the lists. Come on, let's go blow a bundle at the supermarket. Did you know Chase is coming home for three weeks?"

"No! Why? Don't tell me he got fired!" For all their similarity in size, Aurelia had trouble keeping up with her friend's energetic stride.

"Outbreak of some mysterious stomach bug. They're having to shut down temporarily and wait for a clean bill of health from the state board of something or other. Why not get him to teach you to drive while he's laid off?"

Aurelia mulled that one over as they filled two grocery carts. It would save money, but it might put a serious strain on a good friendship. She knew instinctively that she wouldn't be a natural when it came to driving. Still, she'd give it some thought.

Just why it was so important that she learn to drive, Aurelia couldn't have said; she only knew that it was. Something to do with her ongoing struggle for independence, probably. Whether or not she could ever afford a car was immaterial. She might look soft and ineffectual on the outside, but there was iron in her backbone, and if she had to go mining for it, she would!

Over the following week Aurelia learned the rudiments of starting, steering, shifting, and stopping. With the seat of Chase's feisty red compact moved forward to accommodate her shorter legs, she learned which was the brake and which was the clutch, and she wished a hundred times that Chase had opted for an automatic transmission. There was so much to learn, and she had to fight a tendency to panic when the gears made that terrible screeching noise. After the first look at Chase's agonized face, she kept her eyes glued straight ahead. Poor Chase; she'd never be able to repay him for this sacrifice.

They practiced daily after the school buses had finished their rounds, and Aurelia told herself that if she ever managed to pass her driving test and get a license, she'd never be frightened of anything again. If she could control half a ton of cold steel with a jillion horsepower behind it, she could darn well handle a hundred pounds of timid, quaking female flesh. She clenched her teeth and concentrated on staying alive for an hour or so each day, and then drove them to her house where she soothed her jangled nerves by cooking dinner for them both.

Mornings were devoted to writing. She applied herself doggedly, sticking to facts, dates, and logistics.

Later on she'd have to make some attempt to blend the two manuscripts, but at the moment the task was beyond her. For Jo she felt nothing more than an abstract sort of interest. As for Jed—well, the less she thought about him, the better off she'd be. He'd obviously decided to leave her alone, but the very fact that he didn't bother her bothered her. It bothered her enormously.

She had just ripped another ruined page from the typewriter and crumpled it up when the phone rang. Chase was due any minute and her writing had gone sour from the minute she had happened to glance at Jo's picture. It had been Jed's face she had seen. She picked up the receiver and snapped a terse greeting.

It was Jed. "I'm coming by to see you," he announced bluntly.

"I'm just leaving."

"Stay there. I'll be there in fifteen minutes."

"Jed, didn't you hear me?" She heard Chase drive up and sound the horn, and she waved distractedly to him through the window. Then, scowling at the picture on the mantel, she pressed the phone against her ear. Who the devil did he think he was—avoiding her like the plague for almost a week and then asking, no, *telling* her to stay put! "I'm going out—now! Chase is waiting for me. You can call me later if you have anything to say." She hung up before he could reply, shivering from the waves of animosity that seemed to come right through the very lines.

They drove along the parkway for a few miles. She could handle the lower speed limit and the relative straightness more comfortably than fifty-five on steep, curving mountain roads. When her knuckles no longer showed white, Chase told her to turn off at the next intersection, and they spent the following hour on an unused back road practicing several more intricate maneuvers. Chase set out eight empty milk cartons, and after several attempts Aurelia managed to parallel park without knocking over a single carton.

When she had done it three times in succession, Chase called it a day. Aurelia breathed a sigh of relief, but the minute she relaxed the tight control she had maintained over her mind all afternoon, the image of a darkly bearded visage rose up to mock her. Swearing softly under her breath, she switched on the engine, rammed the gear noisily into reverse, and backed out of her parking place, toppling five of the forgotten cartons in the process.

She managed to put Jed out of her mind long enough to drive them safely home, and then she ran two wheels into the culvert beside her driveway when she saw the familiar deep green car parked in front of her house.

Jed got up from the swing and stretched lazily, looking dark and dangerous and stunningly attractive, and Aurelia closed her eyes and rested her forehead briefly against the top of the steering wheel.

"Climb out, honey," Chase offered, patiently withholding any comment at her latest disastrous maneuver. "I'll back it out. Looks like we've got company for dinner."

"He's not staying," she declared grimly.

"Care to make a bet?"

She climbed awkwardly out of the tilted vehicle and stepped back, carefully keeping her face averted from the man on her porch. Her fingers were trembling and her palms were damp, but that, of course, was understandable considering that she had just driven them into a ditch. It had nothing to do with Jed. Nor did the jackhammer rhythm of her pulses!

* * *

An hour later Chase mopped up the last of the beef stew with his sixth biscuit and tilted his chair back with a fatuous grin. "That was the pass that Kubacek fumbled and Galanos recovered. After that, it was no-man's-land. Madder'n hell! I thought they were going to dismember the quarterback right then and there."

They had talked football incessantly while Aurelia rammed the biscuits in the oven to brown and dished up the delectable melange of beef, vegetables, wine, and herbs. She had placed individual salads before them, plopped the oil and vinegar on the table, and wielded the pepper grinder furiously over everything but the biscuits. Tightlipped, she had accepted their absentminded blessings when she sneezed at her own recklessness.

And *still* they had gone right on discussing sports, favoring her with an occasional preoccupied smile as they buttered another biscuit and reached for the homemade apple jelly.

"Just stack 'em, honey, and I'll help with them later on," Jed murmured blandly as he turned to follow Chase into the parlor.

Aurelia endangered three place settings of Bristol Rose as she stacked them beside the sink, and Jed's wicked black brows lifted in feigned concern.

"Are you upset about something? Come to think of it, you looked a little riled when you drove up. I guess I didn't leave you enough room to park—sorry about that."

"You know darned well I'm upset about something, and it has nothing to do with driving! You barge in here as if you had every right, and interrupt and my—my date with Chase. You have the hide of a rhinoceros!"

The slow smile that spread over his bearded face

only added to her feeling of frustration. "And you have the hide of a rose petal," he returned genially. "But we'll talk about that later, after Junior's been sent home to bed." He eased through the door before she could throw the bowl she was holding. He was doing it deliberately. The man was deliberately setting out to aggravate her, and Lord knows he was succeeding!

And it didn't make sense. Why should a perfectly rational adult go out of his way to alienate another perfectly rational adult with whom he had only the most prosaic business relationship? In ten years of working in the publishing business, she'd met all kinds. Doctors were notoriously difficult to deal with, and doctors who fancied themselves as writers were even worse. She had managed to work with them effectively—even the few who had tried to promote a more intimate relationship with her—without once becoming personally involved.

So why couldn't she deal with Jed Dancey? Was it because she had admitted to herself that she was in love with him? Good Lord, if ever a woman had learned how to put her emotions into cold storage and ignore them until they went away, she had. Could love be so very different from grief, or fear, or pain? Was she going to have to go through it all still another time—the aching loss, the anguish, the tediously slow healing process spiked with miserable setbacks?

Chase left at a quarter to ten. Aurelia had scoured every surface in the kitchen except the floor. She had scraped out the rest of the stew for Sigh and his friends on the tiny back porch, and at nine fifteen she could no longer find any excuse not to join the men in the parlor.

Carefully avoiding the real issue, she whipped up her irritation at being excluded from the conversation.

You'd think she was the hired help! You'd think this was Jed's home and he was entertaining one of his own friends, instead of barging in unwanted and stealing the attention of hers. And Chase was no better. He had really burst into full bloom under Jed's careful cultivation—but at least he had an excuse. Sports was his life's work. Jed was too old to be reliving past glories. Besides being rude and ungrateful, they were both too old to be so wrapped up in childish games.

What game *was* Jed playing? Lingering just outside the back door, Aurelia watched the cats crouching around the basin of scraps while her mind went over the past few hours. Somehow Jed had taken command from the first. He had directed the conversation, claiming all of Chase's attention for himself and letting the poor boy go on and on until Aurelia could have screamed from sheer boredom. And then, just when she was ready to jump up and shove them both out the door, he had turned an "I told you so" look on her that had slowly kindled into a smile, and she had melted.

Talk about games! She had not only been utterly trounced, but disqualified and thrown off the field as well—and she still didn't know what game they were playing!

Even before she heard the soft click of the back door, she felt his presence. "Sulking?" he asked softly. "Chase said to tell you good night, and that he'd pick you up tomorrow at the same time. I told him not to bother."

"You told him what?" she exploded.

"If you want to learn to drive, I'll teach you. No point in taking lessons from someone with minimal qualifications when expert instruction is available."

She turned to stare at him, startled to discover that he was so close to her. Moving back a step, she marveled, "No wonder you're so big. It would take a blimp just to house your ego!"

"There's a subtle difference between ego and self-confidence, but we won't go into that just now." Without seeming to move, he loomed closer.

She backed up another step. "We won't go into anything now," she corrected him. "I've fed you and listened to your inane chatter until my head's splitting, and I've had about all of your glorious self-confidence I can stomach at one sitting!"

"Boring, wasn't he?" Jed grinned. "He's probably excellent at his job though, poor kid."

"Wasn't *he! Poor kid!* Look, I don't know what gives you the right to be so condescending, but when it comes to boring, you can call it a draw!"

"Ah, but you see, he was sincerely boring. I was only pretending."

"You mean you were egging poor Chase on to boast about every yard he ever gained since he tripped and fell across his first goal line? Oh, God, that's even worse! *Why?* Just tell me why you bothered." Her hands lifted to her temples. The headache she had exaggerated a moment ago was now a throbbing reality.

He shrugged, a look of concern replacing the slightly smug amusement of a moment before. "Come on inside. I can take care of that headache for you."

"There's just no end to your talents, is there? Tell me, do you also walk on water?" She watched the dull color seep up above the line of his beard, and she felt even more wretched, if that were possible. "Oh, Jed, it's just this headache. And that's no excuse for rudeness."

"Honey, you couldn't be rude if your life depended on it. Now come on inside and let me try to repay you for an excellent dinner. What did you season that stew with, anyway? It had a little something extra that reminded me of Mexico for some reason, but I could swear it wasn't chili."

Distracted, she followed him inside. "Don't tell me you cook, too," she grumbled as Sigh darted between them unnoticed.

He steered her into the parlor and adjusted the three-way lamp to its lowest power. "I'm not very good yet," he admitted with suspect modesty, "but I have hopes. After all, I can't very well uproot my housekeeper every time I want to come south for a vacation."

"It was cilantro," she admitted, allowing herself to be led to the settee and pushed gently back against the cushions. Jed moved behind her, resting his hands lightly on her shoulders at the base of her neck. As his fingers began to knead, her head went back and her eyes closed reluctantly. She shouldn't. It was dangerous. She couldn't trust him to stop with merely massaging the tension from her head and shoulders. She couldn't trust herself to make him stop.

"Maybe I'd better just take a couple of aspirin and go to bed," she temporized.

"Relax," he rasped softly. His hands moved rhythmically on the sides of her face, his thumbs resting just under the angle of her jaw, and she wondered how he knew she had been clenching her teeth until her jaws ached. "I'm not going to bite," he reassured her.

Soft miracles began to happen to her. Her bones started to dissolve until she felt like purring. Another minute and she'd be lulled into believing that those magic hands were unattached to any human agent—

and that was where the danger hid. Her head lolled slowly on her neck as the hands clasped her brow and the back of her head and eased into a lifting, rotating motion.

Was it really all that dangerous? Chances were he'd pat her on the head and say good night in a few minutes. . . . But what if he didn't? What if those hands—ahhhh, they were back at her nape, stroking, slipping down inside the neck of her mauve jersey blouse to soothe away the sudden tension in her spine. What if those hands—and Jed—had other ideas? What then? Would it be so very wrong to let him stay?

Wordlessly he moved around to sit beside her. Lulled by his spell, Aurelia was slow to react, and he reached for her, pulling her gently against his chest. "Let me work on your back now. Wearing your hackles up for so long is tough on you, hmmm?" Without waiting for the protest she felt obligated to issue, he stroked the tense muscles along her spine. A thread of unease began to uncurl inside her, but Aurelia pushed it away. It was her dream—she'd dream it her way and let tomorrow take care of itself. At least he wasn't reaching down the neck of her blouse now; his hands slithered the soft knit fabric over the satiny surface of her slip as his fingers loosened the knots of her muscles.

"How's the headache?" he murmured in a solicitous rumble.

She adjusted her position slightly so that her head nestled more securely in the hollow of his shoulder. "Mmmm, it's marvelous."

"These tensions have a way of building up, don't they?" he whispered agreeably, and she made an acquiescent sound at the back of her throat as she felt the smooth hardness of his palm sloping over her shoulder. . . . There was no fabric between them now. Had he gone up from below, or down from the top? Did it really matter? She was still only dreaming.

She caught the scent of wool and tobacco and a musky-spicy sweetness that stimulated appetites she didn't even know she had. Reacting instinctively, she touched the tip of her tongue to the skin above the collar of his black wool shirt, and it was as if she had set fire to him.

"God, woman, you'd better know what you're doing," he growled, and somehow she found herself lying on her back, with Jed's face hovering inches above hers. The force of their combined heartbeats was almost audible in the intense silence of the small room. Before she could gather her senses, his mouth came down on hers, and the taste of him intoxicated her beyond all further reason.

He held back nothing. Her soft lips were crushed mercilessly as he bore her down into the cushions. His teeth raked the tender inside of her bottom lip and then his tongue assuaged the hurt and inflicted tender wounds of its own. The dream fragmented and fell apart as her own driving needs took control. Nothing had prepared her for those. How could she have imagined the spiraling pattern of desire—his touch, her response; her response, his reaction. How could she have made allowances for that? As her own arousal triggered an aggressively masculine thrust, she allowed her hands to follow their own dreams. Gone was any thought of holding back, of preserving that last illusion, of sparing herself his look of disgust when he saw the network of scars on her back.

She kissed him back feverishly, her ardor lending her a spurious expertise she was only half aware of. Even as his fingers opened her blouse and moved up to conquer the curves of her breasts, her own hands were tugging at the buttons of his shirt, wanting to feel the solid flesh of him against her bare skin. In the dense thicket of body hair, her hands curled convulsively. She felt the hard pinpoints beneath her fingertips, pinpoints that stiffened at her touch. Above her, Jed jerked and gasped out an oath, and for an instant she bore the full weight of his body. Then, as he expelled a shuddering breath, he raised himself up and lifted her shoulders just long enough to divest her of the silken blouse. "Still too many clothes," he grated, going to work on the catch of her bra under the creamy satin slip.

"Jed, not here in the parlor," she managed, twisting slightly so that he could loosen the scrap of lace. He tossed it aside and lowered the straps of her slip, and something inside her slammed up against her ribcage at the sight of that hungry look on his face.

"The parlor! God, sweetheart, next I'll be trying to find my way into your hoopskirt. If I can make it, there's a better place for what I have in mind."

Not yet, she cried silently. A flicker of uncertainty slipped between them, and she searched his face for . . . for what? He raised himself up, and the gleam of his ebony eyes was clearly visible, even in the shadowy glow of the small lamp. This was her chance to escape. She watched it come and go in the time it took Jed to lower his mouth to her breast and take one small, pale tip between his lips. Her hand slipped inside his shirt to clutch frantically at the hard, damp flesh of his muscular back as wave after wave of suffocating excitement shook her.

"Jed . . . I've never—" She broke off as his touch feathered along the sensitive length of her inner thigh.

"Neither have I, darling," he whispered, brushing the sensitized flesh of her breast with his beard as he lifted his face to look at her. "I've never—*ever*—

wanted a woman as badly as I want you right this moment. You feel it, too, don't you? I can see it in your eyes, in the way your lips look. I can feel it in the way your heart beats"—he placed one hand on her body, his thumb brushing her breast while his little finger circled her navel—"right here, and in the way your breath comes out in little sobs. I can smell it mingling with the flowers in your perfume." He groaned, lowering his mouth to her throat again.

He gathered her in his arms and stood, sweat glistening on the satiny skin of his shoulders as he gazed down at her softly. "You won't be sorry, Aurelia," he promised her.

Chapter Ten

Some small fragment of common sense began to shrill a warning inside her head as Jed shouldered open the door of her bedroom. Aurelia closed her ears to it. Still holding her in his arms, he leaned against the door and allowed his gaze to rove from the ivory-painted, wrought-iron bed with its delicate candlewick spread, to the dainty dressing table and the graceful highboy she had painted to match.

Still held high in his arms, she followed his glance. It seemed to her that his aggressive masculinity actually sent shock waves ricocheting through the rose-sprigged, sachet-scented atmosphere, threatening the fragile huddle of appointments on her dresser, stirring the eyelet embroidered curtains like a gale-force wind. She waited.

For a moment he simply stood there, like a darkly powerful throwback to an age of piracy, and Aurelia held her breath. If anything happened to shatter this moment, it would never come again. Please, she prayed fervently, don't let me wake up now. Just this once, let me dream the sweetest dream of all, and I'll never ask for more.

Two long strides took him to the edge of her bed, and he lowered her gently and then stood over her, savoring her with his fathomless eyes. His hands moved with slow deliberation to her waistband, and the heather-pink skirt ceased to be a barrier. Her slip went next, leaving her only a garter belt, her stockings, and a pair of lacy beige briefs, and she braced herself as Jed's practiced fingers began to unfasten her hose.

And then, inexplicably, the shimmering tension disintegrated. One minute her heart was threatening to explode, the next minute it lay like a cold weight in her chest. Her mind tried to snatch back the receding waves of suffocating pleasure that had been building in her body, hurling her headlong toward the point of no return, but they were simply gone, replaced by a baffling sort of numbness.

And then the numbness was swept away by a bewildering sense of embarrassment. She closed her eyes and turned her face aside, willing herself to disappear. Oh, God, how mortifying! Frantically she wondered if she could go through with it anyway. Could she pretend well enough to get it over with and get rid of him? She could feel his puzzled thoughts bombarding her through her closed eyelids. What must he think of her?

What had gone wrong? Had her brain picked up some subliminal message that signified a lapse of interest on his part? Was it something she had done?

He must have caught a glimpse of her back. It had to be that. And she had picked up on his shock, his disgust, and her own body had reacted accordingly. In an unconscious movement that was purely defensive, she pushed her shoulders deeper into the softness of the mattress.

Swallowing the bitterness that arose in her throat, she resolved to rescue his pride. She could get him off the hook before he was forced to blurt out some unconvincing excuse. At least she could do that much for him. "I can't, Jed," she said bleakly. "I'm sorry."

His hand froze in the process of unfastening his belt. His gaze narrowed on her, and then, very deliberately, he lifted her and moved her to one side of the bed and lowered himself beside her. "Look at me, Aurelia," he commanded softly. Oh, God, why couldn't he just leave her alone? Did he have to taunt her with her inadequacies? Maybe she was simply frigid. It was bad enough that it had happened; he didn't have to analyze it to death!

When she continued to stare miserably at the wall, he hooked a finger around her chin and pulled her face toward him. She shut her eyes.

"No, don't slip away from me—I can't follow you there. Aurelia? What is it, sweetheart? Are you still angry with me?"

Angry! Oh, dear God, anger was such a paltry emotion compared to what she was feeling. The protest died in her throat. To what she *had* been feeling. At the moment she felt absolutely nothing. Something inside her had simply shut down, switched off, and if Jed hadn't caused it with his unconscious reaction to her scars, then she had no idea what or why. What did she know about such things? How could he expect her to explain something she didn't even understand herself?

Her eyes flashed accusingly into the shadowed depths of his puzzled gaze. He had to be pretending. Didn't he even guess the power he had over her? Couldn't he tell that she had been his for the taking? One touch of his hand on her body, and suddenly nothing mattered—not her scars, not Rae, not even the fact that afterward she'd probably spend the rest of her life hungry for what she couldn't have.

He was still waiting for an explanation, and there was none she could give him. Gathering her courage, she opened her mouth to speak just as he turned away. She gazed at him hopelessly. He was lying on his back beside her, his head resting on his crossed arms as he stared up at the ceiling. If he'd pulled out a cigar and lighted it, she wouldn't have been surprised, he looked so completely relaxed. With the beard, she couldn't even tell if his jaw was clenched.

Was he still waiting or had he fallen asleep? She continued to stare at him until he turned his head. His eyes were totally without expression now, and she cringed inwardly, wishing he'd yell at her, swear at her—do something other than just . . . ignore her.

And then, searching his face for a clue to what he was feeling, she saw a small pulse beating rapidly in the center of his bottom lip. Without thinking, she lifted a tentative finger and touched it.

As if her gesture released a tightly coiled spring inside him, Jed's breath exploded in one long, heavy sigh. He seemed to wilt before her very eyes, his head falling back heavily to the pillow beside her.

"Jed, I'm sorry," she blurted. He gave no indication of having heard her, and she felt like crawling under the bed.

The familiar sound of Sigh's claws climbing the bedspread broke the tense silence, and Aurelia watched through wretched eyes as the kitten leaped onto the bed between them. Absently Jed scooped the animal up in one hand and rumpled his ears. She watched, mesmerized, as he held the playful cat until claws and teeth were soothed into docility. He did it so well, the taming. Why hadn't he tried it on her? Had he just not cared enough to bother?

Well, darned if she was going to apologize again, she decided in a sudden rush of resentment. Here she was, lying in bed with the man, nude except for a few scraps of nylon, and all he could do was stare at the ceiling and pet the cat!

Then he began to speak, his voice a low, troubled murmur. Waves of remorse washed over her as he said, "Don't apologize, Aurelia. Accept my apologies, if anything. To be perfectly frank, I've been determined to get you into bed for some time now—which should come as no great surprise to you," he added wryly. "Remember, I warned you that I have a tendency to forge full steam ahead once I make up my mind to something. Only I'm discovering that what works in business doesn't necessarily cut it when it comes to more personal matters."

The air was growing distinctly chilly and Aurelia was beginning to shiver, but she couldn't have moved to cover herself if her life depended on it. She swallowed convulsively and concentrated on the words Jed was speaking.

"You're perfectly entitled to choose where and when and with whom you go to bed, Aurelia, and if you don't want to pursue that sort of relationship with me, then there's not a hell of a lot I can do about it, within the bounds of decency." His voice edged off into bitter amusement. "Except to regret your lamentable lack of taste in men."

Some of the tension began to drain from her spine and she took a deep, shuddering breath. She had to say *some*thing . . . but what? Did Amy Vanderbilt have a set of rules to cover such occasions? "Jed, please don't think it's anything personal," she began,

and the sound of his harsh laughter tore right through
her. She froze in confusion.

"Personal? Of course not. I use all those highly
advertised grooming products, so how could it be
anything personal?" He dropped the cat, who darted
from the room, and then he sighed heavily. "Sorry. I
seem determined to make an ass of myself tonight."

The hint of vulnerability was her undoing. Jed
Dancey—the tough, much sought after communications tycoon who had more sophistication in the tip of
his little finger than she had in her whole body—Jed
Dancey, apologizing twice in one night?

She could have wept. Her burning eyes were tightly
shut, but she felt him get off the bed. He couldn't be
leaving, not like this, not with everything unresolved
between them. She opened her eyes in time to see him
shove his arms into his shirt. His back was to her, and
he started fastening the buttons as he moved toward
the door. She couldn't let him go like this.

"Jed—" She managed to get the one word out, and
then she choked up. He halted and turned an enigmatic look on her, and she shook her head silently,
unable to get the words past the constriction in her
throat. With a small, inarticulate sound, she rolled
over on her stomach and buried her head under the
pillow.

Look, damn you. Look your fill! The scars were a
part of her, and if he couldn't face it, they'd both
better know it now. At least they wouldn't make
the same mistake again—and he'd understand
why she couldn't just undress and go to bed with
a man, confident that he would still find her attractive.

She waited an agonizing eternity. Was he so thoroughly revolted that he couldn't find words? He was
still there; she could feel his eyes on her. *Damn you,*

why don't you say something? Anything! Don't just stand there and pity me.

The soft snick of the closing door struck her like a bludgeon. Whatever she had expected, it hadn't been this. Disbelievingly, she pulled her head from under the pillow and peered over her shoulder. He had gone. Just like that, without even trying to be tactful, he had left.

She gave a low, wounded cry and then buried her face in the pillow again and wept.

It was amazing how much work a person could get done given a strong enough motivation. The house shone, the yard was devoid of a single leaf, and it was only eight twenty-five in the morning. Aurelia still had the whole day ahead of her to write. Work was marvelous therapy; hadn't she proven that to herself over and over again? Long walks in the country wouldn't do it—too much time to reflect. Reading wouldn't do it—no matter how captivating the printed word, there were times when her attention simply couldn't be focused on someone else's plot. But just let her get her hands busy and her body moving, and her mind shifted into a sort of limbo. There was no past, no future, only the task at hand.

And the task, at the moment, was to chart the chronology of Jo's story. Pity she knew so little of his early life. She glanced at the mantel and then back again; all three pictures had been put away. She had no need of them now. Instead she had the facts—or at least the facts concerning his term of service in the Confederate army. They were all there in the three diaries, only she had somehow managed to waltz her way right past them as if they were of no importance at all. Maybe Jed was right to doubt her abilities as an objective, unbiased biographer.

Before he joined the army Jo had probably farmed. There were so many references to nature and to growing things, and Mary had mentioned hog butchering, rendering, and "putting by" sweet potatoes and apples. She must have moved back to live with her own family after Jo had joined up. Her letters were full of references to her father.

By late afternoon of the third day Aurelia had collated factual notes with the more introspective study she had done before, and come up with two really sound chapters. What's more, she'd challenge anyone to find fault with them.

If anyone was interested. So far, she had had little indication of interest beyond the vague threat of a deadline. That had come and gone unnoticed, indicating that either Jed had lost interest, or he trusted her to finish the job unsupervised. Either way, she supposed she was lucky. She could have jeopardized the whole thing with her silly theatrics the other night.

For the first time she allowed her thoughts to range back to that mortifying experience. What had she expected? That he'd throw himself down on his knees and swear it didn't make any difference? That he adored her, scars and all? At least he'd been tactful enough to ignore her melodramatic gesture and leave quietly, pretending he hadn't even looked.

Carol called just before Aurelia went to bed to ask if she could take over the shop for a day or so. The day after her mother had gone back to Baltimore, Drew started having problems with a nonexistent malady, and the baby sitter didn't seem able to cope with it.

Aurelia yelped. "She's sick? Is she in the hospital? What's wrong, Carol? For goodness sake, tell me!"

"I told you," Carol said calmly. "Mama says it's colic and my very enlightened pediatrician says there's no such thing as colic."

"So? *So?*"

"Great scott, Aurelia, even I know better than that. I grew up on a farm, remember? Cows get colic. Horses get colic. I've drenched many a sick—"

"Carol, I don't care about cows and horses. It's Drew I'm worried about!"

"Don't sweat it, honey," Carol said inelegantly. "Poor little thing's just got gas, but she bawls nonstop for about two hours at a stretch, and my sitter just comes unglued. I should have gotten an experienced woman instead of a girl just out of high school, but who can pick and choose?"

It was arranged that Aurelia would open the shop and stay until two, when Drew was usually settled for her nap. "Schedule subject to change at a moment's notice, of course," Carol warned her. "She may decide to howl in the afternoon instead."

"I can't believe you can be so unfeeling," Aurelia accused.

"Honey, all my babies are gassy. It's the foods I eat while I'm nursing. The twins were so colicky I swear Henry and I once went three months without once having . . . you know."

Aurelia hung up the phone and reached down to stroke Sigh's arched back. "Mother Nature sure plays havoc with Mother Nature," she murmured. Sometimes she was inclined to think it was all one vast, overrated joke—love, marriage, sex.

She stared wistfully at her half-filled bookshelf and thought about the couples she knew, the special, intimate little looks and catch words she had intercepted between them. Bill Voncannon made fun of Mitzi's freckles and obviously adored every one of them, and Mitzi cracked jokes about intelligent looking high, *high* foreheads, but her eyes had a sort of melted-butter look in them as they followed Bill's lanky, baldheaded progress across a room. And as for Carol and Henry, after seventeen years they were still openly crazy about each other.

"I guess that leaves you and me, Sigh," she murmured, absently scratching the kitten's orange ears.

She was on her way out the door the next morning when the phone rang. She had half expected to hear from Chase. Surely he'd get in touch before he returned to Asheville.

"Hello," she panted, kicking the door shut behind her as the cat attempted to get back in the house.

"Aurelia?" The sound of that raspy baritone sent her into shock. "I meant to call you—about the book, that is—but I had to fly up to New York for a couple of days." He paused, and she waited, wondering abstractedly if her heart could actually slam up against her ribcage. "Aurelia? Are you still there?"

"Where else would I be?"

"You tell me," he retorted dryly. She could almost see the derisive expression on that lean, bearded face. "Look, if you're not busy, I'd like to come around and glance over what you've done so far. About the deadline—the January deadline, that is—forget it. Take as long as you need, all right?"

"January first will be just fine. And now, if you don't mind, I'm on my way out."

"Out! Out where?"

The unnaturally meek tone he had started out with was beginning to sound slightly frayed at the edges, she noted with satisfaction. "I'm on my way to the antique shop—not that it's any business of yours. And I really am running late, so good-bye." She hung up without giving him a chance to argue. After locking the front door behind her, she buttoned her pearl-gray suedecloth coat and told herself that that was one way to have the last word.

She should have known it wouldn't end there. He was waiting on the front porch of the long rustic building. "How did you get here before I did?" she demanded, obscurely glad she had dressed in one of her more becoming outfits. The flattering navy blue with its touches of ecru lace might distract his mind from what lay underneath.

"I called from the service station," he answered laconically, levering himself from the split-rail banister as she came up the three steps. "Don't hang up on me again, Aurelia."

Ramming the key in the door, she scowled at him. "I seem to recall a few times when you slammed the phone down in my ear!"

"When did I ever do that?" he demanded in offended tones. He followed her inside and as she shucked off her coat, he took it from her and tossed it onto the loveseat.

Aurelia picked it up again, hung it carefully on a hanger, and marched across to the coatrack. Her heels rang out sharply on the bare plank floors, underlining her indignation. "I don't happen to remember the day, but believe me, you did it! And now, if you'll excuse me, I'd like to get to work."

He insisted on helping her. When she lifted the basket of pears and apples from the table to put it outside, he tried to take it from her hands. She evaded him, her lips tightening impatiently. With the iron pot of pine cones, though, he won out. It really was heavy, and before she could even get it up off the floor he removed it from her straining grasp.

"Damn it, Aurelia, don't be so stubborn. The thing

weighs more than you do and you've got no business trying to lift it."

"Oh, thanks for your tender solicitude. What am I supposed to do when I've got fifteen pounds of groceries and a twenty-five-pound bag of kitty litter to carry into the house? Sit on the porch and look helpless until some big, macho creature comes along to rescue me? For your information, women have been handling heavy bags of groceries and—and heavy children, and heavy baskets of wet laundry ever since some chivalrous Stone Age gentleman with a club in his hand dragged a female into his cave and put her to work. So don't worry about me, will you? I got along just fine for thirty years without your help, and I think I can survive the next thirty."

His voice was deadly calm. "You might not even survive the next thirty seconds, woman. Now sit down and listen to what I have to say before I lose my patience with you."

It had been a long time since Aurelia had so regretted her lack of height. Not even four-inch heels could bring her up to a level where she could intimidate six feet, two inches of solid muscle and pigheadedness. Shrouding herself with icy dignity, she sat carefully on the edge of the antique velvet loveseat, crossing her ankles primly and resting her hands in her lap—a picture of composure that was as counterfeit as the Tiffany-type lampshade Grace Bradham had mistakenly taken in on consignment.

Jed pulled up the matching chair as if it weighed no more than a few ounces and sat down in front of her. He was wearing an Irish wool turtlenecked sweater with lean black trousers, and when he sat, the fabric stretched tautly over the powerful muscles of his thighs. Aurelia forced her gaze to remain pinned to a spot somewhere over his left shoulder, thankful that he couldn't read her mind.

"Two things. First, about the other night," he commenced, and her eyes flew to his grimly determined face with a look of dismay. "Don't interrupt," he ordered before she could open her mouth. "I'm sorry about what happened—that I upset you. When I went there, I had no intention of . . . well, all right, maybe I did, but I want you to know that from now on, you'll be perfectly safe with me, Aurelia. Which brings me to item two."

Perfectly safe! How dare he pretend that he was only concerned with her welfare. Aurelia's eyes blazed as offended pride stiffened her spine. Of all the contemptible, hypocritical, insincere—

She watched a series of perplexing expressions flicker across his face. He shifted his weight in the chair, as if in discomfort, and looked almost guilty.

Conveniently forgetting her own part in that abortive seduction, Aurelia waited with grim satisfaction for him to continue. She saw his eyes slide away from hers; then he seemed to gather himself determinedly.

"Do you realize you're doing your friends, the Claiborns, a disservice?"

Her jaw dropped in delicate disbelief. "What disservice?" she demanded skeptically.

"The disservice of preventing them from selling their house."

By the time the first customer appeared at the door, Jed had succeeded in convincing her that it was only out of loyalty to her that Henry had refused the offers for the rented house. With farm profits down and expenses way up, with the twins' increasing needs and the new baby to consider, he was strapped for cash. He had borrowed up to the hilt, and it was only because Aurelia had so recently moved into the place and put so much time and effort into refurbishing it that he was reluctant to sell it.

"But Carol said—but she should have told me! Jed, are you positive?" she pleaded, and then, casting a distracted glance at the woman who had interrupted with a question, "Yes, Mrs. Oakley, that's the Geisha Girl pattern. It's a berry set, but one of the small bowls is missing." She turned back to Jed. "I would have understood if she'd only explained."

"Honey, Carol didn't want you feel obligated to leave. Henry mentioned it to me after some fellow in pink pants made him an offer at the Voncannons' party."

Once again Aurelia was aware of that same odd sequence of expressions—as if Jed had somehow taken on Henry's guilt, and his subsequent determination to go through with the sale, regardless of the inconvenience to her. It was absurd, of course. She had to be imagining his discomfort, but . . .

As the full import hit her, all thought of Jed's strange reaction fell away. Her house. Her *home*. Her very first home! They had only lived in the house on Faculty Row two years when . . . and after that, there was Adam's house, and after that, the furnished room. It had almost come to feel like home after a while, even though she had hated the Grand Rapids veneer and the musty smell that no amount of cleaning and airing could ever disperse.

In just a few months she had made the farmhouse hers. She had painted every single room inside; she'd even borrowed a ladder and painted the gingerbread trim. She had chosen every stick of furniture and spent hours rearranging it. It was *hers,* she wailed silently. Henry might have inherited it along with the rest of the farm, but she had made it a home.

"What will Sigh think? Where will he bring his friends?" she demanded with distraught irrelevancy, a slight tremor in her voice.

"Oh, honey—" Jed reached out to her and then drew back. Some of the misery inside her shifted slightly as she took in his own distress. He seemed genuinely concerned.

Aurelia's gaze fell away again as she absorbed the full import of Jed's news. Where would she go? How would she even get there? How long did she have before she had to get out? Oh, God, there were so many things to consider. She felt—she felt *naked*.

Staring woodenly at her twisting fingers, she let her mind run unchecked for a few moments, and then she called it back. Falling apart wouldn't help. If she had to depend on her own resources, the sooner she got started, the better. She'd done it before. Who knows, maybe one improved with practice, she thought a little wildly.

Jed remained silent, and if that silence held a certain quality of watchful tension, Aurelia didn't notice. Mrs. Oakley continued to browse, but she could have walked out with half the merchandise and Aurelia wouldn't have noticed.

Buying the house herself was out of the question, even if there was no man in pink pants with a prior offer. And if she offered to move out so that they could sell it, both Carol and Henry would feel obligated to protest.

Deep in thought, she ran her fingers through her hair distractedly, oblivious to the look of distress on Jed's face as he watched her every move. It had been only a fluke that she had found this small community and the house that was so perfect for her in the first place. A friend of a friend in Atlanta had mentioned having rented a gem of a house in Meadows-of-Dan for a summer, and Aurelia had fallen in love with the name before she ever saw the place.

Jed leaned forward. He opened his mouth to speak and then closed it again. *All right, you bastard, you started this—now you're going to go through with it.* Oh, he had been so clever, taking that bit of information and twisting it to his own use. Sure, Claiborn would like to sell. Sure, money was tight for farmers this year, but that wife of his had him in the palm of her hand. . . . No, he'd done the right thing. It had been his only chance—tumble her out of her nest and then stand by to catch her when she fell. And now that he'd shaken her tree, it was too late to back off.

"I've given it considerable thought, Aurelia, and I think I've hit on a solution," Jed said quietly, jerking her attention back into the present.

What solution? Did he plan to buy it for her out of the goodness of his heart? Out of pity? She schooled her features to a composure she was far from feeling. "I'm sure I can find another house, but thanks for your concern."

Mrs. Oakley walked out empty handed, promising to come again, and Jed swore succinctly. "Where? How will you get there? Pack up your typewriter, your cat, and your furniture and hit the parkway with your thumb out? Be reasonable for once in your life, Aurelia. I'm trying to help you."

She faced him with a regal lift of her chin. The nostrils of her upturned nose had whitened, but that was the only visible sign of the panic that was growing inside her. That house was *not* her sole security, she told herself desperately. Even if she were cast adrift again, with no real job, no family, no home, she wouldn't go under. Under the circumstances, she couldn't turn to Carol or any of their mutual friends, and she wasn't ready to go hat in hand back to Adam and Diana. That particular bridge was still far too shaky.

"Rae will be staying on until the end of the week, and after that I can send down a woman from the main office if you're afraid to stay by yourself."

She blinked in confusion. "What? What are you talking about?" Her mind had been too busy winnowing through the facts to pay attention to what Jed was saying.

"I said," he repeated carefully, "you can live in my house for as long as you need to while you look around for somewhere that suits you better. It's not completely furnished yet, and it's not exactly your style, but it would give you a base of operations, a place to park your cat and store your furniture while you scout around." He sounded almost diffident when he added, "I don't like going off and leaving it empty—it's not good for a house, so you'd be doing me a favor."

Her instinctive doubts must have shown, for he went on hurriedly to say, "I promise not to . . . bother you again, Aurelia. Besides, being on the site might give you added inspiration to get on with the book."

He turned away, unable to meet her eyes. Damn it, why had he gotten mixed up in this business in the first place? It would have blown over if he hadn't decided to butt in. He'd hurt her; he'd damn near knocked the props right out from under her! Somehow it hadn't occurred to him that she'd take it so hard. It was only a house. People changed houses these days as often as they changed shirts.

Was it possible that three weeks had already passed since the day when her house of cards had come tumbling down around her ears? It had all borne a dreadful similarity to the last time she had been forced to pull up stakes and start over. She'd had far less in the way of security, either financial or emotional, in that instance, but she'd made it. She could do it again.

Jed had been invaluable, in more ways than one, after an initial clash. At first he had been so impatient she'd threatened to cancel the whole deal. He had practically insisted on shutting up the shop, dragging her off, and hiring a truck so that she could move that very day. She had put her foot down. Once she had explained her reasons, he had had the grace to back down. It had given her an enormous sense of satisfaction, winning a fight with him, even when it concerned the terms of the favor he was doing her.

Especially when it concerned the favor he was doing her! If she had knuckled under and allowed him to call all the shots right from the beginning, it simply wouldn't have worked; she'd have been forced to make other arrangements. Evidently Jed had recognized that fact. When she explained to him that her rent was paid up until the end of the month, and that she had every intention of staying on until then, and that furthermore, she had to work at the shop for as long as Carol needed her, or at least until the colic crisis was over, he had reluctantly backed down. The gleam that had flashed briefly in his eye could have been admiration for her gumption, or it might even have been amusement. She didn't care. She might have been forced to accept his help, but at least she had accepted it on her terms.

After carefully explaining to Carol and Henry that she really needed to be on location to finish the book, and that Jed had offered his house rent-free for an indefinite period, she had set about making plans. She didn't have all that much to pack, but even so, it took time.

Carol had argued briefly, but it had been impossible to miss the look of relief that had flashed between her and Henry. Thank the Lord Jed had intervened! The thought of inadvertently standing between her friends and the solution to their financial woes made her cringe.

She finished out the week at the shop, and by that time Drew was once again amenable enough for the baby sitter. Mitzi Voncannon had begged to be allowed to work part-time in exchange for merchandise. "I've just been looking for an excuse to get out of the house," she exclaimed, caressing a Coralene carafe and its matching tumbler. She had recently discovered Tumble-Ups and could hardly wait to get started on a new collection.

Jed had gone back to New York, promising to return a few days before the end of the month. Chase was back at school, and as his weekends were tied up with games, she probably wouldn't see much of him in the foreseeable future. There was only one bit of unfinished business.

"All I need is one more session to brush up for the road test, and then I'll be ready to take my exam," Aurelia told Carol as she and Mitzi helped close up the shop for the day. "Chase picked up a copy of the driver's manual for me, and I've practically memorized it. Besides, if I wait, my learner's permit will expire—not to mention my nerve."

Mitzi volunteered her services, introducing her to the wonders of an automatic transmission, which, as it turned out, was a blessing. On the day before Jed was due back, Aurelia took her driver's test and passed with flying colors. "Thank the Lord for those two hours in your car, Mitzi. Great scott, do you realize how much agony I'd have been spared if I'd known I didn't have to do all that noisy clutching and shifting on the exam? I hope I never see another stick shift as long as I live! From now on, four-in-the-floor just means Sigh knocked over the condiment stand again!''

Now, installed in Jed's massive glass-and-stone house on top of Dancey Hill, Aurelia considered her situation. Granted, Jed had finally gotten his way about her moving in with him, but he'd hardly been there to gloat over it since the first day. He had hauled her belongings and showed her where she could store her furniture. "Scatter the stuff around if you want. I'm not locked into any particular decorating scheme. Just so long as you're comfortable."

Then he had flown back to New York. He'd called several times, repeating his offer of a companion, but the last thing Aurelia wanted was some strange woman hovering over her to see that she didn't vandalize the place.

All in all, she'd call it a draw. Once more she found herself dependent on someone else for the roof over her head, but it was a purely temporary measure. The ego-undermining effect was more than balanced out by the small rectangle of laminated plastic she now carried proudly in her billfold. She was authorized to operate a motor vehicle. Of course, she was as far as ever from owning one, but that was beside the point; she was one small step closer to independence. It was the euphoria from that knowledge that gave her the nerve to live in this house, beholden to a man like Jed Dancey, until she could find another place to live.

On Friday, Jed drove in from the airport just before dark. Aurelia, concentrating on the microwave cookbook in her hand, whirled at the sound of a key in the door and stared. "Jed? What are you doing here? You might have warned me!" she snapped, uncomfortably aware of her fluffy, peach-colored bathrobe. She looked awful! He wasn't supposed to be here, anyway. He'd given her the run of his house, and she'd grown so comfortable she'd let down her guard. And now he had to barge in and find her not even dressed.

She had written until dark, forgetting to turn up the thermostat when the day's heat followed the sun over the mountain, and then been forced to stand under a steamy shower for ages to thaw out her fingers and feet. After that she had resumed her cautious experiments in the kitchen. Carol swore by her microwave oven; Mitzi insisted she couldn't cook without one. Aurelia was determined not to be left behind a second time when it came to coping with the marvels of modern technology.

She continued to glare at him where he stood in the doorway, an expression of strained patience on his face. In a deceptively mild tone he said, "It is my house, you know." He dropped his bag to the floor and stretched, and Aurelia noticed for the first time how pale and tired he looked.

Guilt mingled with chagrin and something stronger, something that had her averting her eyes from those broad shoulders that narrowed down to a muscular leanness. "Sorry, I guess I'm still a little nervous. I'm not used to being responsible for all this . . ." She gestured vaguely at the gleaming appliances built into the cherry-paneled kitchen.

"I offered you a companion." He tugged at the already loosened tie and unbuttoned another button on his rumpled white shirt. He looked different wearing a three-piece suit, even with the waistcoat and shirt undone and the black-figured tie dangling. He nodded at the cookbook in her hand. "If you're cooking, how about doubling the recipe. I skipped lunch so I could finish up in time to catch an earlier flight."

"Oh, but—well, you probably know more about this contraption than I do. I just thought I'd experiment a little. I've had baked potatoes for breakfast twice, but that's as far as I've ventured."

He came and peered over her shoulder. "Hmmm . . . radionics. This ought to be right up my alley. So far my cooking has been limited to opening cans and boiling water. The pictures in that cookbook look tempting enough, but the intermediate steps are pretty much of a mystery to me. I told the designer to put in everything a kitchen needs and not bother me with details—I eat out a lot in New York."

His nearness was having a decided effect on her breathing apparatus, and Aurelia tried to edge away. He was tired and hungry, and she shouldn't be thinking about the things she was thinking about. The scent of tobacco, good woolens, leather, and a faint spicy after-shave seemed to act as a catalyst on her brain, triggering areas she thought had been safely laid to rest.

"Tell you what," he murmured, his breath stirring the hair she had piled untidily on top of her head while she showered. "Let me clean up and change and we'll collaborate. You do the mixing, I'll do the transmitting. Deal?"

She eyed him warily, finding nothing at all to object to in his guileless smile. His beard had been trimmed a bit since she had last seen him, making him look less like a pirate and more like a tired professional man.

"Deal," she agreed. "Carol came by and took me shopping, so I've got the basics—bacon, eggs, butter, bread, that sort of thing. Not very exciting, I'm afraid."

"Have you looked in the freezer? I had Rae fill it while she was here, and I temporarily depleted the stock of a supermarket in Stuart one day last month."

At the reminder of the woman with whom he'd probably dined—and Lord knows what else—for the past week, Aurelia came down to earth with a thud. "How is Rae?"

"Fine. Sends her regards. Says if you want to run up to New York for a fling, you're welcome to stay with her for a few days."

He headed for the door, shedding his clothes as he went, and Aurelia buried her nose in the colorful cookbook. *That* would be the day. She liked Rae, she even admired her, but one did not run up to New York for a few days when one had a limited amount of money deposited in an interest-bearing account, which one doled out very sparingly for the necessities of life. She had just received her fall royalty check from Max—hardly enough to raise the hunting instincts of the IRS. Even added to the residue of her last advance, it meant she was going to have to make every penny count until she finished the book, was paid the rest of her fee, and took on another commission.

Thank goodness she had learned to shop wisely. She had had to augment her sketchy wardrobe when she had gone to work in Atlanta, and she had shopped the sales for quality and timeless, flattering styles. She had also learned how to care for her things so that she was still wearing clothes she had bought that first year. She might never really be *in* style, but then, she'd never be that far out of it, either.

Forcefully directing her mind away from nebulous thoughts of beards and money and Rae and elderly bathrobes, she concentrated on her growing hunger pangs. After placing the cookbook on the sparkling white counter, she crossed to the freezer and opened it. "Good Lord, I could live for a year on all this," she muttered, her eyes skimming over stacked packages of Alaskan king crab, palmetto hearts, and stuffed quail. She had stored her few items in the huge, bare refrigerator, huddling them well apart from the bottle of horseradish and the two cans of imported beer Jed had left.

She had already peeped into the custom-built cherry cabinets, closing the doors firmly on cans of smoked oysters, clam chowder, beef Stroganoff, and several cans of flaked coconut. Not that she was even tempted to raid his cache. For the short time she was here, she was determined not even to add to the cost of his utilities, which was why she had tackled the energy-efficient microwave in the first place. She was conscious of every luxurious degree of heat, every tick of the power meter, when she was cooking her simple meals or using her electric typewriter.

If he was hungry, she'd do her best to feed him. She owed him that much, but that was the extent of it. She had her emotions under control now, and it was up to her to see that they stayed that way, temptation or no temptation.

At least, she thought bitterly, hurrying to her room to change into the long-sleeved woolen dress she had worn earlier, any temptation would be on her side only. Whatever Jed had thought after seeing her back, he'd be kind enough to keep it to himself. If they both pretended that embarrassing episode had never happened, there was no reason they shouldn't spend an occasional day together in relative peace. At least until she finished the job and found herself somewhere else to stay.

In fact, once this book was done, she might look into moving closer to Adam and Diana and the children. Birmingham was too large to suit her, but there were lots of small towns within visiting distance. She could have the pleasure of watching her niece and nephew grow up.

Chapter Eleven

*J*ed allowed the hot water to course over his body for several minutes before he reached for the ball of sandlewood soap. God, he was tired! It had been a push, but he'd caught up on all the work he'd neglected by hanging around here those extra weeks, as well as tried to anticipate anything that might come up in the immediate future. It was a damned good thing he'd gone back when he had—and not just because it was the only way to keep him from breaking his word to *her*. Rass and the others at the office were topnotch, but there always came a point when they'd back off and wait for him to step in. Maybe if he gave Rassmussen a little more clout, plus the responsibility to go with it—pull Belvins out of legal to second him—Rassmussen would get over this tendency to sit on his hands until things got almost to the breaking point.

Slathering suds over his chest, Jed tuned out the office, the threatened strike, and the mess in Trenton. Blakely could act for him in Trenton, and it looked as if the union was ready to back down. They didn't have a leg to stand on in this particular case, and if Rass had stepped in at the beginning, it never would have gotten as far as it had.

With a mixture of emotions that was becoming increasingly familiar to him of late, Jed turned his attention to the kitchen, where that irritating, fascinating little creature was waiting for him.

Waiting for him! Wouldn't he like to think so. She'd stood there in that fuzzy pink wrapper, with those crocheted dabs on her feet and those ridiculous glasses sliding off her nose, and glared at him as if he were an intruder in his own house. And it had been all he could do to keep his hands off her. Nothing had changed: she still twisted him up inside and left him baffled and wanting and mad as hell besides.

Damn it, if he weren't afraid of sounding like an absolute idiot, he'd bring things out into the open with her. He might have risked it anyway, if she hadn't as much as told him it was no go. He couldn't remember ever coming so close to taking a woman against her will . . .

No matter how angry she made him, no matter how stubborn and unreasonable she was, he knew he'd cut off his hand before he'd ever harm a hair on her head. And if that didn't make him sound like a first-class, maudlin fool, there was the fact that one way or another, he was going to keep her here. He didn't know how. He didn't even know why, but he was going to keep her there, even if she never allowed him to lay a finger on her.

Hell, he might as well—she'd ruined him for other women. When he'd dropped by Rae's place a couple of nights ago, it had been with the full intention of stoking the old fires again. He'd had some idea that having another woman might get his mind off Aurelia. It might even have worked, he thought with a bitter twist of a smile, except that he hadn't got it off the ground. On his way out Rae had offered him a stiff drink and a few trenchant words of advice, and then slammed the door with unmistakable finality.

In love? Him? For an intelligent woman, Rae had sounded more like some soppy advice-to-the-lovelorn columnist. Damn it, if there'd been anything to this "love" business, he'd have found out about it long before now. A man didn't reach his age, knowing as many women as he had, without having at least caught a mild case of the mythical malady.

He'd been extensively exposed over a long period of time; he hadn't caught the disease; ergo, the disease did not exist. Either that or he was immune to it. The results were the same in either case. And if he were inclined to want to experiment and discover just how strong his immunity was, he had only to recall the way Aurelia had spoken his name, in that quiet, desperate little voice, just before she'd turned her head away from him.

He's been rejected before, but it had never been quite so painful. Hell, it had damn near killed him! He'd had to steel himself not to beg, and it had taken every ounce of willpower he possessed to get up and walk out of there without finishing what he had started.

Aurelia was at the counter poring over the cook-book when Jed came in. She'd tucked a towel under the belt of her maroon knit dress, as he didn't possess anything faintly resembling an apron. In fact, there was quite a bit in the way of kitchen equipment he didn't possess. She'd been forced to drag in a box of her own things to augment the basic set of cookware and the handful of implements she'd found there.

"Have you come to any tasty conclusions about

dinner?" he asked. Blue highlights glistened in his damp hair under the recessed fluorescent fixture, and Aurelia slid her reading glasses back on her nose to blur the image of too much magnificent masculinity, as revealed by the clinging fit of his lean gray flannels and his black knit shirt.

"If we thaw steaks in the microwave, then you can grill them while I bake potatoes. Eight minutes to bake, five to stand afterward, which will give me time enough to put together a salad."

"Sounds plausible. I'll get out the beef and the wine. Claret, Chianti, or Burgundy?"

"You choose. I won't know the difference. Where do you hide your salad bowls?"

"Do I have any? I had the cabinetmaker get his wife to pick up a few pots and pans and whatever else a kitchen needed. Must be around here somewhere." He started opening and closing cabinets and Aurelia hid her smile as she began to scrub two of the largest potatoes.

"So that explains those dishes. I couldn't imagine anyone with the good taste to design a house like this fancying plates like those. I unpacked some of my own. I hope you're not offended." There was something inherently disarming about sharing such a domestic scene with a man; she'd better take pains not to allow herself to be disarmed.

Jed slammed the last cabinet shut and braced his narrow hips against the butcher's table to watch her prick the skins of the potatoes. "I didn't know you were prejudiced against pink plates with yellow and purple roses on them. The cabinetmaker's wife probably shopped for days to find something that remarkable." He seemed fascinated by the small movements of her hands until she looked up and caught his eyes on her. Then, muttering something unintelligible, he stalked across the room to the freezer and began to rummage around in the contents.

The steaks were superb, the potatoes done to perfection, and the simple salad was flawlessly dressed with just the right combination of oil, wine vinegar, and freshly ground pepper. They ate from Aurelia's delicately faded china, with Sigh waiting impatiently under the kitchen table for the scraps.

Jed cut off a sliver of rare beef and handed it down to the waiting cat. "First thing tomorrow, let's go shopping for some new dishes and a couple of platters big enough so that the steak doesn't hang off the edges. Do you like pewter?"

"I like pewter just fine, but first thing tomorrow I'm going to be writing. Also second thing, and probably third thing, as well. I still have a long way to go and I'd like to finish well before the deadline so I can get settled somewhere before I tackle my next project."

His features tightened perceptibly. "You can't work all the time."

"Why not?" she retorted with calm logic.

"Because there are other things in life besides work, damn it!" Throwing his napkin on the table, he tipped back his chair, crossed his arms, and glared at her. And then the arms unfolded and the chair struck the brick-tiled floor with a thud. "That's precisely the sort of thing I swore I wouldn't do, isn't it?" He sighed heavily, his rueful expression asking her pardon.

"Never mind." Aurelia patted her lips with the napkin and stood, gathering her plates and the stainless flatware the cabinetmaker's wife had selected. It was every bit as dreadful as the china. "I'll move my writing table into the bedroom and you can come and go to suit yourself without even knowing I'm in the house."

He lifted one derisive brow. "Would you care to bet on that?"

"I'm afraid it is a bit noisy. I guess I could always write in longhand while you're around." She wished there were some tactful way she could ask how long he planned to stay. He might not know she was in the house, but she was going to have all sorts of trouble keeping her mind on work knowing he was prowling around nearby. Maybe he could chop wood outdoors or something.

Stacking the dishes beside the sink, she said tentatively, "If you're going shopping for steak plates, there are a few other things you might want to pick up. A long-handled fork, a butcher knife, a cooking spoon, and a couple of corkscrews don't exactly add up to a well-equipped kitchen." She ran water in the stainless steel sink. "I could give you a list."

"I'd better wait until you can take a break and go with me. Hey, you're not washing those things, are you?" He nodded tiredly to the sink, which was rapidly filling with mounds of hot suds, and then stretched his arms over his head and smothered a yawn.

Aurelia watched, fascinated, as his shirttail pulled free of his belt, revealing a flat, hair-patterned section of flesh. "It's the usual practice, I believe." Her voice sounded slightly strained, even to her own ears, but perhaps he wouldn't notice. He'd probably forgotten what she looked like, much less sounded like.

He gestured impatiently around the well-appointed room. "One of these contraptions is supposed to be a dishwasher. Use it. You've got better things to do with your time than to spend it messing about in the kitchen."

Lowering her face over the billowing suds, Aurelia said a little grimly, "I've worked on the book a full eight hours today. That's as much as I can do without getting stale. Now, if you'll excuse me, I'll get these done so I can go to bed. I like to keep early hours, because I do my best writing in the mornings. And thank you very much for the steak and the wine. I enjoyed it."

His knowledge of profanity easily outdistanced hers. He gave vent to a few highly original phrases and then turned, striding from the room. Aurelia winced as the saloon-type doors clattered behind him, and then, before she could echo his sentiments, he was back again, glaring at her as if considering the most efficient form of mayhem.

While she stood there, up to her elbows in soap-suds, he opened his mouth, closed it, took a deep breath, and then opened it again to say, "Aurelia, I'm glad you enjoyed the steak. I enjoyed the potatoes and the salad and the coffee. I enjoyed the salad dressing and the butter on the potatoes. I also enjoyed your company—" The tight control he had started out with began to unravel. "And I'd damn well like to enjoy a bit more of it before you scuttle off to bed like some damned churchmouse! Now leave those things where they are and come have a drink with me. Do you understand?!"

A mouse again! What was it about her that reminded everyone of mice? Flinging suds across the floor, Aurelia jerked her hands out and planted them firmly on her hips. "If you can't speak to me without swearing, then please refrain from speaking at all. I refuse to leave my dishes in the sink overnight, and I refuse to use a noisy dishwasher. I do *not* want a drink, and I do *not* plan to sit on that monstrous piece of furniture and watch you scowl at me while *you* have a drink. And furthermore, I am not a mouse of any kind or description! Is that understood? Have I made myself clear?"

All signs of tiredness and pallor disappeared from Jed's face. A ruddy stain crept up under the thick dark beard and mustache and his eyes blazed at her. Aurelia watched, mesmerized, as the small pulse began to flicker in the center of his bottom lip, and another one at his temple. Had she pushed him too far? She was alone with him; there was no one else living within miles. What did she really know about the man, anyway?

She watched in reluctant admiration as he deliberately took control of his emotions. The flush faded, leaving him even paler than before. His eyes lost that blazing quality and looked merely tired. His voice, when he finally spoke, held a hollow note of defeat.

"All right, Aurelia, what is it that you *do* want? Just tell me, and if it's within my power to grant it, it's yours."

There. He had laid it on the line. If she cared for him at all, if there was the slightest chance that she could ever care for him, then the door was open for her. He'd left it wide open; all she had to do was give him a sign, and he'd take it from there.

Aurelia stared back at him in dismay. What do I want? Oh, God, don't you even know? Haven't you guessed? I want all this. Her mind encompassed the cozy domestic scene, the table for two in the kitchen, the large single couch overlooking a moonlit valley below, the bedroom with one king-sized bed, one rock fireplace, and nothing more.

I want *us*, she wailed inwardly.

"Since you asked," she said in a deliberately expressionless tone, "I'd like to be allowed to finish my chores without any more tirades, and then go to bed.

Tomorrow I'd like to be allowed to work uninterrupted until I take my morning break, at which time, if you have anything to say to me, I'd like to be allowed to hear it without having my ears continually assaulted by profanity. If that's too much to ask, then perhaps we'd better make other arrangements about my staying here."

Turning away to hide the agony of longing in her eyes, she scrubbed at the delicate stylized design on the ivory plate. After a while, when she heard him turn and leave the room, her shoulders sagged, every muscle aching from the effort it took to keep from hurling herself into his arms. *And if you believe all that gibberish, then you're as hopeless as I am.*

"Mail call," Jed announced with cautious friendliness when Aurelia shut off her typewriter and emerged from the room she had hastily claimed as her workroom.

Until he had come home, she had worked in the big living room, finding that she enjoyed being able to stare out into nothingness whenever she looked up from the keyboard. This morning, before he was even awake, she had moved her things back into one of the unused bedrooms—at least she supposed it was a bedroom. Among all the unfurnished rooms, there were only two beds in the entire house; Jed's and the one Aurelia had taken—the one Rae had used. If she had actually used it.

"Mail for me?"

He tossed several items on the improvised coffee table. "Auction sale Saturday week—household goods and farm implements. If it's white tie, we can't go. I didn't come prepared. Oh, yes, for Miss Aurelia Rose Kenner, one letter and two important looking documents." He held one of the colorful catalogs to the light and peered closer with exaggerated interest. "Good Lord! Twenty to fifty percent off on office supplies? And take a look at this one—two golden delicious apple trees for the price of one, *plus* a bonus of five forsythia seedlings if you order within thirty days."

Her smile broke through of its own accord. "I'd better hurry and pawn my diamond tiara again. I can't afford to pass up a deal like that, can I?" She reached for her letter, frowning as she studied the half-familiar handwriting. Diana had always called her Aurelia Rose; she had often joked about the southern penchant for double names, swearing that she was going to name her first son Jimmy George Adam.

"There's one way to find out," Jed said softly.

She looked up at the half-teasing words to find his gaze still on her—dark, enigmatic, but not unkind. Perhaps last night's little confrontation had cleared the air between them. They had both managed a weak joke or two, and she found she could actually stand within a few feet of him this morning and not reach out to touch him. That was progress, wasn't it?

"Right," she muttered, slitting the envelope. It was just a note, but it was from Diana, congratulating her on the Larson book. The book had come out eleven months ago, but that didn't matter. Aurelia recognized the gesture for what it was—an olive branch. She looked up, her eyes brimming, to find Jed's gaze still on her. Disconcerted by the puzzling intensity of his expression, she rushed into an explanation. "It's from my sister-in-law, Adam's wife. We've been . . . I suppose you could say we've been estranged for some time now, and . . ." She lifted her shoulders helplessly, a tremulous smile on her lips.

The smile faded as she watched the change that came over Jed's face. His color seemed to vanish right under her eyes. "Adam? Adam is your brother?" he repeated very carefully, and then she understood.

"I'm afraid so. I might have explained if you'd—"

His head lifted in cold disdain. "Forget it. You don't owe me any explanations. Why should you think I'd even be interested?" He turned on his heel and stalked across the echoing floor, slamming out the front door into the drizzling rain that had started only moments before.

Throwing a socket wrench to the ground, Jed swore under his breath. What the hell ailed him, tearing into her like that? Finding out that the man he'd thought was her lover was actually her brother should have had him crowing from the rooftop. Instead it had twisted his gut another turn and he'd taken it out on her! So there wasn't a man in her life, if you discount-ed Jamison—and he was easy enough to discount. A lightweight. She needed someone with more on the ball than that baby-faced jock.

All right, so why had he flown off the handle that way? Could it be because now there was no excuse for her having rejected him—except for the inescapable one that she just wasn't interested? Hell, he'd known that before! He'd known it ever since she had frozen up on him and then deliberately turned her back on him. It was as effective a way as he'd seen to tell a man that he just didn't turn you on.

She'd be the rare type to go in for fidelity if she really cared for a man; he'd be willing to swear to that. And just when he'd accepted the face-saving theory that she'd remembered the redhead just in time and backed out for that reason, she blew his rationalization all to hell and gone! So it wasn't the competition, not unless she had a third prospect hidden out somewhere, and all his hunting instincts told him otherwise. Which left the field empty.

Add up the odds, Dancey: You're reasonably young, reasonably successful, reasonably decent looking. You've got two homes, a steady income, and your table manners will pass muster in all but the very best watering holes. So why not? What have you got to lose? Whether or not the stubborn little witch will admit it, she needs a husband. She needs someone to look after her so that she doesn't have to worry about where she's going to live and how she's going to pay the rent. She needs someone to curl up against in bed when the snow climbs halfway up the mountain and the days are only a few hours long.

She needs you, damn it! Only how the devil do you go about proving it to her?

All Saturday it seemed as if they were both tiptoeing around the borders of a fragile armistice. Aurelia stayed glued to her typewriter, even though her concentration was shot. Jed had insisted on bringing her gear back into the living room, and then he'd spent the rest of the day in the kitchen experimenting with the microwave or outside working on an old wreck of a Jeep.

Lunch had been another joint affair. They were both overly polite, and Aurelia wondered if Jed were as tempted as she was to laugh at the absurd formality with which they ate their hot dogs with sauerkraut and mustard.

By dinnertime she had produced three pages of inanities, which she crumpled and threw to the floor out of habit. Sigh was in his element in the large, empty rooms. He bowled with balls of paper, one crocheted slipper, and a pine cone that had unaccountably found its way inside.

A few hours after lunch Jed came tromping through the front door, moisture glistening on his bare head, clutching one hand with the other. Aurelia rose and crossed to meet him, words of concern forming on her lips, only to back away again at the thunderous look on his face.

"The d—the screwdriver slipped," he'd muttered. "Don't worry, I'll live."

He looked as if he rather regretted it, and she was almost ready to let him deal with it alone. If he wanted to go out in the rain and work on a rusty old motor, then who was she to protest? And if his filthy temper made him careless, then he got no more than he deserved.

She couldn't do it. "Jed, let me see it." Steeling herself for an ugly gash, she marched across the room and took hold of his arm, tugging it down to where she could survey the damage. He was holding a scrap of filthy rag over it and she tried to edge it away before she thought better of it. "Come on, let's get you to the bathroom where I can clean you up enough to see what's needed." He was pale under a fine film of perspiration, but he followed her meekly.

"Here, sit. Lean against me if you feel faint, but I've got to get this rag off and see if we need any stitches." Holding his wrist, she adjusted the water to a lukewarm stream and urged his hand under it. "This might sting a little," she muttered.

It was impossible to see what was what under the grease and smeared blood. Gingerly, she rubbed soap around the base of his thumb, taking care not to start the bleeding again. Then, frowning, she turned his hand over and searched the back for the real wound.

Jed's head sagged onto her stomach and she resisted the impulse to hug him to her. "Jed, this can't be it. It doesn't look very serious."

It was about an inch long, but it didn't look very deep. It might have hurt like the devil if he'd done it with a screwdriver, but it was only a scratch. She leaned over and looked at his closed eyes. "Jed? What about your tetanus?"

"I'm up to date," he managed between clenched teeth. Bless him, he still looked pale.

"Then I'll dab on some antiseptic and bandage you up and you can lie down for a while," she said gently. Oh, how the mighty have fallen. She took her time applying far more bandage than the wound required. After she was finished, she returned to her work.

With a muttered oath, she switched off her typewriter some time later and glared at the meaningless words before her. She'd gotten up to the summer of 1864, when Jo was at Petersburg. Grant was throwing everything at them; soldiers were being killed, and women and children dressed in little more than rags were practically starving, and all she could think of was a small wound inflicted on a hand through sheer carelessness.

"How'd the writing go today?" Jed asked with studied casualness as they met in the kitchen to commence dinner preparations. Aurelia slammed a pan down on the counter. She was embarrassed by the lack of progress she'd made, and she didn't care to be reminded of it.

"So-so. Did you get the Jeep running?"

"More or less. It ran well enough a few weeks back to pass inspection, but it's still temperamental. I forgot! There's a package in my car. My lawyer sent it over yesterday just before I left; said it had been dropped off at the firm that had handled the estate by some repair outfit. A bookbinder or something. A year and a half overdue. Probably another stack of diaries, from the feel of it. He didn't open it and I forgot about it."

Aurelia suppressed a groan of dismay. Through steady plodding, she was just over two-thirds finished with the project. All she needed now was a few missing volumes that would throw the whole works out of kilter. "Thanks, I'll check it out," she mumbled, hoping Jed would overlook her lack of enthusiasm.

"Later," he specified. "Meanwhile, the next sound you hear will be my stomach rumbling. What'll it be? Steaks again? Or would you prefer . . . ah . . ." He stood at the door of the freezer and scanned the menu. "Seafood, game birds, or some of these frozen concoctions in a sauce?"

They settled on a recipe that had intrigued Aurelia simply because it had looked so attractive in the cookbook, and she allocated the various tasks. Jed remained docile—suspiciously so. Her eyes kept being drawn to where he was busily dicing celery and onions and scraped carrots, his bandaged thumb held ostentatiously aloof. She had half expected him to fling down the paring knife and stalk out of the room by now.

At one point he grumbled something about his fingers being better at finding their way around a microchip than at chopping up rabbit food. When she glanced up, he was glaring at a tiny nick on the tip of his index finger.

"Wounded again?" she inquired, suppressing a smile at the sight of his massive shoulders hunched over a mass of badly hacked up vegetables.

"The damned knife—I mean the blasted thing's too dull to cut hot butter."

"Oh, good," she cooed softly. "Then you won't hurt yourself with it."

He came up from the table in one swift surge, looming over her threateningly. "Item one, woman: A dull knife is far more dangerous than a sharp one. Item two: A hungry man is far more dangerous than a well-fed one. Item three: If I see another smirk on your face, I won't be responsible for my actions or your safety. Is that understood?" He waited, glowering at her from a distance of a few inches away, and Aurelia thought her neck would break from bending backward to face him down. As it was, her lips were trembling. If she ever let go, it would be disastrous— she'd be giggling hysterically and they'd probably end up killing each other.

This time she rejoined him in the living room after she had cleared away the debris in the kitchen. His good behavior didn't extend to offering to help her with the washing up, she noticed, but she had to forgive him that. He had bent over backward to keep a civil tongue in his head all during the delectable dinner of wine and butter-basted squab stuffed with braised vegetables and served on a bed of wild rice. Jed had selected a white Burgundy, and by the time she had finished her second glass, Aurelia decided she liked it even better than the red variety.

He hadn't sworn once, nor had he lost his temper. And, she had to admit, the provocation had been there if he'd been looking for it. For some reason she'd been unable to keep from testing him. Subtle taunts, obscure non sequiturs that had led once or twice to a suspicious glare. She had countered each glare with an innocent look, and he'd subsided.

Jed had promised Irish coffee for dessert, and she watched expectantly as he assembled the ingredients. She'd had Mexican coffee, and Costa Rican, plus a few specialty blends, but this was a new one for her.

"Is that whiskey?" she asked uncertainly.

"The best Irish," he assured her. He measured and poured and then reached for a bowl of cream.

"I didn't know it was going to be an alcoholic drink."

His look was as bland as the bowl of whipped cream she had provided him with at his request. "The caffeine counteracts the intoxicating effect of the whiskey. You don't think I'd try anything underhanded, do you?"

She returned his look uncertainly. Was he getting his own back after her outrageous remarks about beards and the fragile masculine ego? She had only been quoting an article she'd read somewhere. Well, misquoting, to be more accurate. At the time he'd appeared to take her words at face value.

"Here, try this," he urged, handing her a slender, double-handled mug. She sipped cautiously. It was smooth, intriguing, and altogether delicious. Smiling at him over the rim, she said, "I like it."

She finished her first and he poured her another while they discussed what sort of furniture would look best in the long, high-ceilinged living room. Aurelia grew expansive with her ideas, and Jed leaned back at his end of the sofa and watched her, a warm smile hovering just beyond the reach of his lips.

"It has to be on the grand scale," she informed him very seriously. "*Every*thing. Even the ashtrays . . . 'specially those. But not all square and angular and masculine." She shook her head judiciously. "A lit-tle touch of softness—a nice oriental rug in one of those melony shades, maybe a piece of alabaster over there where the light will shine through it."

"Or possibly a piece of cranberry glass," he murmured so softly that she wasn't certain she'd heard him. "Something warm and feminine to balance the contemporary design. Hmmm, I think you're absolutely right," he agreed gravely. "While I'm down here in the heart of furniture country, maybe I'll look in on a few showrooms, and if I can persuade someone to advise me on antiques, I might even pick up one or two nice old pieces. I think you're right about mixing it up; the place looks pretty barren as it stands. What do they call it, yin and yang? A balance of masculine and feminine, old and new, might take the curse off all these hard surfaces."

"I could help you," she offered eagerly, leaning forward to peer into his face. He was reclining against the overstuffed arm of the sofa, and there was nothing at all threatening in his expression. All the same, alarm bells suddenly began to clang in Aurelia's head, and she drew back, her reactions slowed just enough so that her empty mug caught the edge of a cushion and crashed to the floor.

Almost before the shattered pieces had stopped spinning, Sigh was on the scene to take charge of them. Aurelia cried out, reaching down to retrieve a segment with the double handles still intact, and Jed touched her arm and drew her back up on the sofa.

"You'll cut yourself," he remonstrated gently. "It's in the stars. Haven't I been slicing myself up all day long? Mercury is looking cross-eyed at Mars, or some such business, according to my secretary. She won't sharpen a pencil without consulting her astrological chart."

Distracted, Aurelia began to apologize profusely, and he raised a finger to her lips, shutting off the flow of regrets.

"Hush, hush now, honey. It's just an old cup. We still have three more left—one for you, one for me, and one to break. Only next time it's my turn."

"Oh, Jed, don't be so nice to me," she sniffed. "It makes me nervous. I didn't want to cost you anything

—staying here I mean, electricity and water and . . . and I think I might be drunk. Do you think so?"

He stared down into her anxious face—obsidian meeting smoky topaz—and sighed heavily as a newly kindled spark was reluctantly extinguished in his eyes. "No, honey, I don't think you're drunk. But maybe for both our sakes, you'd better go to bed. If it clears up tomorrow, we'll look around for old Jo's cave. A little fresh air will clear up any collywobbles and you'll be right as rain."

And if you stay here one minute more, he thought grimly, gazing up at me through those eyes of yours, I'll go with you, and this time there won't be any turning back.

He brought the package in from the car while she was in the bathroom. It was on the cricket table she'd placed beside her bed. Wrapped in brown paper, tied with string, it was diary-sized, but thicker, much, much thicker.

"Oh, golly, it'll take me another six months to finish now," she sighed.

Reluctantly, she sat on the edge of the bed and untied the string. It had been tied in a neat bow, and it occurred to her that a man who sealed a package that ways instead of using tape would be just the sort to deliver it a year and a half late.

It was a Bible, a newly covered Bible, and she stared blankly down at the Morocco binding with its plain gilt lettering. On top of it was a handwritten invoice from R. Squires, bookbinder, marked "Paid in Advance."

Inside the front cover the silky, tissue-thin paper told the story of generations of readers. The corners were creased, some of them actually ragged. Aurelia turned carefully to the back, certain of what she'd find there. Two pages, illuminated in the old style with angels and scrolls, recorded the births, marriages, and deaths of the offspring of Ethelbert Dozier and Rebecca Jones Dancey. Aurelia stared down at the blurred pages for long minutes before she reached for her glasses.

She read both pages carefully and then began to search through the heavy volume for more data. That couldn't be all. It didn't fit; something was missing somewhere. She pushed her glasses back up on her nose, crossed her legs, tucked her nightgown over her feet, and started at the beginning once more. Muttering under her breath, she re-read the list of offspring of Ethelbert and Rebecca. The first son was named John Stevens Jones Dancey. Then came a daughter, stillborn, and another son who died at age fourteen months. Then two more daughters, both of whom later died childless. Poor Ethelbert and Rebecca. And then they had had another son. Jocephus Ezra Dozier Dancey. Her Jo.

The next entry was the marriage of Jo's older brother, John. He had married Rachel Morris and they had had four children. John died at age thirty-six. Aurelia stared at the five words written so long ago in the cramped handwriting. *A tree fell on him.* A man was born; he grew up. He fell in love, married, and fathered four children. Had he been a stern father? Had he spoiled them? What kind of a man was he that his life and death could be summed up in a few bleak words?

Drawing her mind back to the present puzzle, Aurelia went back to the beginning and read through the page of statistics from one end to the other, searching for a certain name. Once again she reached the inevitable conclusion. Uncrossing her legs, she pushed her damp, tangled hair back from her face and got up off the bed.

"Jed?" she called tentatively, stepping out into the hall, and then, "Jed! Jed, you've got to see this!"

His light was still on. His door was ajar, and unthinking, she opened it further, Bible in hand, and said, "Jed, there's something wrong. Jo wasn't married to—"

She stopped short. Her voice trailed off as she stared at him. He held a towel over his arm, and aside from that, he was completely naked. As if he were made of steel and her eyes were magnets, she stood frozen to the spot, her whole being absorbing the stunning beauty of his perfectly proportioned body.

It was Jed who broke the spell. "You were saying?" he prompted, his voice registering the heightened tension.

She began to back away, the heavy book clutched in front of her as if it were a shield. "Later," she mumbled. "I'll tell you later." She backed out, spilling incoherent words of apology, and her face flamed miserably as she dashed into her own room and slammed the door. Not even the thickness of two heavy doors was enough to extinguish the visual memory. Her skin was burning, her heart was racing, and her mind was busily processing all sorts of tantalizing information.

When the knock on her door came a few minutes later, she was in bed. The light was out, and the covers were pulled up over her head.

"Aurelia?" Jed called softly. "I'm decent now. What was it you had to tell me?"

"Just go away, will you?"

"Aurelia? I can't sleep when I'm curious. What was so important that you couldn't wait to tell me?"

She sighed and flipped the covers back. There was no point in both of them lying awake all night. The devil finds work for idle minds, or hands—or both, she reminded herself resignedly. She'd talk to him, though she wasn't about to invite him in.

She made a deliberate effort to keep her tone unemotional, and she succeeded at first. "Jo married his brother John's widow, Rebecca. He was only twenty-one, and she was thirty-four." Her flat tone gave way to despair. "Jed, she lost her husband and exactly six months later to the day, she married Jo! What about Mary? Think what they must have felt when he was forced to marry his brother's widow just because there was nobody else to take care of them. He was an honorable man, and look where it got him!" she wailed. Her eyes were on the closed door, but she was seeing again all those lovely, poignant letters. Mary had poured out her heart, but she had never once complained about the separation.

"I thought it was the war that separated them," she said brokenly, "but it wasn't. No wonder poor Jo enlisted. And do you realize," she exclaimed to the shut door, "that it was only the war that allowed Jo and Mary to write to each other? That's all they ever had—the letters. And Jed, they had been lovers! But they couldn't have corresponded with him living in the house with a wife and four children.

"Jed? Are you still there? Do you hear me? They *stayed* married for years and years, and I can't find a word about Mary! I don't even know who she was."

Silence. Then, when she thought he had gone away, he said softly, "And that bothers you?"

"Well, of course it bothers me."

"What difference does it make who Mary was? Aurelia, may I come in? I hate trying to carry on a conversation through a door."

"Oh, go to bed. It doesn't mean anything to you. You didn't even know him. Good night."

"You can't sleep if you're all tensed up," he insisted gently.

"I am *not* all tensed up! Just leave me alone and let me go to sleep. Please," she added in a small voice. After a moment she heard the soft footfalls move away from her door, and she turned over and poked a fist into her pillow.

Poor Jo. Poor Rebecca and poor Mary and poor Jo. Dutifully, she added John's name to the list. Her mind churned over the elements of the long-buried triangle, but she could come to no happy conclusion. Jo had evidently done what he felt he had to in order to look after his brother's family.

His sense of duty had made him sacrifice any chance of happiness with Mary. They had obviously been lovers, probably planned to marry, then John had died, leaving a helpless family, and the war had intervened. No wonder Jo had joined the army before he had to. It must have been awful to love one woman and be forced to marry someone else. And there had never been a word of remonstrance or regret in Mary's letters. They had each accepted their roles and taken what small happiness they could.

For several moments Aurelia allowed herself to ache for the three of them—for poor John, as well. And then her mind turned inward, to a more intimate pain, the pain of being with Jed and not being able to reach out and touch him. It was like seeing him through a powerful telescope. There were times when he seemed so close, but it was all just a cruel illusion.

Chapter Twelve

$\mathcal{B}$y the time Aurelia woke up, the sun had already risen high enough to scatter bountious handfuls of diamonds over a carpet of wet, fallen leaves. It was one of those late October days for which the mountains had been created, and she greeted it with a painful squint. Cool blue light dazzled its way invitingly across the polished floor of her bedroom. She rubbed her unfocused eyes and groaned, but by the time she'd splashed her face with water, icy from the deep-bored well, and stretched the kinks out of her body, she was ready to face breakfast. The night's nebulous worries seemed to have dissipated under the spell of the morning's clear sunshine.

Jed was already in the kitchen. He wore a yellow towel tucked apronwise into the belt of his old flannels, and his black wool shirt was halfway open. Aurelia felt something inside her tilt dangerously as she was reminded of that unencumbered view she had had of him last night. Before embarrassment could overtake the initial quickening of her senses, however, he looked up with a warm, uncomplicated grin.

"I remembered you said you liked baked potatoes

for breakfast," he greeted her, and she peered warily past him to the kitchen table. It hadn't been a matter of preference—it had been before she'd unearthed the microwave cookbook. The instructions manual she had found inside the oven had used baked potatoes as an example.

"That's it? Baked potatoes?" she asked dubiously.

"You're about to experience an example of what man is capable of accomplishing when confronted by a new gadget and a pantry full of supplies. I call it Fancy Dancey Potatoes."

The coffee was superb; the Fancy Dancey Potatoes . . . interesting. In fact, parts of them were delicious.

"But pickles? Chopped hot pickles?" she murmured wonderingly as she forked aside several ounces of melted cheese.

"Hot pickles, bacon, smoked oysters, shad roe, catsup, cheese, and—what's that label say?" He tipped his chair back until the legs creaked alarmingly and reached for the empty jar. "Sauce Béarnaise."

There was something to be said for being confronted with Fancy Dancey Potatoes before one even had one's wits about one. It did away with any tendency toward self-consciousness. And after an evening rife with embarrassing episodes, that was no small accomplishment. They discussed possible variations— Aurelia tactfully refrained from calling them "improvements"—and before the unorthodox meal was finished, they were laughing as though her slight inebriation, the discovery of a remote personal tragedy, and the subsequent nude encounter had never occurred.

"I'd omit the catsup and pickles, and probably the shad roe, too," she ventured.

"Hmmmm . . . you may be right. It was pretty

much overpowered, I guess. What about sour cream instead of catsup next time? And maybe chopped raw onions instead of pickles?"

Aurelia finished her coffee and as much of the colorful concoction as she could manage. She wouldn't allow herself to think of a next time. If she was smart, there wouldn't be one.

They spent the next hour exploring the grounds. Jed had already covered them fairly extensively, and he led her to what he theorized had been Jo's cave, a shallow crevice that had been largely filled in by falling boulders and scrubby undergrowth.

"It was probably much deeper back then. A lot of erosion can take place in the space of a hundred and fifty years or so." He moved to stand behind her, casting a shadow across the granite face of the hillside that swallowed up her own much smaller one.

Staring at the jumble of rocks and weeds, Aurelia thought sadly that even old tragedies had a way of eroding, given time. Jo's had. Hers had. She made a deliberate effort to stretch her mind back to a time when a small boy had found adventure by hiding out in this very cave. She gave up when she found she couldn't picture the face beneath the beard.

Instead her thoughts shifted back to the night when she'd accompanied her parents to the annual faculty banquet. Both she and her mother had new dresses for the occasion. Hers was the first really grown-up one she'd ever had, and she'd just come from the ladies' room, where she'd added a touch more lipstick to that her mother had allowed, and was on her way back to the table when she suddenly found herself swept up in a towering, surging tide of humanity, a tide that had snatched her up and carried her away from her parents, carried her roughly for a few feet and then cast her heedlessly down again. Fortunately she'd been pushed beneath the table that had held the coffee service, and she'd cowered there until she lost consciousness.

Even now she could see the solid wall of flesh—the elbows and the shifting waves of silk-clad backs and bosoms, the stiff white shirtfronts and mothball-scented dinner jackets. There had been no faces; that was the dreadful part of it, and later there had been the terrifying forest of legs and feet. For years afterward she could still hear the sounds and even smell the mixture of spilled coffee, perfume, and smoke, but it had gradually lost its power to frighten her. And now it was all just a dimly remembered dream.

"Aurelia?"

She turned to see Jed watching her intently, and suddenly she was intoxicated by the sheer brilliance of the day. In the black wool shirt, with the sun glistening down on his raven-dark hair and beard, he was magnificent. She felt the last remnants of the past disintegrate. As a surge of indefinable longing threatened to dim the sun, she countered it by spinning on her heel and flinging a challenge over her shoulder. "Race you to the top of the hill!"

Jed's legs were much longer than hers, but Aurelia had the advantage of surprise. In her one pair of jeans, a pink turtleneck sweater, and a pair of red sneakers, she scrambled fleetly up the rugged, uneven slope, grasping chunks of granite to pull herself up when the incline grew steeper. The sun had dried what it had touched of the rocks, but there were still slippery places—cool, damp, mossy areas that smelled of earth and decaying leaves.

"Slow down before you break something irreplacable," Jed called after her. He was several yards behind her, gaining fast, but the memory of his recent tumble had obviously given him a healthy respect for the treacherous terrain.

There was something intoxicating about the whole situation. Fleeting snatches of memory flickered once more through Aurelia's mind as she twisted agilely around a sharp outcropping and cast a taunting grin over her shoulder. Summer evenings when she was thirteen, fourteen, just beginning to unfurl her womanly wings. Band concerts on the square at dusk, girls in twos and threes prancing past swaggering boys, casting self-conscious looks over their shoulders and giggling as they tried to appear nonchalant. She felt like a teenager again—which was absurd!

"I'm warning you, woman, when I catch you—" Jed broke off as he rounded the outcropping just behind her.

"*If* you catch me," she flung at him, laughing. From the corner of her eye she caught sight of a relatively clear stretch that angled off toward the house. Spinning away from the rocky slope, she took the leaf-covered hillside at a hard run, clutching her sides as she gasped for air.

It was too easy. The path was almost flat, tilting only slightly over the contour of the hillside, but there were a few small rocks hidden under the carpet of slick, wet leaves. Aurelia stepped on one of these, skidded wildly as she tried to regain her balance, and then both feet flew out from under her and she landed on her back.

He was beside her instantly, dropping to his knees and reaching down to where she lay gasping dazedly. "Aurelia—damn it, girl, I warned you!"

"Thanks for the tender concern," she panted, blinking up at his ferocious scowl.

"Tender concern, hell! I ought to take you over my knee and tenderize your behind. What does it take to teach you a lesson?"

She began to move her limbs experimentally. Her breath was still tearing at her lungs, but that was more from the uphill run than from the tumble. There were times when short legs weren't such a disadvantage after all, she consoled herself. At least she hadn't far to fall. "If you're through threatening me, do you think you could move aside so I could get up? A few of these pebbles feel as if they might be alive."

He touched her shoulders gingerly, allowing his hands to trail down to her wrists before lifting away. "Are you sure nothing's broken?"

"Well, my dignity's a little chipped around the edges, but other than that . . ." She waited for him to help her to her feet, and when no help seemed forthcoming, she rolled over onto her knees and scrambled up. It was only when she turned around and saw the expression on his face that she understood. It was pained, distressed—even agonized. The one thing it wasn't, was sympathetic.

Oh, God, he couldn't even bring himself to touch her. She had heard of people who were put off by physical imperfections, but hers didn't even show! Still, the chipped cranberry glass, his remarks about poor Sigh—she might have known he wouldn't be able to handle her extensive scarring. She *had* known. She'd known since the night he had walked out of her bedroom, but she'd foolishly allowed herself to relax her guard, and now she was going to pay for it. The bruises she had suffered in her ignominious pratfall were nothing compared to the pain of being rejected for a second time.

Tugging her sweater down in the back, she began to plod up the path toward the house. It wasn't going to work. She'd simply have to make other arrangements, because it was *not* going to work.

Jed followed a few paces behind her, a helpless look on his face. His eyes moved expressively over her narrow back—ramrod straight and still plastered with wet leaves—and on the rounded little bottom that swung in sympathetic harmony with her angry steps.

Damn it, it just wouldn't work! He'd thought he could handle it, thought he could take it at an easy pace and bring her around, but there were too many pitfalls. Last night had been one.

One, hell—last night had been half a dozen! The whole time she'd sat across the table from him, making those outrageous remarks with a perfectly straight face and watching him for a reaction—it was the first time he'd seen her sense of humor come to the surface so clearly. If he hadn't been afraid of scaring her back into her shell, he'd have taken her up on a few of those cracks. The next time he'd give her a run for her money!

And then later, when she'd leaned toward him with that owlish look and offered her services as a decorator, it had been all he could do to keep from pulling her onto his lap and kissing the very breath from her. She'd had just enough to drink so that her inhibitions were down, for once—what the devil was a melony rug, anyway? Whatever it was, she could have it. She could have anything he owned, and if he didn't own it, he'd get it for her.

He paced the long bare expanse of floor before the glass wall, wondering what she was doing in there. He'd ordered her to peel down and see if she had done any real damage, and the look she'd given him would have frozen the river Styx. It was a good thing she didn't know just how close he had come to stripping her down then and there, and not for any medical purposes, either! If she could have read his mind, she'd have been in the next county by now.

And speaking of stripping, there was that odd little episode last night. She'd been upset, all right; it had really jolted her to discover that her hero wasn't above a spot of hanky-panky, wife or no wife. She took it all to heart, this business between old Jocephus and Mary. He'd glanced at some of the letters, and he had to admit it was pretty potent stuff. And come to think of it, some of the feelings described weren't all that farfetched. In one letter he dimly recalled, the mysterious Mary could have been describing the way he had felt when he'd glanced up last night on his way to the shower and seen Aurelia standing there in his doorway, her hair all over her shoulders and that nightgown curving around her hills and valleys.

That had been tricky. Damn, he must have more control than he'd suspected. Thank the Lord for the towel! And that was another thing: Swearing had gotten to be second nature to him at this point in his life, but he was going to have to ease off a little. Maybe if he let her see that he was trying to smooth off a few rough edges, she'd warm up a little.

But if she did warm up, even a little, he was apt to forget all his self-imposed restraints and rush things again, and there'd go the whole ball game!

Could any woman be worth it? He shook his head and moved restlessly across to the small bookshelf to stare down with unseeing eyes at her handful of reference books. He could buy her a library full of reference books. He could buy her a word processor, hire her a typist, whatever she needed to make her work easier.

He found himself thinking of all the things he'd like to buy for her and it occurred to him that he'd never had the slightest desire to buy anything for anyone else. Oh, a few dinners, show tickets, flowers, and maybe the occasional piece of jewelry. Nor had his motives been particularly unselfish in any of those cases.

Nor was it in this case, he admitted ruefully. He wanted something, wanted it badly, and he wasn't above a touch of bribery if that was what it took. He reached out and removed a well-worn book from the second shelf. A Descartes dictionary. God, how long had it been since he'd seen one of these? Philosophy 101, wasn't it? Old Dr. Thurlow.

He flipped through the pages and his forefinger came to rest at the L's. "Logic," he murmured, his finger pausing at one of the briefer definitions. "'According to the laws of true logic, one ought never to ask of a thing, *if it is,* unless one knows first *what it is.*'"

"Well put, old fellow," he muttered. "So first we define *what* it is." His finger moved to the next category, which happened to be Love, and he read aloud. "'[Sensual or sensuous love] is nothing other than a confused thought excited in the soul by some movement of the nerves, which inclines it to the other, clearer thought of which rational love consists.'"

He replaced the book and tugged thoughtfully at his beard and turned to stare out the window. "So there is something rational about it, after all. That's comforting to know, at least."

At a sound from the doorway, he turned. She was standing there looking as if she'd lost her last friend, and he fought to resist the urge to go and gather her in his arms. Instead he offered her coffee.

"In fact, I think a touch of the Irish might not be a bad idea. You've had a shock, you know." The shock she'd had had been nothing to the shock he'd just been jolted with. It had taken a man who had lived a hundred and fifty years ago to get them together; it had taken a man who had lived in the early part of the seventeenth century to point out the fact that he was in love for the first time in his life. It was strictly up to him now to figure out what to do about it.

"Just a small tad of whiskey, please," she directed, holding out her coffee cup. It was strictly medicinal, she assured herself—she wasn't embarking on a lifetime of dissolution. She was shaken, both physically and emotionally. There were no bruises to show for what ailed her, only a soreness in the region of her heart that no amount of whiskey could assuage. Still, one had to go through the motions.

"You mentioned going back to New York tomorrow?" she assayed brightly. Only after she settled herself into the bentwood rocker she had dragged into the living room the week before did Jed lower himself onto the king-sized sofa. As handsome as it was, she always felt dwarfed by its massiveness. Her feet didn't even touch the floor.

"I hate to run off and leave you here alone again, but I have a meeting I can't dodge. I'm considering opening up shop here in this area, possibly with Bill Voncannon."

"Radio telephones? I noticed you had one in your car."

"Yes, well, having it and using it are two different things around here. These mountains present a different sort of situation. We'd have to go into the topography pretty thoroughly before we settled on repeater locations, but it's a challenge. Different thing altogether from operating in downtown Manhattan—downtown anywhere, for that matter. Buildings don't block transmission like mountains do, even though a few of them are shielded."

"And you enjoy being challenged," she suggested, hooking a foot up beside her in the cane-bottomed rocker.

"And I enjoy being challenged," he repeated, leveling an ambiguous look at her from under the shadow of his thick brows.

Restlessness caused her to squirm, and she lowered her foot to the floor again. "I think, if you don't mind, I'd better get some work done. I try to do at least ten pages a day, but if it bothers you, I'll carry my things to the bedroom again."

He stood, ramming his hands into his hip pockets. "I'll be outdoors. Work anywhere you want to," he said shortly. He glared at her, wondering how a man was supposed to bring up the fact that he loved a woman. Over breakfast? Pass the salt, please, and oh, yes—I love you. Over coffee? One lump or two? Do you know I'm so damned much in love with you I can't see straight? Do you take cream?

He stalked out of the room. His stomach was churning and he suspected it was the breakfast. Or maybe it was heartburn. Was love supposed to give you indigestion? At this rate he might as well forget the meeting tomorrow. If he couldn't keep his head under control any better than this, he'd just better stay here and fight it out, win or lose.

To think that he'd been functionally crippled by a little thing half his size, half his weight, with nothing more lethal than a certain way of looking at him, a certain way of carrying herself, as if she were holding up her skirts to keep from soiling them on the rest of the world.

On the other hand, if he stayed, he was going to bring matters to a head, one way or another. And if he barged into something carelessly, he could blow the whole deal. Maybe he'd better be on his best behavior tonight—a pleasant dinner, a little light conversation. He'd ask about her family, get her talking about herself, and then he'd kiss her good night. One kiss. That was all. He'd take off early for the airport, and maybe call tomorrow night just to see how she was faring. No, too soon. Make that Wednesday night. That should show enough restraint to relax her guard. Then, next weekend . . .

Meanwhile, at least he'd take care of these leaves before he left. She could break her neck slipping on these things and there'd be no one around to look after her.

Aurelia applied herself doggedly to facts and figures. So many infantry, so many cavalry, so many miles to travel. So much dysentery, so much mud to clog gun barrels, bog down feet, immobilize cannons . . .

She lifted her face to gaze out over the valley. Jed had gone outside hours ago. What was he doing? She hadn't heard him drive off, but she hadn't heard the clink of tools, either. He wasn't working on the Jeep; she'd have heard him swearing if he'd been nearby.

A smile unraveled the frown on her face. He was fierce, wasn't he? Fierce looking and fierce sounding, but underneath it all, there were unsuspected soft spots. If it weren't for the scars she carried, they might have come together. Who knows, he might even have come to love her in time. Stranger things had happened.

But she had seen the look on his face. He'd dropped down beside her out there on the side of the hill and reached out for her, and she'd seen him hesitate. He'd had to force himself to touch her. Good

Lord, what would he have done if she'd really needed help? Worn gloves? Cut himself a ten-foot pole?

Just before she switched off her typewriter to go shower and change for dinner, she caught a drift of smoke and tightened up instinctively. It was leaf smoke, fragrant actually, and she'd smelled it often enough over the years, but it still made her uneasy—smoke of any sort.

Dinner was another joint affair, with Jed grilling chops and Aurelia microwaving winter squash and butterbeans. They concocted the salad together, and she restrained him from getting too creative with the dressing. It had been fun, and they'd laughed together, but she couldn't help noticing the way he avoided touching her, and that, in turn, made her responses a bit stiff. As the evening wore on, she found herself withdrawing into her old shell.

He had offered to build a fire in the fireplace even though the spark arrester he'd ordered wasn't installed, and she'd told him hastily not to bother on her account. After that, he seemed to grow more and more morose, and shortly after ten she had given up and said good night. She didn't quite know what she'd expected, or at least hoped for, from his last night home, but it hadn't been a stilted discourse on the vagaries of line-of-sight radio transmission in mountainous terrain.

She had opened her window before crawling under the down-filled comforter that someone had provided along with the rest of the linens. She rather suspected Rae was the instrument in this case; the color harmonies were too subtle to have been chosen by anyone who selected pink, yellow, and purple dishes.

And after all, why not? Rae would probably be choosing the rest of the furnishings one of these days.

And when that day came, she'd take care to be long gone, even if she had to move in with Adam and Diana again.

The pungent smell of damp burned leaves drifted in through the window as sleep claimed her. It followed her into her dreams, calling up half-forgotten images of bonfires, of football games and pumpkins and Saturday mornings in the back yard of their Faculty Row home. And then, imperceptibly, the focus began to shift. She stirred in her sleep, struggling to force a sound of protest through lax jaws.

"Aurelia! Aurelia, wake up! Wake up, honey, you're having a bad dream."

The rough urgency of Jed's voice penetrated the suffocating weight of her nightmare and she blinked into the half darkness. Light was streaming in through the open door, gleaming on the broad shoulders that bent over her.

"Jed?" The sound was barely audible, but it was definitely a sound. She was profoundly relieved that her voice worked at all. She'd been screaming and screaming and no sound had come out, no one had found her. "Oh, Jed, don't leave me here!"

"I won't leave you, sweetheart, I won't ever leave you." His arms came around her then, and she clung to the security of his solid warmth, burying her face in his throat. She could feel the pulse, the pounding of his heart, and it seemed to her that the rate doubled in the instant it took her to go from dream to reality.

He was touching her. He was holding her, comforting her, his hands on her back as if he didn't care about the scars, as if he'd forgotten their existence. And oh, God, she wasn't going to remind him! If he'd forgotten, even for a minute, she was foolish enough and selfish enough to steal that minute for herself, to savor it for as long as she lived.

His lips were in her hair, his beard brushing against her forehead, and afterward she never knew who made the first move. All she knew was the taste and the feel of his lips, warm and soft and demanding on hers. The last remnant of terror faded as he began deliberately, with exquisite gentleness, to search out every sensitive nerve ending in her neck. His tongue traced the delicate pattern of her ear and then began to inch downward, and long before he reached the curve of her shoulder, she was shuddering uncontrollably. The flicker of his tongue stroked the pulse points at the base of her throat and she gasped his name.

"Easy, love, I won't hurt you," he whispered hoarsely. In spite of the incredible things he was doing to her, she reacted instinctively to the reassuring note in his voice. Nor did she protest when he followed her down into the soft warm cocoon of her bed, and when he slid the straps of her gown from her shoulders, she shifted to make it easier.

Very slowly, and with consummate skill, he undressed her. Not once did he seem to hurry. It was as though they had all the time in the world, as if they were bound up together in some sweet dream of fulfillment. She was trembling before her gown ever slithered to the floor, her breath catching in her throat as wave after wave of raw desire racked her body.

He knew each secret source of pleasure, and he touched them all, one after the other. And each touch was followed by a slow, lingering kiss. Without speaking a word, he led her slowly, tenderly, until she lay twisting helplessly, begging him with every unconscious gesture to quench this raging wildfire inside her.

His pajama pants joined her gown on the floor, and he drew her down on top of him, gentling her with soft, incoherent sounds and soothing touches. With the infinitesimal portion of her brain that was still functioning, Aurelia recognized the care he was taking, had taken all along, not to hurt her. He was enormously strong, and he was powerfully aroused. He could have taken her at any moment and she'd only have helped him, but he had held back.

His fingers combed through her hair, then moved on to stroke her back, her hips, as if he found the texture of her skin incredibly fascinating. If he'd gone too fast, if he'd even tried to talk to her at first, she might have frozen up again, but he hadn't. From a state of senseless terror, he'd gentled her until she was totally without fear, totally susceptible to his touch, his spell. His hands eased down over her hips to cup her to him, and her legs trembled as she felt the brush of his strong, sensitive fingers. Just for an instant she stiffened—no one had ever touched her there. Her reaction did not go unnoticed. He turned them both carefully so that she was no longer on top of him, but on her side, facing him, and he held her so that she could have pulled away if she'd wanted to. He watched her face searchingly. Then, seemingly reassured, he murmured, "I was afraid you'd crush me."

She could feel his soft laughter in her very bones, and she smiled at the absurdity of his words. But she didn't speak, not yet. It was still all too new to her. She might still be dreaming; he might vanish if she spoke. Carefully, he inserted one of his hair-roughened legs between hers, and then he brought her hand up to his mouth and buried a kiss in her palm, tucking both hands—her small one in his larger one—between them, between their hearts. She could feel the double thunder, see it at his temple, at the base of his throat, and in that place in his bottom lip that pounded when he was stirred.

"I think you'd better kiss me," he whispered huskily. "I can't last much longer."

In spite of the easygoing request, he was trembling, and the tension in him transmitted itself to Aurelia. She moved so that her parted lips were against his shoulder. Her tongue emerged to taste the slight saltiness of his skin and then, lifting her head, she pushed her mouth through his beard to find the angle of his jaw, and she kissed it, marveling at the oddly erotic feel of the stiff, crinkly hairs. Drawing herself up through his arms until she gained access, she kissed his eyes, one after the other, and the lean hollow of his cheeks. She kissed his temple, and the corner of his mouth, and then, last of all, she let her mouth open tentatively over his lips, conscious of a fleeting moment of uncertainty.

She didn't know how to kiss a man. She only knew how to be kissed, but this was different. He expected her to take the initiative, and she was oddly shy, strangely uncertain, and then a heady feeling of power overcame her and she extended the tip of her tongue to trace the curved line between his lips.

It was too much, too much. He couldn't hold out much longer. Groaning, he took control of the kiss, at the same time easing one of her slender thighs up over his hips. She was so small, so fragile. God, he'd never felt so clumsy! His hands moved over her, cupping her to him, echoing the rhythm set by his tongue, and then, when she was clinging, her own hands searching his chest for the pleasure points, he let his lips leave her mouth and seek the sweetness of her small, perfect breasts. The taste of her was enough to drive him insane; he'd never get enough of it . . . of her.

Leaning away in order to lose himself in the fragrant hills only brought her pelvis into closer contact, and he fought for control, thankful that he was no longer an impatient twenty-year-old. He'd follow her lead, take her only when she was ready, if it killed him.

"Oh, God, precious," his agonized words grated on her ear, "make it soon. Soon . . ."

As if the words and the emotion struggling to get through his voice triggered a release in her, Aurelia moved to bring herself into stunning contact with Jed's relentless masculinity. The rest seemed to happen of its own accord. She was conscious of an aching, driving hunger, a compulsion more powerful than anything she could ever have conceived of, and then she was a part of him, guided by his hands, lifted, held, her body joyously celebrated in the most miraculous way of all.

He handled her as if she were infinitely fragile, infinitely precious, and the strain of his control showed in his face. Looming over her, he managed to hang on to his sanity long enough to be certain he hadn't hurt her, and then, when sanity was no longer a remote possibility, he carried her with him to the top.

Perhaps she said the words; perhaps he said them. They seemed to shimmer in the ringing silence, but afterward she couldn't be certain. In the cosmic clarity that followed, she watched while a million glittering mirrors shattered and drifted slowly back to earth. Fascinated, hypnotized, she gazed at them through closed eyelids and smiled, secure in the arms that held her in a warm cocoon of love.

Chapter Thirteen

*U*nder the steady pelting of rain that beat against the windows, Aurelia's dream gradually disintegrated. Groaning, she rolled over to look at the clock and then sat up stiffly, drawing her knees up and resting her arms on them. When full remembrance hit her, she buried her face in her arms. He wasn't there beside her now; she'd have known it without even looking. The warmth emanating from the pillow beside her was Sigh's. He was at his most playful this time of day, as he teased her into getting his breakfast.

Awareness came in soft-edged fragments. Her back was sore; she was sore in every inch of her body. She had fallen yesterday. And then, last night . . .

Warm blood coursed swiftly to her face as she recalled in intimate detail the events of the previous night. It was no dream. It would have taken far more knowledge and experience for her to have dreamed what had happened last night.

Her smile widened to a complacent grin. "This is silly," she muttered to the cat beside her. Vainly she attempted to school herself to some degree of sobriety before she had to face Jed again. How did he feel this morning? Regretful?

Oh, Lord, she hoped not. The grin flickered uncertainly and then faded as she wondered why he hadn't stayed the night with her. Maybe he had. Maybe he was even now making coffee, and in a minute he'd shoulder his way into her room, bringing coffee and that heart-melting smile of his.

In which case she wanted to be ready, her teeth brushed, her face washed, and her hair brushed into seemingly careless disarray. That was cheating, of course. Sooner or later he had to discover what she looked like first thing in the morning. Her old insecurities weren't quite laid to rest, though, and she'd rather make it later. Turning to the cat, who was swatting at the do-not-remove tag on her pillow, she said "Go ask Jed for some milk."

Of course, he was supposed to be back in New York this morning, but there were later flights. His business wouldn't fall apart if he strolled in a little late for once. After a leisurely breakfast she could help him pack, and then later . . . much, much later . . . she could see him off.

The uncarpeted floor was cold under her bare feet as she scooted into the bathroom and turned on the hot water faucet. A long, hot soak would be heavenly, but she wanted to be back in bed if Jed brought in coffee. She confronted her image in the steamy mirror. Except for a rather fatuous smile, she didn't look any different. Her mouth was slightly swollen, perhaps, and there was a softness in her eyes that hadn't been there before. All in all, she decided, love was pretty flattering. And as Jed had a beard, she didn't even have to worry about having her face scratched by morning stubble.

What if Jed was cooking his Fancy Dancey Potatoes

for breakfast? A word of caution might be in order . . .

And then again, maybe it wouldn't. If Jed liked it, she'd learn to like it. He'd been so incredibly gentle last night, so absolutely, marvelously . . . *wonderful!* Her eyes softened in remembrance. How could anyone so strong and forceful be so tender and patient? He'd made her feel truly cherished. He'd taken away her nightmare and replaced it with. . . . She smiled softly to herself and closed her eyes, reliving a magic she had never, in her wildest moments, imagined.

Some of the smugness faded from her lingering smile when she stepped back into her bedroom to find it still empty. Halfway under the bed, Jed's pajama pants were entangled with her gown. That was sure proof that she hadn't merely dreamed it all.

But of course she hadn't. Moving briskly, she dressed in her heather-pink skirt and the mauve jersey blouse. Jed had a business to run, after all. Just because—she shouldn't have assumed that—

Well, at any rate, he wouldn't be bringing her breakfast in bed. He'd be cramming his clothes into a suitcase and wondering if she'd have the coffee made in time for him to have a cup to go.

God, what an idiot she was! By the time she'd brushed her hair and twisted it up into a swirl on top of her head, her cheeks were flushed enough so that a touch of lipgloss was all she needed. The sparkle of her eyes couldn't possibly be enhanced by makeup, not today. Not after last night. If she glowed anymore, Jed might be tempted to hang a lampshade over her head.

She tried the kitchen first. It was empty. Frowning slightly, Aurelia retraced her steps to Jed's bedroom door. It was shut, and even as her hand closed over the knob, she hesitated. A hollow sort of uncertainty touched her and she turned away. Moving stiffly, she went to the front door, and then to the back. The car was gone. Only then did she return to his bedroom.

The bed was neatly made up. Inside his closet were a pair of desert boots, the old flannels, and the black jeans. No three-piece suit, no cordovans, and no suitcase and no briefcase. He was gone. A small sound of protest escaped her before her mouth clamped shut again.

He must have left her a note. If he'd waked early in time to drive to the airport in Roanoke, he probably thought he was being considerate in not waking her. She looked in the living room first. Her typing table; the coffee table. There weren't many places for a note to hide. Next she tried the kitchen. The stove? The coffee maker? She even glanced in the microwave oven. His puckish sense of humor just might have led him to . . .

Ten minutes later she was forced to accept the truth. Jed had got up from her bed, dressed, and taken himself off without so much as a word. No "I'll be seeing you," no "Thanks for the memory"—no *nothing*.

Aurelia forced herself to go through the motions of making coffee. Then, sitting in the bentwood rocker in front of the broad living room window, she stared out at the dismal rain and began a cool, rational analysis of the facts. It lasted less than a minute, and then she was swearing inexpertly, condemning Jed, his motives, and his immediate ancestry.

She condemned his heartless lack of morals, but most of all she condemned herself and the foolish romanticism that had led her into the trap. He had given her fair warning, and she'd been too stupidly blind to take it at face value. Hadn't he told her weeks ago that he was going to get her into his bed?

Well, he'd succeeded. She hoped he'd enjoyed it, because it would be the last time. She slammed her cup carelessly onto the makeshift coffee table, picked up the rocking chair, and headed for the unused room at the end of the hall. Her steps echoed purposefully on the bare floors as she returned for her typewriter, and then she collected the rest of her belongings, scowling as she ruthlessly sorted them into two groups —those she could leave behind temporarily and those she had to take with her.

By eleven o'clock she was done. She'd probably made mistakes. She'd been too upset to think clearly, but she'd just have to live with them until Henry could collect the rest of her things and forward them to her.

By the time she'd carted her largest suitcase, the typewriter, and Sigh's assorted equipment out to the Jeep, her plans were in good order. She was disheveled and hungry, but she felt enormously better after the physical exertion. From past experience she'd learned that work was a panacea. Now that the fine edge of fury was dulled, maybe she could settle down long enough to make a few calls.

Dialing quickly, she tapped her foot and waited. Never again would she ridicule intuition. It had to be something of that sort that had urged her to secure a driver's license after all these years.

Max answered on the third ring. His was not one of the Madison Avenue type agencies, with receptionists, flocks of secretaries, and a head of busy agents.

"Max, I blew it," she announced bluntly. She went on to explain that she'd found it impossible to work with Jed Dancey, and that if and when he wanted to make other arrangements, she'd turn over her papers to whomever succeeded her. "And now I need another job. Have you got anything, just *any*thing to tide me over?"

"Why do I let you do this to me?" Max protested plaintively. "You do realize that this isn't the way our relationship is supposed to work, don't you? I'm not an employment agency." But he went on to tell her about a new bimonthly magazine that needed quasi-medical articles. "The sort of thing you did in Atlanta, but with a popular slant. The pay's a sack of beans, but it could lead to something."

There was an editorial opening for a large automotive trade journal and any number of possibilities for technical writers in the computer industry. "I think I could land you another ghosting job, one that could net us both a bundle, but it'll be rough. She's a dragon—a stage mother type whose daughter went off the deep end. She's got an axe to grind, and she'll name names. We'll have to go over the contract with a fine-tooth comb to protect ourselves from lawsuits, but if you're willing to gamble, I'll see what I can do."

It was settled. Max was to get the particulars and she'd contact him within a week. Her next call was to Adam. There was no one at home. She bit off a fingernail and frowned absently at the instrument in her hand. Blast! She hated to call him at work, and she didn't even know where Diana worked these days. The housekeeper was probably out with the children, and Aurelia didn't want to talk to her, anyway.

She'd give it another fifteen minutes, and then she'd try again. If there was no one home, she'd just have to call from farther down the road and warn them that she was about to descend on them temporarily. Next, she'd leave a note telling Jed he could collect his Jeep at the bus station. There'd be a certain amount of satisfaction in writing it. At least *she'd* have the courtesy not to simply pack her bags and walk out without a word.

It was an ungainly load. The cart carrier was larger

than her suitcase. Jed had bought it for her when he'd moved her from Meadows-of-Dan. There was the litter box, too, an enormous covered affair, also courtesy of Jed, that took up half the back seat. She only hoped the bus driver was an accommodating sort, because there was really nothing she could leave behind, not even the twenty-five-pound bag of litter she'd opened just yesterday. Diana wasn't a cat fancier, and it was going to be up to Aurelia to see that she and Sigh remained as unobtrusive and inoffensive as possible until she located another place to stay.

Everything looked depressingly gray and wet, and the rain was still coming down in half-hearted flurries. Thank goodness the windshield wipers worked. Now, if she could only figure out how to start this creature . . .

It cranked on the second try. The muffler no longer muffled, and the vibrations actually rattled her teeth, but at least it ran. "Settle down, darling," she reassured the uneasy cat in-the cage beside her. "From here on it's downhill all the way."

"Oh . . . my . . . God," Aurelia moaned, resting her forehead against the steering wheel. "It's just not fair. I don't deserve this."

Jed's hands reached through the open door to lift her down and paused to rake the kitty litter from her hair and shoulders. "I hope to hell this isn't what I think it is," he growled. "Lift your head up; let me see. How bad is it?"

She shook his hands from her arms and lifted her head to glower at him. A shower of tiny pellets cascaded to the pavement and quickly darkened in the rain. "There's nothing the matter with me. Kindly remove your hands from my arms."

"I'll kindly remove your arms from your body if you don't tell me what the hell you think you're doing. What's the idea of barreling down this mountain in the rain? Didn't I tell you this damned Jeep wasn't safe?"

"Stop swearing at me! I wasn't brought up in a—in a gutter!"

"From the looks of you, I'd say you were brought up in a cat house—in the literal sense of the word. Now, where were you going? And it had better be good."

"I was going home." The words came instinctively, and she hadn't time to qualify them before he had caught her by the shoulders, lowering his face to within inches of hers.

"Your home is with me," he ground out with frightening intensity. "Don't ever—*ever*—forget it. If it's no more than a bedroll and a campfire, it's still your home, for as long as I have the power to provide for you."

Only then did she notice how haggard he looked. There were beads of moisture on his unnaturally pale forehead that had nothing to do with the rain, and not even the punishing strength of his grip could hide the tremor that shook his hands.

"Jed?" she whispered uncertainly. "I thought you'd gone."

"I had. I left before daylight this morning, got as far as Washington and jumped ship, caught another flight, and burned up the highway getting back here." His face seemed to crumple before her eyes. "I just couldn't do it, Aurelia. I couldn't stay away from you, not after last night, not after what you told me."

"You couldn't?" she echoed wonderingly. His words echoed in her mind. So she *had* told him. Had he answered her? She didn't have the nerve to ask, but he was back. That must mean something. "Jed, what if I'd missed you!"

"Thank the good Lord you did! I aged ten years when I saw you rattling down the hill at breakneck speed in that old wreck. I was ready to go over the edge when you swerved into the drive-out and came to rest halfway up that bank. Oh, sweetheart—" He shook his head slowly, leading her over to where the Jaguar rested at a rakish angle. "You're going to have to take it easy on me. I'm not in condition to chase you around these mountains, either on foot or on wheels."

"Get Sigh," Aurelia reminded him as he closed the door and started around to the driver's side. "And my typewriter, please. It's the green box."

The typewriter was stashed on the floor, and then the cat was retrieved, along with the most vital pieces of his equipment. Jed eased the car back onto the wetly gleaming pavement and proceeded slowly up the hill. The shoulders of his trench coat were saturated, and rain glistened in his hair and beard like beads of jet. Aurelia squirmed miserably in her gray suedecloth raincoat as pellets of cat litter worked their way down her spine. This was not the way a joyous reconciliation was supposed to go.

She darted a look at Jed's scowl of concentration. If they had any sort of future together, she was going to have to stop expecting the moon. Even if he loved her, she'd have to do without the flowery declarations and constant reassurances. Jed simply wasn't the type.

Half an hour later she emerged from her room, clean and warm and dressed in her fuzzy peach-colored bathrobe. She'd left it behind because it took up half a suitcase, and now she had reason to be glad. Most of her clothes were still out in the Jeep.

Jed was waiting for her. The frown on his face lifted

momentarily as she entered the room, and then lowered again. "You could have been killed," he accused, and then, before she could formulate a reply, he was across the room, reaching for her, burying his face in her hair and whispering her name over and over.

"Aurelia, sweetest heart, how could you do that to me? It ruins me to think you were leaving without a single word."

She struggled to escape his crushing embrace. "Wait a minute. Wa-ait a minute. Who left whom? I woke up this morning and you were simply gone."

"You knew I had a meeting scheduled for eleven. Didn't you get my note?"

"What note?"

"The note I left on your pillow. I watched you while you slept for almost half an hour, trying to psych myself into waking you up. There was so much I wanted to tell you; I didn't know where to begin. Finally I figured I'd do better to try and write it down without you there to distract me. It took me so long to come up with the right words, I damned near missed my plane."

She bent back to gaze levelly into his face, shaken to see the fine flush rising on his cheeks. "There wasn't any note, Jed. I looked. I searched everywhere," Aurelia said slowly. The import of his words was just now beginning to seep into the cold hollows of her body to root out the doubts, and she searched his eyes for reassurance.

"Of course there was a note," he protested indignantly. "Do you think I'd just leave you without a word? Good Lord, Aurelia, do you honestly think I'm that insensitive?"

She didn't know what to think any longer. Everything in her whole life had taught her to be cautious, not to take anything for granted. She'd built up her defenses and had them flattened too many times, and now she was almost afraid to reach out and take the risk.

"Aurelia, honey, I did write it. I sweated blood over the thing—believe me, it's not the sort of thing I can just dash off. I put it on your pillow where you'd see it as soon as you woke up." He smiled, his eyes narrowing lazily as they moved over her anxious features. "Did you know you purr when you sleep? Not a snore, just a little whisper, like—"

With dawning comprehension, they stared at each other. "Sigh."

"He was playing on the pillow," she began, her words tumbling over Jed's.

"I should have known better than to trust a one-eyed half Siamese."

"I'll look under the bed." She was torn between a desire to find Jed's note and a reluctance to leave the shelter of his arms.

Jed led her over to the enormous sofa and settled her onto his lap, drawing her back into his arms so that her head was cradled in the hollow of his shoulder. "Not yet," he murmured deeply. "I don't want to be around when you find the thing. If I remember correctly, I was using some pretty high-flown prose by the time I got going good, and now I'm scared you'll laugh."

Aiming a spontaneous kiss that missed its mark and landed on the side of his mustache, Aurelia laughed shakily. There was more than a hint of unsteadiness in her voice when she said. "Oh, darling, I don't care if you only signed your name, as long as you wrote *something*. I thought you just didn't . . . that you weren't . . ." She gave up when her voice threatened to cave in under an overload of emotion.

"In love with you? That I didn't worship you? Adore you? Is that it? For God's sake, Aurelia, what have I been trying to tell you? Until you said the words last night, I thought I didn't stand a chance. Hell—I mean there, you see? That's just one of the things I'm talking about," he said with helpless exasperation. "I've had to learn a whole new language just to talk to you, sweetheart, and I'm still pretty bad at it. You'll just have to be patient with me."

Growing confidence gave way to boldness, and she ran a hand inside his shirt and brushed her palm over the coarse silk hair, glorying in the series of shudders that shook his solid frame. "Maybe we can study together," she teased.

"When it comes to homework, though, I have a few ideas of my own," he warned her gruffly. He shifted enough to tug his shirttail out, and then he went to work on hers. "We start with the simple, four-letter word, love. Watch my lips. I *love* you, Aurelia. Now you try it. Go ahead, use it in a sentence. As in, I, Aurelia, love you, Jed, et cetera, et cetera."

Her laughter threatened to edge over into tears before she could steer it back on track. "What are all those et ceteras? Is that the same as fine print?" Her arms were around his waist now, and her fingers played daring games with the sleek, resilient muscles of his back.

"I was hoping you wouldn't ask. Do I have to spell it out to you?" An indulgent smile teased the corners of his mouth.

"I think maybe you'd better," she prompted softly.

"Start making allowances," he warned. "I'm strictly a novice when it comes to this sort of thing. To begin with, I didn't know what the h—what love was. That's not to say I haven't known a lot of women."

In every sense of the word, Aurelia thought, growing more secure by the moment as she gazed up at the magnificent creature who was holding her as if he'd never let her go. She laughed delightedly and reached up to tangle her fingers in his beard. "Go on, you're doing fine. We were up to your lovelife—start from there." Her fingertips traced the angular contour of his jaw, reveling in her freedom to do so.

"Yes, well, that's just it. It had nothing to do with love. I could have sworn that there was no such thing, but there's no other way to explain what happened to me. Suddenly, about a month ago, I started paying attention to things that had passed over my head for years. Those letters—Mary's letters to Jocephus— they started making sense to me. That's when I began to wonder. Didn't you notice? Couldn't you tell? Lord knows, I was floundering around like a fish out of water."

She snuggled deeper into the arms that held her, knowing in her burgeoning wisdom that her movements were having a decided effect on Jed. "You're too good at keeping secrets. I never even guessed. . . . Jed," she said, some of the anxiety seeping back into her voice, "about that night when . . . when I froze up. I don't know what happened. I think maybe it was nervousness about . . . you know. I thought I'd die when you walked out. After you'd seen them, I mean."

"Whoa, back up a little, honey. After I walked out when? After I saw what?"

She twisted her head up to give him a stern look, wishing he'd come into focus more clearly. She was either going to have to take a lot on faith, or figure out some way to keep from steaming up her glasses. "After you walked out when you first saw my scars," she forced herself to say.

"After I saw what scars?"

Even without her glasses, she couldn't mistake the puzzlement in his voice. "The scars on my back. The burns—the skin grafts."

Slowly he shook his head. One of his hands was absently stroking her back, and it paused momentarily and then resumed its leisurely motion. "Sweetheart, there's nothing the matter with my eyes. I've seen your back. If there are any scars there, they're on the inside."

She twisted around again and leaned away enough to catch the pained look on his face.

"Aurelia, can you sit still for three minutes?" he said. "Remind me to teach you a little basic biology."

"No, I can't. I want you to pull down my bathrobe and look—look closely." She was busy tugging at the sash, wondering how she could manage to lower the back without baring herself in the front. She had nothing at all on underneath, but somehow it didn't seem at all important as Jed's hands slipped the heavy pile fabric down her arms.

"Now take a good look. If there's anything there that—that you object to, then I want to know now. Because . . . because it's important to me, Jed," she finished earnestly.

He leaned her forward, allowing the heavy robe to fall to her waist. She clutched at the two ends of the sash, wondering how one could feel paralyzed and stimulated at the same time. "All right, now let's see what we've got here." He angled her toward the single light and she swallowed convulsively, trembling as she felt his warm breath strike her naked skin.

"Well? *Well?*" she prompted impatiently. The tip of a finger trailed across her shoulders, down beside her spine, and then around her sides, to the pale softness of her breasts, and without thinking she covered the long, hard fingers with her hand, pressing them deeply into her flesh.

"There's no cat litter here, you'll be delighted to know. Were you by any chance talking about this tiny little trail of pink and silver lines?" He brushed his fingers across her lower back. "Looks like embroidery to me. Now, tell me, love, why should I settle for plain when I can have fancy?" The featherlight touch moved up to her shoulders and out onto the backs of her arms to produce a rush of tremors.

"That's it? That's all? No redness?" Why hadn't she been able to believe what she knew had been true?

"Darling, I'm a sorry bargain in some ways, but I'll never lie to you. What happened to make you think your back was scarred?"

She didn't want to go into that now. Somehow it no longer seemed quite real. Not when a more compelling reality—the reality of Jed's love—was filling her to overflowing. But he was entitled to an explanation. "When I was almost fifteen," she said in a small, tense voice, "my parents and I were at a banquet." She went on to outline the sequence of events that had shaped her life, had made her doubt fate and herself to the point where even now, she could hardly believe in her good fortune.

"I was afraid of crowds, afraid of short sleeves, afraid of depending on anyone but myself. Oh, Jed, I was a real mess. You're right, most of the scars were on the inside, only how could I know? I was too stupid, too foolish to—"

Jed touched her lips with a gentle finger to still the flow of words. She lifted her eyes to his and was shaken by what she saw. Behind the moisture that shimmered there, was all the love in the world—and it was hers. With a total lack of self-consciousness,

Aurelia lifted her arms and wrapped them around his neck. His soft beard brushed over her shoulders, and her back was bare to his scrutiny, but she didn't care. Secure in the knowledge of his love, nothing mattered except that they were together.

Against the graying hair at his temple, she whispered, "I wish I could think of some new and splendid way to say I love you, but I just don't know any words. You'll just have to take me on faith."

"Sweetheart, I'll take you on faith, on Tuesdays, and any other way either one of us can figure out—starting now."

His kiss was incredibly gentle, a communication that went far beyond mere words. After a long time he lifted his head and said softly, "This next one's for Jocephus and Mary. After that, they're all mine."

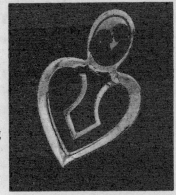

MORE ROMANCE FOR
A SPECIAL WAY TO RELAX
$1.95 each

2 ☐ Hastings	21 ☐ Hastings	41 ☐ Halston	60 ☐ Thorne
3 ☐ Dixon	22 ☐ Howard	42 ☐ Drummond	61 ☐ Beckman
4 ☐ Vitek	23 ☐ Charles	43 ☐ Shaw	62 ☐ Bright
5 ☐ Converse	24 ☐ Dixon	44 ☐ Eden	63 ☐ Wallace
6 ☐ Douglass	25 ☐ Hardy	45 ☐ Charles	64 ☐ Converse
7 ☐ Stanford	26 ☐ Scott	46 ☐ Howard	65 ☐ Cates
8 ☐ Halston	27 ☐ Wisdom	47 ☐ Stephens	66 ☐ Mikels
9 ☐ Baxter	28 ☐ Ripy	48 ☐ Ferrell	67 ☐ Shaw
10 ☐ Thiels	29 ☐ Bergen	49 ☐ Hastings	68 ☐ Sinclair
11 ☐ Thornton	30 ☐ Stephens	50 ☐ Browning	69 ☐ Dalton
12 ☐ Sinclair	31 ☐ Baxter	51 ☐ Trent	70 ☐ Clare
13 ☐ Beckman	32 ☐ Douglass	52 ☐ Sinclair	71 ☐ Skillern
14 ☐ Keene	33 ☐ Palmer	53 ☐ Thomas	72 ☐ Belmont
15 ☐ James	35 ☐ James	54 ☐ Hohl	73 ☐ Taylor
16 ☐ Carr	36 ☐ Dailey	55 ☐ Stanford	74 ☐ Wisdom
17 ☐ John	37 ☐ Stanford	56 ☐ Wallace	75 ☐ John
18 ☐ Hamilton	38 ☐ John	57 ☐ Thornton	76 ☐ Ripy
19 ☐ Shaw	39 ☐ Milan	58 ☐ Douglass	77 ☐ Bergen
20 ☐ Musgrave	40 ☐ Converse	59 ☐ Roberts	78 ☐ Gladstone

MORE ROMANCE FOR
A SPECIAL WAY TO RELAX

$2.25 each

79 ☐ Hastings	89 ☐ Meriwether	99 ☐ Dixon	109 ☐ Beckman
80 ☐ Douglass	90 ☐ Justin	100 ☐ Roberts	110 ☐ Browning
81 ☐ Thornton	91 ☐ Stanford	101 ☐ Bergen	111 ☐ Thorne
82 ☐ McKenna	92 ☐ Hamilton	102 ☐ Wallace	112 ☐ Belmont
83 ☐ Major	93 ☐ Lacey	103 ☐ Taylor	113 ☐ Camp
84 ☐ Stephens	94 ☐ Barrie	104 ☐ Wallace	114 ☐ Ripy
85 ☐ Beckman	95 ☐ Doyle	105 ☐ Sinclair	
86 ☐ Halston	96 ☐ Baxter	106 ☐ John	
87 ☐ Dixon	97 ☐ Shaw	107 ☐ Ross	
88 ☐ Saxon	98 ☐ Hurley	108 ☐ Stephens	

LOOK FOR A THISTLE IN THE SPRING
BY LINDA SHAW AVAILABLE IN OCTOBER
AND
A WOMAN OF DARING BY ABRA TAYLOR
IN NOVEMBER.

SILHOUETTE SPECIAL EDITION, Department SE/2
1230 Avenue of the Americas
New York, NY 10020

Please send me the books I have checked above. I am enclosing $_____
(please add 50¢ to cover postage and handling. NYS and NYC residents
please add appropriate sales tax). Send check or money order—no cash or
C.O.D.'s please. Allow six weeks for delivery.

NAME _____

ADDRESS _____

CITY _____ STATE/ZIP _____

Silhouette **Romance**

15-Day Free Trial Offer
6 Silhouette Romances

6 Silhouette Romances, free for 15 days! We'll send you 6 new Silhouette Romances to keep for 15 days, absolutely free! If you decide not to keep them, send them back to us. You pay nothing.

Free Home Delivery. But if you enjoy them as much as we think you will, keep them by paying the invoice enclosed with your free trial shipment. We'll pay all shipping and handling charges. You get the convenience of Home Delivery and we pay the postage and handling charge each month.

Don't miss a copy. The Silhouette Book Club is the way to make sure you'll be able to receive every new romance we publish before they're sold out. There is no minimum number of books to buy and you can cancel at any time.

This offer expires April 30, 1984

Silhouette Book Club, Dept. SRSE 7K
120 Brighton Road, Clifton, NJ 07012

Please send me 6 Silhouette Romances to keep for 15 days, absolutely free. I understand I am not obligated to join the Silhouette Book Club unless I decide to keep them.

NAME_____

ADDRESS_____

CITY_____ STATE_____ ZIP_____

READERS' COMMENTS ON SILHOUETTE SPECIAL EDITIONS: